He Said Never

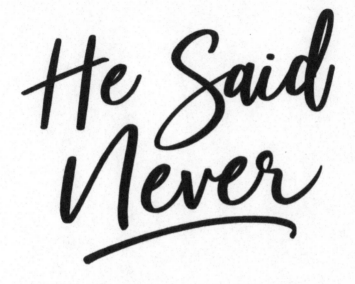

RUTH CARDELLO

Published by Montlake, Seattle

www.apub.com

Amazon, the Amazon logo, and Montlake are trademarks of Amazon.com, Inc., or its affiliates.

ISBN-13: 9781542026185
ISBN-10: 1542026180

Cover design by Eileen Carey

Printed in the United States of America

This book is dedicated to my friend Jen.
Without you,
and your ability to bring order after chaos,
this book would never have been possible.

Don't miss a thing!

www.ruthcardello.com

Sign up for Ruth's newsletter:
Yes, let's stay in touch!
https://forms.aweber.com/form/00/819443400.htm

Join Ruth's private fan group:
www.facebook.com/groups/ruthiesroadies

Follow Ruth on Goodreads:
www.goodreads.com/author/show/4820876.Ruth_Cardello

CHAPTER ONE

—

RILEY

Again?

From a small table in the corner of a coffee shop in Lockton, Massachusetts, I checked the time on my phone and compared it to the clock on the wall. My date was seriously late—the kind of late that didn't leave much doubt about whether or not he was coming.

I've been stood up—again.

I don't get it. We clicked. He was interested enough to ask for my number. He asked me to meet here; I didn't ask him. Is it me? Something I said?

Two months. Three different men. Three no-shows. It was enough to shake any woman's confidence. Normally the first call I made would have been to my best friend, Teagan, but she'd recently gotten engaged and had headed off to Italy to celebrate and meet more of her fiancé Gian's family. She deserved uninterrupted time to simply enjoy the experience.

Italy! A few months earlier I wouldn't have been able to imagine either of us going anywhere we couldn't drive to. So much had changed since Gian Romano had come into Teagan's T-shirt printshop looking for me. My head was still spinning from how different our lives had become.

I grew up in a tough suburb of Boston, still had an apartment there a floor above my mother's. I always felt safe in my neighborhood, but everyone I grew up with was one paycheck away from not being able to pay the rent. The area could get a little dicey after dark, but we all looked out for each other. None of them knew that I had my own driver now. A driver. Me.

It still felt unreal.

I'd only agreed to having one because it was important to my new-found brother, Dominic Corisi, a man who just happened to be richer than God and more than a little paranoid when it came to security. We'd recently discovered that we were related and were still figuring each other out. I sent a text to my driver: Mr. Tuttle. You there?

I'm paid to always be.

Could you come inside?

Of course.

A few minutes later, Mr. Tuttle walked into the shop and looked around until he located me. He removed his hat as he made his way to my table. His salt-and-pepper hair was short and neatly styled. His suit was immaculate. He had a hired-soldier presence about him that made most men take a step back, but the more time I spent with him, the less he intimidated me. I was pretty sure underneath that dead-eyed stare he was a big softie. "Is there something you require, Miss Ragsdale?"

The truth was, I just didn't want to be alone. "Could you sit with me?"

He hesitated. "Is something wrong?"

Hands waving in the air, I said, "No. No. What could be?"

After clearing his throat, he took the seat across from me. "Would you like me to call someone?"

"No. It's nothing serious." I leaned forward and lowered my voice. "I've been stood up again. Steve Wercherlinker, or whatever his last name is, apparently wasn't interested in sharing a coffee with me."

Mr. Tuttle lifted and dropped his shoulders without meeting my gaze. "I'm sorry to hear that."

I waved my hand again. "It's okay. I mean, what can I do, right?"

Mr. Tuttle kept his silence.

"I'm usually pretty good with people, but lately I'm second-guessing myself." I brought both of my hands to my temples. "Do you think this is happening because I'm not being honest with people? Do I have 'liar' stamped on my forehead?" It would have been nice if Mr. Tuttle had said no, but I kept going anyway. "I want to be honest. I just don't want to disappoint anyone. My mother is afraid of Dominic—she gets upset if I even mention his name. I promised I'd have nothing to do with him, but how could I keep that promise? He's my brother."

In response to Mr. Tuttle's continued silence, I added, "You'd think Kal would be on my side, but he isn't. He thinks Mom is right and that nothing good will come from getting to know the Corisis. So much for twins thinking alike. Kal and I agree on next to nothing lately, and that was never us. He's ignoring my calls now because he says listening to me talk about the Corisis just pisses him off. He thinks my loyalty should be to my mother and not to family we never even knew we had. Do you think he's right?"

Nothing.

I nodded. "You're right, it's probably too complicated for you to have an answer. I just don't know if I'm doing anything right lately." I slumped in my chair. "I can't even get a man to show up for a date. What's that about?"

Mr. Tuttle stood. "Miss Ragsdale, I just want to drive, you understand? I don't want any problems."

"Problems?"

"It's better if I don't know too much."

"Too much about what?" I rose to my feet as well and followed him as he made his way across the coffee shop toward the door. "I don't understand."

He paused to look down at me with absolutely no emotion in his expression. "If there's nothing else, I'll be with the car."

People like me, I thought. *I genuinely like most people, and they know it. Friendship, as well as finding dates, has always been as easy as that for me.*

Mr. Tuttle was a tougher nut to crack, and I was seriously beginning to question if I'd lost my mojo. I stood there after his departure wondering if I should apologize or let the matter drop.

"Excuse me," a male voice said behind me.

It was a deliciously deep voice, the kind no woman would mind waking up to. I turned slowly, fully prepared for the face and body to not live up to the promise of his voice. It wasn't the voice of my would-be date; it was better. Everything about him was better. Tall. Dark hair. Dark eyes. Square jaw. A lick-worthy muscular neck. *Holy crap.*

Insta-lust. I felt wonderfully breathless and tingly.

Until I remembered the last three men who'd asked me out. I'd been attracted to them, albeit not on this level, but the last thing I needed was to set myself up for another disappointment before I figured out what I was doing wrong. "Stop right there. Sure, you're beautiful." I leaned in and took a whiff of him. "And you smell amazing, but I already know where this will go. I'll say something witty. You'll counter with a pickup line. We'll exchange numbers and you'll call. We'll talk all night and you'll ask me out, but that's as far as it'll go. I'll be right back here waiting for you to show up, but you won't. Why? Is it me? Is it you? I don't know. Maybe men are just asshats."

The amusement in his eyes irritated me, because I wasn't trying to be funny. He pointed behind me. "Not an asshat, just someone trying to order a coffee."

I glanced behind me at the line to the register. He hadn't come over to talk to me. I was blocking his way. I stepped aside. "Sorry." As soon as the word came out of my mouth, I knew it didn't fit how I felt. I was still too irritated with men in general to be sorry. "No, I'm not sorry. You would have stood me up too."

As he went to walk past me, he paused and lowered his head so he was next to my ear. His breath tickled my neck. "Sadly, we shall never know."

Our eyes met, and there was a definite sizzle in the air. I'd dated plenty of men in my life, had sex with one or two—okay, five, but three of them were disappointing enough to not be worth mentioning. *Does it count as sex if you don't orgasm? I say no.*

Something about this man made me certain he didn't fumble and rush. It might have been wishful thinking, but as I stared up into his chiseled face, I saw the desire I felt reflected in his eyes. I always believed in fate and things working out the way they were supposed to. He might have been the reason it didn't work out with the other men.

He straightened, gave me one more lingering look, shook his head, then turned to the register to place his order. *Or not.*

Teagan getting engaged is messing with my mind. The poor man just wants a coffee.

I told my feet to move, but they didn't. There was no comparison between him and any of the men I'd been with. Not in the looks department. Not in how he made my body hum with anticipation.

He ordered his coffee, then moved down the counter to the pickup area. His shoes were expensive, and his jeans looked as new as the blue oxford button-down shirt he was wearing. His attire reminded me of my niece Judy's when she was attempting to blend in to a crowd. I wondered about his reason for being in my hometown.

The barista called out, "Gavin!" And the man stepped forward to get his drink.

Gavin. The name fit him. A strong name. One I could imagine calling out as I came. My cheeks warmed at the thought. *Thank God mind reading isn't a thing.*

He turned. Our eyes met again, and he frowned. I should have looked away, but I couldn't. In a heartbeat he was towering over me. "What's your name?" he demanded.

Whoa. Straightforward. Almost impatient. Kind of sexy. "Riley."

"Are you employed?"

It was my turn to frown. My employment status was a sore subject with me. Definitely not a subject I wanted to discuss with someone like him. "I'm currently between jobs." It was true. I'd worked at Teagan's printshop, but that job was quickly coming to an end as Teagan reshuffled her life to make room for Gian. Teagan not only believed I was now beyond having financial issues, but she also expected me to be headed off to college soon. Dominic had offered to pay for any school I chose, but I'd already accepted more from him than I was comfortable with.

Until recently, I had also been working part time as a paid bridesmaid. Yes, as I'd told my mom many times, "That's a thing." But I had natural lags between gigs. I didn't advertise—brides contacted me, and when the work was there, it was quite profitable. Much like my love life, that career was experiencing a dry spell.

Gavin was looking me over again, and having his sustained attention was doing funny things to my ability to think straight. "Do you have friends?"

It was such an odd question that I laughed. "Doesn't everyone?"

Rather than answering me, he simply held my gaze. "Single?"

Strange, but he was hot enough that I was willing to at least hear him out. "Yes."

"Willing to sign a nondisclosure?"

"No." Two months ago I would have been shocked at the request, but everyone who worked for Dominic signed one. Mr. Tuttle was no exception. Rich people were weird about stuff like that. He had to have money. Or I looked like someone who was seriously in need of a job. Or both.

I looked down. Sure, my jeans were worn, and my shirt was as well, but not because I didn't have others. It just happened to be my favorite shirt. I always liked to take things slow with men, test things out before I brought out the cleavage.

I searched his face. He wasn't looking at me like he was considering hiring me . . .

Unless it was for something on the kinky side. I didn't walk on the wild side, but that didn't make me less curious about if he did. "Why? What are you looking for?"

He shook his head and sighed. "Nothing that makes any damn sense."

For just a moment, I thought he would say something more. He stood there, looking down at me like he wanted to, and I held my breath. No matter what he wanted, my answer would be no. Most likely. As we gazed into each other's eyes, I sensed something in him—a yearning? Not in a sexual sense, although the air was charged with our mutual attraction. No, something was weighing on him, something he wasn't sure how to handle.

I knew that feeling well.

I wished I knew what he was struggling with. Maybe, like me, all he needed was someone to talk to. I could be that for him.

My heart was beating wildly in my chest when he turned on his heel and began to walk away. I called out his name. "Gavin!"

He paused but didn't turn back.

"I hope you find it—whatever it is you're looking for."

He continued walking with no acknowledgment that he'd heard me.

I made my way to the parking lot, where Mr. Tuttle was waiting for me. He opened the back door for me as I approached.

"Home, James," I said.

"Benjamin," Mr. Tuttle said as I slid into the back seat. "But I prefer Mr. Tuttle." He closed the door and walked around to the driver's side.

As soon as he was inside the car as well, I said, "About earlier. I'm sorry."

Our eyes met in the rearview mirror. "You're a nice woman, but you have to be careful. We all do."

I wanted to ask him what he meant by that, but he'd already looked away, and I didn't want to add to the awkwardness of the night. "I will be."

He cleared his throat. "Lockton or Back Bay?"

I slumped down in the seat. That was the big question, wasn't it? I was straddling two worlds, trying to please the people in both. Eventually something would have to give. "My Lockton apartment, please."

"Absolutely."

As we pulled away from the curb, I turned to see if Gavin was outside the coffee shop watching me leave, but he wasn't. What a strange man—gorgeous, but obviously troubled.

Look who's talking.

I always considered myself a pretty stable person. Kal and I were raised by a mother who had always struggled with her health. It instilled in us both a strong sense of family as well as a good work ethic.

Life was never easy, but at least it made sense. Our mother lived in constant pain that past surgeries had promised to alleviate but hadn't. Her newest doctor said he had a solution, but it was costly. Kal and I worked two, sometimes three jobs, with the goal of paying off her older medical bills so we could afford to sign on for more.

Gian's appearance in my life and his declaration that I shared a biological parent with Dominic changed everything. It also opened a door to questions my mother had always discouraged us from asking. Who was our biological father? Why didn't she want to talk about him? How had she hurt her back?

It wasn't easy to hear that my biological father, Antonio Corisi, was the one who'd hurt my mother and that he was a married man when he did it. Although he was long dead, my mother was still dealing with the aftereffects of his abuse.

So much of what I'd thought I knew about my life had been a lie. I'd always thought my mother was a private woman, an introvert. To hear that it had been fear that had kept her in had shaken me. The more I learned about my father, the more I was relieved he was dead. I didn't have hate in my heart for anyone, but I could have hated him.

When I asked her why she never went after Antonio legally, tears filled her eyes. "Some people," she said with memories darkening her eyes, "are so rich they're above the law. Promise me you'll have nothing to do with the Corisis."

I made that promise, but only to comfort her. I understood her fears, but I'd just discovered I not only had two brothers and a sister but also nephews and nieces. And they wanted to know me.

As soon as Dominic discovered we existed, he reached out to both Kal and me. Kal wasn't interested, but I went to meet Dominic. He said he wanted to be part of our lives, and he'd spent the last two months showing me how much he meant that.

My mother's hospital bills were paid off—supposedly by a government program. Our insurance company suddenly decided to cover the cost of my mother's next surgery in full. Dominic claimed he wasn't responsible for either, but I knew he was. Our father's sins were not his to atone for, but that didn't stop him from trying to.

Coming back to the present, I said aloud, "Guess what, Mr. Tuttle? I met the most interesting man in the coffee shop just after you left. But don't worry; he didn't ask me out, so it doesn't look like I'll be stood up again this month."

I would have felt better about the joke if my driver had laughed. *Tough crowd.*

I missed Teagan. If she were here, I would have unloaded all my confusion on her, and she would have helped me sort through it.

She'd probably tell me that none of the men who had stood me up mattered. According to her, the only man who mattered was the right one. Easy for her to say—she'd found hers.

She'd also say that not everyone's emotional state was my responsibility. She often accused me of being a people pleaser, like that was a bad thing. I saw nothing wrong with making the happiness of the people I loved a priority.

We wouldn't have been friends if I hadn't been that way when we'd met. I'd been popular in school, while Teagan had struggled to connect with her classmates. Not only did she not have any friends, but she'd also sounded equally lonely outside school. She was brilliant but socially awkward and prone to sleeping during her classes—an easy target for bullies. Defending her had gotten me tossed out of the cool clique, but bringing her home to meet my family had gained me a sister. Given the chance to go back and change anything, I wouldn't. *One real friendship is worth a hundred superficial ones.*

What would she say about the situation with my mother? Probably that not every lie is bad. Teagan as well as Gian were living lives their families knew nothing about. Her T-shirt shop was a front for the top-secret AI programs she hoped would one day save humanity from itself. Gian's wine shop was also a front. He didn't want his family to know he had begun designing and testing high-tech sex toys. Their secrets didn't hurt anyone, and since they'd found each other, they finally had someone to share them with.

My lies were not as harmless. Whenever my mother asked if I'd heard from the Corisis, I said I hadn't. Whenever any of the Corisis asked what my mother thought of them, I said she held no ill feelings toward them, but she needed time to get used to the idea of our families coming together. The truth would hurt both sides of my family, and that put me in a difficult spot.

Unlike Teagan, hiding things weighed on me, and bottling my feelings up was starting to unravel me. I felt like a criminal in a movie who just blurts out a confession. I'd always thought that was ridiculous, but the more I kept things in, the more they threatened to spill out.

I really didn't have to wonder too hard about why Gavin might have chosen to bolt rather than ask me out on the date I'd already assured him he wouldn't show up for. I'd seen the struggle in his eyes; he probably glimpsed the craziness building in mine.

Mr. Tuttle drove me to the corner just before my street, parked, and positioned himself where he could watch me walk to the entrance of my building. "Good night, Miss Ragsdale."

"Good night, Mr. Tuttle."

I headed into my old building and walked up the stairs, because the building's elevator had never been reliable. As I undressed and brushed my teeth, I went over my plans for the next day. In the morning I'd bring my mother breakfast, clean her apartment, and talk about nothing that had mattered to me lately. Would we ever get back to the place where I could look my mother in the eyes and not feel like I was betraying her? I hoped so.

I made myself tea and let my mind fill with images of the hot stranger from the coffee shop. *Gavin.* I curled up on my couch, sipped at my tea, and replayed our brief meeting. What if I hadn't unleashed my crazy on him? What if I'd said yes instead of no to an NDA? It was fun to imagine the possibilities.

Leather suits and whips? I wasn't into that, but considering how my body warmed just at the memory of him, he'd be a tough man to say no to.

He might be married and looking for something on the side. I made a face. I didn't want to think about that possibility.

I turned my thoughts back to more X-rated possibilities and tucked a blanket around myself. Some people were perfectly fine alone. I was happier when I was with someone, but the older I got, the less I wanted to waste my time on relationships that didn't matter.

Seeing Teagan with someone brought me joy, but it also heightened my yearning to have someone of my own. The man I ended up with wouldn't be like Gavin.

No, I couldn't imagine myself with someone who didn't look like he knew how to smile.

So it was a good thing nothing had panned out between us.

CHAPTER TWO

GAVIN

A few days later, I sat on a bench along a cobblestone pier outside my Boston apartment building, watching sailboats pass on the bay. It was a sight I normally missed, because my workday rarely ended before the sun went down. I would still have been at the office if my father hadn't dropped two bombshells on me recently. At sixty-two, my career-driven CEO father had called me into his office to discuss his plans to retire within a year.

It had always been understood that I'd take over our multibillion-dollar family business, but I hadn't imagined that happening for a very long time. He was too sharp, still too much a part of the game, to want to step down. Hamilton Wenham IV was born into money, but that didn't stop him from taking the family company to the next level. He took over his father's shipping company and diversified it, and Wenham Industries became Wenham Global.

My father believed in rewarding hard work and loyalty, and he had no patience for excuses or incompetence. To gain my current position as president of the company, I needed to prove myself by working my way up from an entry-level position.

His lectures laid the foundation for my success. Good enough was never good enough. To lead, I needed to be brighter, stronger, more determined than any adversary. There was no place for weakness when it came to business—or life.

When I started working for the company right after college, my father also hired a young man, Jared Seacrest, who'd graduated from a much less prestigious business school he'd attended on a scholarship. He was the standard my father pitted me against. I thought it would be an easy win.

Being beaten out for promotion after promotion by Jared taught me humility. He consistently arrived at the office before me, left after I did, and worked almost every weekend. Looking back, I saw the rationale behind my father's methods. I grew up with money, and although I saw it as an asset, my father saw it as something that made people complacent. Jared was hungrier than I was, and that meant he prepared better for meetings, put more time into cultivating relationships with our clients, and was overall much more committed than I was in the beginning. Losing to him over and over woke me up. In time, resentment grew into admiration and eventually gratitude.

"Step up or step off" was something my father often said. Competing with Jared pushed me to do just that.

It could have been an ugly situation, but my father also cultivated a friendship between us. He encouraged us to play off each other's strengths rather than try to take each other down. Winning took on a deeper meaning when viewed in a collective manner.

When I began to excel, my father suggested Jared start his own e-commerce company, Seacrest Solutions. It would complement rather than compete with our business. Wenham Global invested generously in and partnered with Seacrest Solutions on many projects. In the industry, our companies were formidable in their own right. When either was challenged, they both pulled together and were indomitable. Despite market fluctuations, both companies were riding high and expanding.

It made no sense that my father would choose now to retire. His whole justification for it sounded like a late-life crisis, but I was doing my best to honor his wishes. He and I had butted heads many times in the past, and I'd often thought he was dead wrong. Things would never be easy between us because, according to him, we were too much alike. What others might've called hardheadedness, we called perseverance.

My phone vibrated. Jared. I accepted the call and put him on speakerphone. "Don't."

He laughed. "Time away from the office has done nothing for your personality, I see."

I didn't dignify his comment with a response. I couldn't even summon anger for how much amusement he was finding in my situation. If our roles were reversed, I likely would have done the same.

In a more serious tone, he said, "I had dinner with your father last night. He explained his reasoning behind temporarily cutting you loose."

"It's only temporary if I fulfill his requirements. Did he tell you what he wants from me? I have six months to get engaged, but not to anyone I'm currently dating. He wants me to find a 'normal' woman."

Jared chuckled. "So no models or heiresses. How can you possibly meet a normal woman? Oh, wait, walk down any street. The world is full of them."

"Very funny. I have no intention of getting married."

"You may change your mind if you expand your circle."

"Oh, I'm fine with meeting new women. I just have no desire to legally bind my life to anyone else's. Not now. Not in the future. Never."

"So what will you do? We both know how Hamilton gets when he thinks he's right. Are you prepared to watch him hand the business over to someone else? He would do it."

"I know he would."

Jared cleared his throat. "For transparency's sake, you need to know he asked me if I would want to buy out Wenham Global if you fail to get engaged. The only caveat was that I fulfill the same requirement."

It wasn't shocking that Jared would be my father's plan B, but that he'd already mentioned it to Jared was not a good sign. I now had another equally pressing question. "What did you say?"

"What do you think?"

"Ours is a multibillion-dollar company that would easily fold into yours. I have no idea."

"That's insulting. I said no."

"Because you know he's off his rocker?"

"No, because I would never do that to you." His claim was a far cry from the insults he'd tossed my way when my father had first hired him, but we'd both grown since then. If it came down to it, would he actually pass on buying our family's company for what would likely be a steal? Only he knew for sure.

"And you don't want to get married either."

He laughed. "There's that as well."

After a brief pause, I said, "My father hasn't been himself since he came back from those two funerals. I understand why Winston's hit him hard—they golfed together on a regular basis. I'm not as clear on why Rutger's funeral pushed him over the edge. I guess the deaths of friends happening so close together was too much."

"It was a wake-up call for him. Hamilton faced his mortality, and that can make a man question if the path he's on is the right one."

"Don't tell me you agree with what he's doing."

"Not at all, but after talking to him, I understand his reasoning. He's rethinking what he wants to do with the time he has left."

"My father is free to live the rest of his life any damn way he wants, as long as we don't all have to go on that ride with him."

"You might not have much of a choice."

I shook my head in disgust. "There's always a choice. I'm not exactly broke. I'll start over if I have to." Better than anyone else, he knew I meant it. The one thing my father had done exceedingly well was to push me beyond fear. It was a trait that served me well in business. Some called me cocky, but that term implied an attitude that was based on ego rather than aptitude.

"With the amount of work you've put into the company, no one would judge you if you fought to gain control of it via a legal battle. He technically didn't have the right to remove you."

Jared was correct. I had heavily invested my own money in the company, and with the right lawyers I might win—not just my position back but my father's as well. It wasn't a scenario I was willing to consider unless my father's behavior began to endanger himself or those around him. For now, he was simply acting irresponsibly. He was missing meetings, forgetting to return calls, and procrastinating on closing deals we had in progress. Normally I would have been in the office, but that was the second bombshell my father had dropped on me: he'd asked me to temporarily step away from our family company. I'd agreed to, because I didn't have much of a choice. That didn't mean I wasn't still very much involved. I had the people nearest him running damage control. It was a complicated situation. My father was a proud man who would be furious if he knew I was propping him up.

"I'm still acting president on paper, just on leave. Two funerals in a row would shake up any man. I'm certain that when my father's head clears, all of this foolishness will end." I wasn't actually certain about that at all, but the truth would have prolonged our discussion of a topic I wanted to wrap up.

"For your sake, I hope so."

"It's the only reason I agreed to take a leave. There is no winning head to head with him—you know that. Confronting him would only push him to do something more drastic to make his point."

"And if the board starts to lose confidence in him?"

"I'll deal with that if it happens, but I don't see this going that far."

"I'm here if you need me. No one wants to see your father's legacy tainted," Jared said.

"If things get ugly, you'll be the first call I make, but let's hope this ends up as nothing more than an unexpected vacation."

"Or that you find your soul mate."

I groaned. "It's all nonsense. He also wants me to find a hobby—an interest completely unrelated to work. He's never had one."

"Maybe that's the point."

"*You* don't have one."

"Hey, hey, this isn't about me."

"Well, it sure as hell isn't about me either. My life is fine just the way it is. Or was."

"He seems to genuinely want you to be happy."

"I *am* happy," I growled. "I'll be happ*ier* as soon as things return to normal."

"Are you at least enjoying your time off?"

"What do you think?"

"I think you should get your ass back to your office, because your father is not doing as well as he'd like us all to believe. He needs you."

"I tried to talk to him. He's making it impossible to be there for him. Doesn't want to see me until I can show up with proof that I'm making progress on his fucking demands."

"Lie."

"You think I haven't considered that? I was in Lockton the other day and asked a complete stranger if she was willing to sign a nondisclosure."

"Lockton? That's certainly throwing a wide net. So, you just went up to the first woman you came across and asked her to sign a nondisclosure?"

"She was gorgeous."

"Well, okay. That makes sense, then. What did she say?"

"She said no." I ran a hand over the back of my neck as images of her flitted through my head. She really had been stunning. Striking black hair. Dark-hazel eyes? No, gray eyes. Classically beautiful features and a tight little body. I remembered how certain she'd been that I would stand her up. Because other men had? What planet were they from? No one I knew would be a moment late to a date with a woman with her looks.

"I like her already."

"It wasn't my best moment. What the hell was I thinking? I wasn't. I sounded like I was looking for a prostitute. Thankfully she doesn't know who I am. Can you imagine that story hitting the news?"

"Why do I have a feeling I'll hear about this woman again?"

"You won't. Now, if there's nothing else you want, I need to return to watching sailboats pass while I question all of my own life choices." I was joking about the last part, but not the first. I was done talking about my father's mental state. I wasn't a worrier—never saw the point—but I was concerned about what the future held for all of us if my father didn't snap back to reality.

"If you want to bring a date home to meet Hamilton, I know several women who could pass for normal, and you wouldn't have to pay them."

"No, you don't, and I've already realized how insane the idea of paying someone to fool my father would be."

"I didn't say it was a good idea. All I'm saying is that if you do decide to go that route, it shouldn't be with a woman you pick up on the street."

"I didn't—whatever. Goodbye, Jared."

In a tone heavy with sarcasm, Jared said, "Piece of advice? If you do see this woman again, try to come across like less of a creeper."

I ended the call to the sound of Jared laughing. It was always annoying when he was right. Not that I would see the woman from the coffee shop again, but in general, I needed to remain calm and rational.

After returning my phone to the breast pocket of my suit, I sat back and closed my eyes. My father was mourning the loss of two friends. He was confused. Lying to him might have proven effective, but he and I had always been brutally honest with each other. There had to be another way.

"Gavin?" a female voice asked.

My eyes flew open, and I rose to my feet as I recognized the voice as one I hadn't expected to hear again. For a second I wondered if I'd drifted off to sleep and conjured her up, but she was wearing far too much clothing for that to be the case. "Riley, right?" I asked, as if there was a chance I might have forgotten her name. Damn, she was even more beautiful than I remembered. She was dressed in white jeans that hugged her curves in a way that sent my heart racing and a striped blue-denim shirt that was unbuttoned just low enough to bring a flush to my cheeks. When she smiled, my mind went completely blank. For an instant there were just the two of us and a pulsing attraction unlike anything I'd felt before.

"I hope I didn't ruin your nap." She tucked her hands into the front pockets of her jeans as she referenced the bench behind me.

"Just soaking up some sun."

"Lunch break?"

I took a moment to decide which course to take. Considering where we'd met, she should have looked out of place in my world, but she had a simple style that transitioned well. Crisp. Clean. Classic. The nondisclosure-fake-fiancée idea might have been off the table, but if she was interested in becoming the manner in which I took my mind off my current situation, I wouldn't throw her out of my bed. "I have the week off."

The wind blew a section of her hair across her face. She tucked it behind one of her ears. She really did have the most incredible eyes. "Well, I hope I didn't disturb you. I was just heading in, recognized you, and thought I should say hello. I'm new to the building."

My eyebrows rose. "You live here?"

"Yes?"

The uncertainty of her response paired with an awkward shrug of her shoulder was briefly confusing. The Terraanum Building boasted some of the most expensive apartments in Boston. When the most likely explanation occurred to me, disappointment followed. "Your boyfriend does," I said with certainty.

"No boyfriend." She blushed and looked away.

So he's married. "I honestly don't care."

Her gaze flew back to meet mine. "Wow. Rude. No wonder you require a nondisclosure. You wouldn't want people spilling the secret that you're an ass." She took a step away.

I should have let her go. I couldn't. Instead I reached out and touched her arm. "What I meant was, your personal life is none of my business."

"That doesn't actually sound any better." She looked down at my hand and frowned. I broke contact.

The world was full of beautiful women. There was no need to steal one from another man. There was something about this one, though, that brought out a territorial side of me I would have said I didn't have. I had to ask: "Is he good to you?"

"Who?" She was either a very good liar or I was misreading the situation.

"The man who owns the apartment you're staying in."

There it was—that frown again. "I own it. Me."

"Generous of him."

Her eyes darkened. "Yes, it was. And unnecessary, because I prefer my place in Lockton—my neighbors are friendlier."

So she'd held on to her old place. That spoke volumes about where she thought things were headed with whoever was payrolling her time in the Terraanum. "Friendly. Is that what he allows you to be when he's not around?" The whole you-would-stand-me-up act had likely been just that . . . something she used to pick up men on the side. Nothing unheard of for a young woman in her situation. Security must have come from looking one man ahead. I hated the idea of her with some old geezer, though. She didn't have the appearance of a gold digger, but perhaps that was her appeal.

Her hands went to her hips. "Why does everything you say sound like an insult?"

She had me there. There was zero chance of things progressing between us now that I knew her deal, so the truth wouldn't make a difference. "I had a different impression of you, and I don't like being wrong."

"I had a different impression of you as well." Her expression turned sad. "I wished you could find whatever it was that would make you happy, but I have to stop worrying so much about what other people are going through. I have the right to be happy too. My decisions, who I choose to spend time with, who I care about, should not affect anyone else's life."

I raised my hands in mock surrender. "I'm not here to judge you."

She stepped closer and tapped me in the chest. "Good, because love shouldn't be like that. It shouldn't come with conditions or guilt. We should be able to all get along." As if realizing the aggressiveness of her stance, she lowered her hand and stepped back. "Sorry. I didn't mean to go off like that."

"Not a problem." It wasn't, but I couldn't say why. I was turned on and completely confused. She'd essentially said she loved her sugar daddy. Why wasn't that enough for me to lose interest in her? "My intention wasn't to upset or insult you."

She shrugged, looking lost for a moment in her own thoughts. She glanced at the building behind her. "You live here too?"

"I do." I also owned the building, but she didn't need to know that.

She gave me another long look, but this time it wasn't just desire I saw in her eyes. There was an openness in her gaze, uncomplicated, warm—drawing me in. Her hand shot out in my direction. "Then let's start over. Hi, I'm Riley Ragsdale. Nice to meet you."

I shook her hand, then continued to hold it. The temptation to brush my lips across hers was almost too strong to resist. I told myself her air of innocence was an act, but I understood why a man might pay a fortune to keep her around. "Nice to meet you, Riley. I'm Gavin Wenham." If she recognized the name, it didn't show in her expression.

I almost felt sorry for the man she was currently with. Whoever he was, she wouldn't be with him long.

CHAPTER THREE

RILEY

When it came to men, I had a type. I gravitated toward ones with easy smiles and upbeat personalities. They tended to come in hot, compliment me until I agreed to see them, then shower me with little gifts. Unlike my super-independent best friend, I liked having a door opened for me. Maybe because I never had a father, I romanticized what a good family man would be like. Teagan and I laughed about our differences, but in the end we agreed that the beauty of the modern world was that she was free to be her and I was free to be me.

The problem with nice guys was that sometimes they were . . . *too nice?*

Before my latest dry spell, I'd dated a wonderful man. Fun. Attentive. Handsome in a conservative way. We shared a lot of laughs, until he broke it off because his sister said she didn't like me. The irony was, his close relationship with his family had been one of the things I'd originally found attractive about him.

What didn't she like about me? There was the neighborhood I grew up in; that my mother was on government aid; and, oh yes, that my brother was an exotic dancer. She'd confused my job as a paid bridesmaid with being an escort. Last insult for the road? She accused me of being after her brother's money because he'd recently paid off the last of his college loans and had been promoted to a bank-manager position.

Life sure was one crazy ride. What would she decide to not like about me if it ever became public knowledge that I was Dominic Corisi's little sister? I was sure I didn't want to know.

Gavin Wenham was *not* a nice man. Confusing—yes. Rude—absolutely. He was not my type at all. There was no sane reason I was standing there, holding his hand longer than I should have, offering to start over.

But I was.

I couldn't help myself. He was attracted to me, that much was obvious, even if he didn't look happy about it. Or, perhaps his unhappiness had nothing to do with me. Either way, I found myself drawn to him. "Did you find what you were looking for?" I asked.

"What?"

"The other day. You said you were looking for something that made no damn sense. I was curious if you'd found it." Was it wrong to hope he hadn't?

"I didn't, but I may have found something better." His thumb moved to caress the inside of my wrist. That's how little it took to send waves of heat cascading through me. No wonder I couldn't walk away. Rude or not, my body was humming for him. If he could get me that excited from such an innocent touch . . .

Stop. I had so much on my mind that I didn't initially understand his comment about who might have purchased my apartment. I heard his questions through the filter of the guilt I felt about being there. My rant was all the pent-up things I wanted to say to my mother. When she'd asked me where I was headed that day, I told her I was meeting a bride in Boston. It was partly true, a lie of omission only, since one of my past clients *had* called and asked to see me. What she didn't need to know was that I'd also made plans to have dinner with my brother Dominic and his family.

As I went over Gavin's questions again, I realized he thought I'd let a man buy the apartment for me. He had no way of knowing my relationship to Dominic, so that left only an insulting assumption about the kind of person he assumed I was. I stepped back and glanced at the towering building behind Gavin. It was a glass monstrosity, cold, proudly dominating the area. I couldn't imagine ever feeling at home in it. My gaze returned to his face. If we'd met at another time in my life, when things weren't already so complicated, I might have been tempted to try to change his opinion of me. I was already at capacity, though, when it came to worrying about what people thought of me. "It was nice to see you again."

"Have dinner with me tonight," he said in a low growl that sent a flush up my neck.

Apparently being a kept woman wasn't a turnoff for him. I tried to summon disgust, but my body had no problem with his questionable moral code. I forced a smile. "Sorry, I already have plans."

"Cancel them."

Bold. Okay, that's hot. But still not happening. I shook my head. "I would, but I don't want to. Goodbye, Gavin Wenham." Without waiting for him to respond, I turned and walked away. I didn't look back to see if he was watching me. I knew he was.

With every step I took, I pushed Gavin further out of my thoughts. There were too many more important things going on in my life to worry about what he thought of me.

I made my way past security at the entrance of the building to an elevator designated for only the top floors. Only the best was good enough for Dominic, even when it came to buying for a sister he'd only recently learned he had. I looked into a facial-recognition camera, and the elevator doors swept open. Somewhere on the bottom of my purse lay a key chain with the simple metal key I used to open my apartment in Lockton. *Teagan would hate this building.* Although she was a tech genius, she didn't trust computers to not take over the world.

Funny how it was possible to love and hate something at the same time. I was grateful for all Dominic wanted to do for me, but I wished he'd heard me when I said I didn't need a place in Boston. His daughter, Judy, told me his generosity was his way of showing how much I meant to him. His daily phone calls would have been enough to do that. With how good he was being to both me and my family, I didn't feel like I could say no. Because of him, my mother was finally going to get the surgery she needed. All he wanted in return was for me to spend more time with him and his family. Did that require my owning one of the best apartments in one of the most exclusive apartment buildings in the city? Couldn't I be his little sister without also having a floor-to-ceiling view of the bay?

When the elevator opened to the white-and-gold-tiled foyer of my apartment, I was conflicted. I stepped out of the elevator and put my purse on a table that probably cost more than the tuition of most four-year colleges.

Nothing in the apartment reflected my taste. It was ultramodern, mostly white, with splashes of color that jarred me every time I caught one out of the corner of my eye. He'd had it decorated for me, and I didn't have the heart to tell him that the word "gaudy" came to mind every time I entered it.

As I looked around, I began to second-guess my decision to meet Eugenia at my place instead of hers. She was by far the wealthiest of the brides I'd worked for. She, the only child of a billionaire real estate developer from out west, had married Edward Thinsley, who was an entirely different kind of wealthy—old Boston money. When I'd first met her, I hadn't understood why anyone with all that money would need to *hire* a bridesmaid, but when I stepped into her life, I found very little to envy. Her father was on his third wife. Her mother was on her second husband. Both were too busy to be bothered with planning their daughter's wedding. Edward's parents didn't approve of Eugenia and yet wanted to be far more involved in deciding every detail of the wedding than any parent should be. Eugenia's friends, if one could call them that, all seemed more concerned about what others thought of them than being there for Eugenia.

Hired bridesmaid? I was more than that. Hired friend, confidante, mediator, and keeper of the tissues for when Eugenia slipped away from the others to have a good cry. She loved Edward, but there wasn't much else in her life that brought her joy. We'd talked on the phone a few times since her wedding, mostly because whenever she called, I felt sorry that she didn't have her own Teagan. Every woman should have at least one ride-or-die girlfriend.

When Eugenia said she wanted to see me, I assumed she wanted to meet where we always had—her home. She didn't. She said what she wanted to discuss with me was a private matter. Could she come to me?

In Lockton? I didn't see how that would work out, so I gave her my Boston address. If she were visiting my other apartment, I would be rushing around putting things away, but I hadn't moved much into this place. The bathroom had a few toiletries. The dresser in the bedroom contained a few articles of clothing. One expensive dress hung in the closet above a matching pair of high heels—all gifts from my niece Judy, who was convinced a woman should always be prepared.

I walked across the pristine white rug and opened the double doors that led to the balcony, letting in a fresh breeze off the water. Inhaling appreciatively, I turned and used the intercom on the wall to call down to the kitchen. I ordered Eugenia's favorite comfort foods along with her favorite brand of bottled water. Wasn't all water the same? Not to people with money.

I couldn't picture her downing a beer with me in my favorite bar. She probably couldn't picture me doing it either. I'd never shown her that side of me because that wasn't what she'd paid for.

Seeing her again would be interesting.

The intercom on the wall announced, "A Mrs. Thinsley is here to see you, Miss Ragsdale."

"Send her up, please," I responded.

I returned to the foyer to greet Eugenia. As she stepped out of the elevator, her smile was tentative. "I'm early. I hope that's okay." Her short hair swung forward as she came to an abrupt stop in front of me. "Casual elegance" was how I would have described her sense of fashion. Each item she wore had likely been tailored to fit her, but her slacks and silk top whispered money rather than screamed it.

"Perfect timing, actually." I almost put my hand out to shake hers, but there was something in her eyes that made me change to a warm hug. "It's so good to see you again."

She hugged me back like we were old friends. "You have no idea how much I've missed you."

Well . . . okay, then. After stepping back, I referenced the living room behind us. "Same. Would you like to sit inside or outside?"

"It's such a beautiful day—let's sit out." We walked together through the open double doors and onto the balcony. "Wow, look at this view. Absolutely stunning. When I saw the address, I imagined a beautiful place, but this is truly impressive."

"Thank you." I wasn't sure what else one would say to that. Thankfully, the intercom buzzed, announcing the arrival of my order. I asked for it to be brought in. When I'd first started using the service, I'd bolted for the door and practically set the table myself, but I was learning. Helping only made it awkward all around. Eugenia and I looked out over the water while the table was set behind us. I waved and mouthed "Thank you" to the familiar staff member. He acknowledged it with a smile and nod. In the building, tipping was done monthly, and Dominic said he would cover it. I had no idea how well Dominic did or didn't tip, but everyone on the staff always seemed happy to help, so I assumed he was generous.

Eugenia gave me a side glance. "I had no idea you had money."

I didn't want to lie, but nor did I want to tell her too much. "I don't, but some of my family does. This was a gift."

She searched my face. "A lot of what didn't make sense before does now. No wonder you weren't intimidated by my mother-in-law. I hated how she spoke to you when she found out I'd hired you. Edward should never have told her. Or I should have lied to him about who you were. I'm sorry I didn't."

"Water under the bridge. How is she treating you?" Eugenia had never been anything but kind to me. I didn't hold her responsible for the lack of class her mother-in-law had displayed.

"Same as before. Edward told her to be nicer to me, but it didn't change anything. She's started calling me his 'first wife'—like she can't wait for him to choose his next." Her bottom lip quivered.

Bitch. I touched her arm. "Miserable people enjoy making other people miserable." I wanted to kick Edward's ass for not doing more to protect his wife. I'd dated enough men, though, who had claimed to care about me but lacked the testicles to go to bat for me. Sadly, I understood how Eugenia felt. "Is that what you wanted to talk to me about?"

"Yes and no." Eugenia looked behind me at the food on the table. "You ordered french onion soup."

"I did."

"My grandmother used to make it for me when I was sick . . . or just sad."

"I remember."

Eugenia burst into tears. "And you ordered it for me."

I rubbed her back and used the same soothing tone that had proven successful at calming her in the weeks leading up to her wedding. "Of course I did. What's wrong, Eugenia?" If she told me Edward was not only spineless but also a cheater, I might have excused myself to go kick his ass.

She straightened, wiped the tears from the corners of her eyes, and said, "I'm pregnant."

I hugged her. "That's wonderful."

"Is it?" She sniffed. "I haven't told Edward yet because I don't want his mother to know. What does that say about our marriage?"

Nothing good, in my mind, but I didn't say that. Instead I took a moment to think of something that might bring her some comfort. "That it's not perfect, but no marriage is."

Her shoulders slumped. "I want to be happy about it. I should be happy, but all I can picture is how I won't be pregnant to the Thinsley standards. Nothing I do is right. What if they treat my child the same way?"

"Edward wouldn't let that happen."

She shook with emotion. "You don't know that."

I don't. "You're right. I'm sorry."

She turned toward me and took one of my hands in hers. "You're the first friend I've had who has been honest with me. Everyone else says what they think I want to hear. I need some of that honesty now. I'm thinking about leaving Edward."

I let out an audible breath. "That's a big decision."

"I know. That's why I need to know if you think it's the right one."

Me? I'd never even been engaged. My mother was proof that it was important to be careful when choosing a partner, but Edward wasn't as bad as my father had been. People said marriage was work and was supposed to be forever. How soon should a person give up when one of them wasn't holding up their end of the deal? They were having a baby. Surely that was a reason to fight even harder for it to work. "Have you considered marriage counseling?"

"Edward doesn't believe in it. Thinsleys don't admit to having weaknesses."

"What does your father think?"

"I can't talk to him about Edward. If he thought he wasn't treating me right, he'd kill him. He's too busy to come visit us, but he'd arrange his funeral."

Yikes. "How pregnant are you?"

"Early enough that most would consider it too soon to share the news with anyone beyond my husband."

I'd spent time with Edward. He wasn't a bad guy and seemed to truly love Eugenia. This was all disappointing to hear. "What if you had this conversation with Edward instead of me? He loves you. He deserves a chance to make things right."

She wrung her hands together. "I don't want him to be better to me only because I'm pregnant. I want him to want to protect me."

As someone who was currently lying to her mother because she didn't want to hurt her, I had a certain amount of sympathy for Edward. But I understood Eugenia's point as well. "I can't tell you what you should do. Only you know that."

Eugenia was quiet for a moment, then said, "Edward says people don't respect people who don't demand to be respected. He thinks how people treat me is my fault."

Edward needs to shut his ignorant mouth. "I don't know what you're looking for me to say, Eugenia."

"Tell me—is it me?" she asked in a broken voice. "If it is, then I shouldn't leave him. I'd be breaking up our family, only to repeat this cycle with someone else I can't figure out how to get to treat me better. I have this fantasy in my head where everyone is happy and getting along. How do I get to that place? I've spent my life trying to make everyone else happy, but I can't live like that anymore. I just don't know how to live any other way."

Her words ricocheted through me. I'd always believed that very little in life happened by chance. People came into each other's lives for a reason. Eugenia and I were in very different places but asking ourselves the same kinds of questions. "I don't, either, but I'm here for you if you need me."

Tears filled her eyes again. "I don't understand why you took the job as my bridesmaid when you clearly don't need the money, but I'm so grateful you did. When I was little, we moved around a lot. I had tutors and nannies, but no real friends. You're the first person I've felt I could be myself with without worrying that you'd judge me."

"You never feel that way with Edward?"

She shrugged. "He doesn't want the real me."

"Then he's a fool. We all doubt ourselves, Eugenia. We all make mistakes, get our feelings hurt by what people say, and hide what we don't want to talk about. Nothing you're saying is crazy—it's just all a symptom of something called being human."

"I wish I were more like you. I heard the way you spoke to my mother-in-law. You're fearless."

I sighed. "It's easy to be that way when it doesn't matter. My mother doesn't know about this apartment or half of what I've been up to lately. I've lied to practically everyone I know because I don't want to upset anyone, but I'm exactly where you are. I don't want to live like that anymore."

"Do you want to talk about it?"

I considered whether laying my problems out for her would help or confuse her more, and decided the only kind of friendship worth having was a real one. "I do. Let's eat, and let me tell you one crazy tale that will have you feeling better about your situation."

She left smiling after our lunch together, but I wished I'd had better answers to her questions—as well as my own.

CHAPTER FOUR

GAVIN

Seated at the bar on the first floor of the Terraanum, I sipped a whiskey I hadn't bothered to ask the name of. Normally it mattered, but my thoughts that evening were far from the drink in my hand.

The ease with which Riley had dismissed my invitation to dinner still irked me. I wasn't under the misconception that every woman on the planet found me attractive, but I hadn't imagined the sexual tension between us. She was interested, so what was holding her back?

Loyalty to the man she supposedly loved? I highly doubted that, or that love had anything to do with their arrangement. I downed more of the whiskey than I meant to and coughed as it burned its way down my throat. "What is this shit?" I asked the bartender.

He looked behind him for the bottle, and I realized he was new. "Braig Club. It's what we serve when someone doesn't specify a brand."

"It's disgusting. Never serve it again."

"Okay, sir." His tone was polite, but I could see he had no idea who I was.

"What's your name?"

His eyes rounded. "Kenyon Sanders."

"Kenyon, I'm sure you're only doing what you were trained to do, and that's the shame of it. For clarification, though, there shouldn't be a top-shelf distinction at this bar. Every liquor back there should be quality. Every drink should remind the customer why they chose to live here. If it doesn't, someone isn't doing their job right, and I'm not happy."

Kenyon visibly swallowed. "Yes, sir."

I wasn't upset with him, just with myself for looking away from the Terraanum long enough for issues in quality to appear. My father made it his business to know the people who worked for him. I'd done the same when I opened the apartment building, but I'd dropped the ball as things at my family's company got busier.

I held out my hand for him to shake. "Gavin Wenham." The kid had a strong handshake I approved of. He was also smart enough to already be pouring me a better drink. "Have you been bartending long?"

"A few months."

"Are you a student?"

He nodded while wiping down the bar with a cloth. "I'm studying dental medicine at Tufts."

"Good school."

He smiled. "Expensive, too, but this job helps. My mother says bartending should count as an internship since it's just another form of anesthetizing."

Smart and funny. He'll go far. I rolled the liquid around in my new glass. A little numbness was what I'd been seeking, but it was losing its appeal. I took out my card and a pen and jotted a quick note on the back of it. "Take this to human resources. We have educational grants for all of our employees, but if you're new, you probably missed the deadline for this year. Tell them we spoke, and they'll help you out. If they say they can't, you have my number."

"Thank you." The man took the card and looked at it like he couldn't believe it. "Thank you so much."

"Just do me a favor. From now on, treat every single patron of this bar as if they were me. Serve them the best, or don't serve them at all."

"Absolutely." He pocketed my card. "I heard this was a good place to work, and I can really see why now. Thanks again."

I took a final sip of my whiskey, choosing to leave the rest, and stood. "You're welcome, Kenyon. Keep up the good work."

I had just exited the bar when I caught a glimpse of black hair and one hell of an ass still in those white jeans that left little to a man's imagination. Sweet torture. Mine wasn't the only head that turned as she made her way across the foyer. Even as I told myself not to, I followed her.

Keith and Bill at the security desk sat up straighter as she passed. She waved to them like they were friends. They waved back with big goofy smiles on their faces, and I shook my head. Exactly how "friendly" was this woman? Both of the security guards had worked for me for years. They were retired military, and I couldn't recall ever seeing them go beyond formal politeness with a resident. At the door, she stopped and exchanged words with the doorman. He was an older gentleman, but even he wasn't immune to her charm. Whatever she said had him laughing and blushing as he opened the door for her.

I had to know. I walked to the door but motioned for the doorman to not open it. Arms folded across my chest, I watched Riley chat with the driver of a limousine before sliding in. He was older, but a wall of muscle nonetheless. I expected to see him smile as well, but his expression remained closed. Did his stiff and formal manner reflect that of his employer?

I fought the urge to run out before the vehicle pulled away and demand that she not go to the man who had sent for her. It was a ridiculous urge that I didn't give in to. Seeing her as happy as she appeared made me wonder if I was wrong to get involved with her at all.

I wasn't interested in anything more than a fuck.

The way she floated through the foyer, laughing and smiling her way to the limo, made me think she might not want to be saved from whatever relationship she was in. I didn't like that thought—not at all.

I really didn't like how much it bothered me that she might be happy with someone else. I was not that guy. I dated, but never anyone exclusively. Jealousy was something I didn't believe in. Who someone had been with before me or who they chose to be with after me had never bothered me. Women were an enjoyable distraction, but never more than that.

So what the hell was wrong with me? Why was I standing at the door of the Terraanum like some lovesick puppy waiting for his person to return? Disgusting. Unacceptable. I turned to the doorman. "What did she say, Fred?"

My question seemed to take him by surprise. "Sorry, sir?"

"Just before you opened the door. What did Miss Ragsdale say to you?"

The blush returned to his face. He touched his tie. "She said blue looks good on me because it brings out the color in my eyes."

I frowned. Fred was in his late sixties and married. His wife would smack him into next week if she saw that smitten expression on his face. I couldn't blame him, though. Riley Ragsdale was making me act foolishly as well. "Did she say where she was going?" I hated that I'd voiced the question, but that didn't mean I didn't listen extra hard for the answer.

Fred glanced toward where the limo had been. "No, but she sure seemed happy about going."

That much was fucking clear. I growled, turned on my heel, and headed toward the elevator to my penthouse apartment. I told myself I didn't care where she was going or who she was meeting.

Once I was seated on my couch, I tried to read over emails, but my thoughts kept returning to Riley Ragsdale. I took out my phone, swiped through my contact list, and hoped one of the women I'd been with recently would tempt me enough to call her for a hookup.

What seemed like an intense interest in a woman I knew almost nothing about was likely more of a byproduct of the uniqueness of my situation. I was frustrated on more than one front, and I had far too much time on my hands to think. I didn't normally have the time or energy to think about much outside my responsibilities at Wenham Global.

But time was all I'd have until my father came to his senses. Time, and the Terraanum. It was one of the few things I'd done on my own with my own money. In the beginning I was invested in every decision, from its design to the hiring of staff. I was never the reflective type, but those were good days. They required me to carve out time here and there for myself, but I enjoyed the process of creating something from the ground up. The demands of my role at my family's business naturally turned my focus, and the ripple effect of that was that the Terraanum bar had started serving bottom-shelf liquor. It had been almost a year since I'd stayed in this penthouse. My apartment on the other side of town was closer to my office at Wenham Global. Staying there was simply more practical. The changes since I'd been away, however, were proof that regardless of the quality of the employee, no one ever cares for someone else's business as well as the owner does. *Things begin to fall apart as soon as one looks away.*

The whole situation had me irritated with myself as well as with the building's management. I sent a text to my top man in charge and told him to gather his team together for an early meeting the next day.

Sex would have been a perfect diversion for the evening. It shouldn't have mattered which partner I chose to have it with. For me to save a woman's number, she had to not only be great in bed, but also drama-free. Any one of the women in my phone were reliable good times who would come over if they were free and know to not spend the night.

Simple.

Easy.

Apparently not what I wanted. I tossed my phone down on the cushion beside me. *What is my problem?*

Riley is good looking, but not better looking than any of the women I could have here tonight. She throws the word "love" around but isn't above trying to meet men on the side. Regardless of what her arrangement is with the man who bought her apartment for her, she's trouble with a capital T.

Why can't I get her out of my thoughts?

I had access to all the building's records. With a few clicks I'd signed in to the main system. *First, Riley Ragsdale, which apartment did your lover buy you?*

All her information was there, including her phone number—not that I would use it. I reread her address, sure it was wrong at first. There were two penthouse apartments in the building. Together they spanned the entire top floor, allowing unobstructed views of the bay on one side as well as the coveted Boston skyline on the other. Only my side was intended to be privately owned. The other was supposed to be kept open as a business perk for visiting politicians, royals, and celebrities associated with Wenham Global.

It had always been listed for sale, but for an amount so high no one in their right mind would ever buy it. Had someone negotiated the price down? If so, whoever okayed that deal wouldn't be employed tomorrow. I looked through the sales documents as well as the funds available in the building's account, and my hands clenched the sides of my laptop.

No mistake—someone had paid the asking price in full.

The purchase had been made via a law office. If I wanted to, I could find out who they represented, but did I want to take things that far?

I knew rich men often kept a woman on the side, but it took a certain level of wealth to keep one in the style that Riley was enjoying. A man like that could cause a lot of trouble, not just for me, but also my father. If she mattered to me, that wouldn't stop me, but . . .

I didn't do relationships.

Was fucking some random woman really worth the drama that would likely follow?

CHAPTER FIVE

RILEY

My thoughts were still on Eugenia as Mr. Tuttle drove me to my brother's home. I lowered the dividing window and moved to sit closer to it.

"Mr. Tuttle?"

"Yes?"

"Are you married?"

"Yes."

"Happily?"

He met my eyes in the rearview mirror. "Yes."

I shifted closer. "Do you mind if I ask you a question?"

His lack of response was a little discouraging, but I was desperate to talk out how Eugenia's marital issues had left me feeling.

I asked, "A friend of mine asked me for advice today, and I didn't know what to say. She's married, and her mother-in-law says hateful things to her. She wants her husband to defend her, but he doesn't. He says it's her fault for not standing up for herself. You're a husband. Is there something she could say to him that would wake him up?"

After a pause, Mr. Tuttle said, "The most dangerous place to wander into is someone else's marriage."

I nodded. "You're right. She came to me, though. And she's pregnant. I didn't know what to say."

He met my gaze again. "Tell her it's time to grow up."

My mouth rounded. I had expected Mr. Tuttle to say something supportive. "She's doing the best she can."

He shrugged and returned his attention to the road.

"She's too nice to defend herself. She wants his family to like her." When Mr. Tuttle didn't respond, I added, "I do want to hear your opinion. I may not agree with it, but I'm asking because I really do want to help her."

He sighed. "If your friend lies down in the road, a car will eventually run over her. She can hate the car, or she can stand up and get out of the road."

"So you think she should leave him?"

"I didn't say that."

"Maybe the driver of the car should watch where she's going."

"Or maybe your friend needs a more realistic view of how roads work."

I don't agree. Families don't have to be like that. "Her husband needs to talk to his mother again."

"Have you ever tried to correct your mother?"

That took a little of the fire out of my fight. I had, and I knew what a futile exercise it could be. "So, you agree with her husband? How people treat a person is their own fault?" I didn't believe my mother deserved how my bio father had treated her. I'd never believe that.

Mr. Tuttle turned to pull into the long driveway that led to my brother's home. "I think your friend's husband is an ass, and his mother sounds jealous of her, but your friend married into that family, so she put herself on that road. My only advice to her would be to not lie down."

He parked and opened the limo door while I was still mulling over his words. "Thank you, Mr. Tuttle, for listening."

"My wife has taught me well." The sudden twinkle in his eye lit up his face, and I was sure he was about to smile.

The front door of the limestone megamansion opened, and my niece Judy ran down the steps to meet me. She hugged me tightly.

I hugged her back just as enthusiastically. Judy Corisi was the oldest of Dominic's children. When I first met her, I struggled to connect with her. Every conversation we had felt like a competition. Judy needed to be the smartest person in the room, and if there was any question as to whether she was, she did outrageous things to prove herself. Teagan saw through Judy's bravado to the insecurities driving them. There was no room for mediocrity in Judy's life. She was expected to excel, and that was a weight that had never been placed on my shoulders. I went from being intimidated by her to feeling protective of her. Although she was twenty, she'd lived a sheltered life. "Hey, I didn't know you'd be here. How are your classes?"

"Amazing," she said with a huge smile. "No one knows who I am. I walk around like a regular person. I've even met people who don't like me. It's everything I hoped it would be."

I rolled my eyes, but not in an unkind way. *Like a regular person? Oh, these Corisis.* The way they saw the world was a consequence of the insulated way they lived. We were all the sum of what we'd experienced, and Judy had lived a life of luxury like few had. "As someone who has been a regular person since birth, I'm glad you're enjoying the experience."

Judy frowned. "Are you making fun of me?"

"Absolutely," I answered without hesitation, but I softened my words with a smile.

It took a moment, but she smiled back. "You know what I meant."

I hugged her again. "I do, but what kind of aunt would I be if I didn't give you shit when you deserve it?"

She mimicked how I'd rolled my eyes skyward, then chuckled. One of Judy's most likable traits was that she wasn't above laughing at herself as well. "Why did I come home tonight? Oh, wait, it was to see you. So I guess I don't mind the shade you throw."

Movement at the door caught my attention, and I waved. Almost eight years old, Judy's little brother was already skipping grades and was considered brilliant, but he was also shy. He waved back without stepping out of the house.

I put my hands on my hips and said cheerfully, "Is that any kind of welcome? Get on down here."

He hesitated, then quickly made his way down the stairs to me as well. "Hi, Riley."

I ducked down to his height and smiled. "Hi, Leonardo. Did you hear about the hotel they just built on the moon? Nice place, but no atmosphere."

The corners of his mouth curled in a smile. "I'll tell that one to my astrophysics tutor. He won't laugh, though. He says humor is the weapon of the unarmed."

If any other child claimed to be studying astrophysics, I would have assumed he was lying, but both Dominic and his wife, Abby, encouraged their children to explore the world and all the knowledge in it freely. Rather than being spoiled by the opportunity, Leonardo seemed to already feel the heavy responsibility of that. We'd only hung out alone a few times, but when we had, we did wild things like fly kites, collect pretty rocks from the beach, and throw sticks into streams to see which would go faster. It was strange to do such mundane activities while Leonardo's bodyguards watched over us, but he seemed to really enjoy himself. "Laughing has definitely helped me stay sane when I was in tough situations I couldn't do anything about. Don't let your tutor's lack of a sense of humor rob you of yours. Life is too short to be taken so seriously. In fact, I'll race you two up the stairs."

Leonardo looked to Judy as if checking if this was okay.

Judy bent in preparation of a sprint. "You're on."

The three of us bolted up the steps. They took the lead near the top, with Leonardo beating Judy, but just barely. We all came to a breathless, laughing stop at the door.

Dominic and Abby met us just inside the door. She gave me a warm hug. Before meeting Dominic, she'd been a teacher, and I could see that. There was a natural warmth to her that always put me at ease.

I hugged Dominic. It would have felt weird if I didn't, but I always wondered if he actually wanted me to. From what I knew about his childhood, it hadn't been an easy one, and because of it, Dominic always appeared on his guard. Abby told me she fell in love with him as soon as she met the kind man behind the growl. I could see that. His resting expression was a harsh one, but when he looked at any member of his family, there was love in his eyes. I saw it even when he looked at me, and it made me wish I'd known of him earlier in our lives. There were times in his life when he must have felt so alone. Kal and I could have been there for him.

"How was the drive?" Abby asked as we made our way deeper into the house.

"Great," I said. "Mr. Tuttle is so nice."

"I'm glad to hear that," Dominic said. "The cook said dinner is ready to serve. Are you hungry?"

"Always."

Abby sent Leonardo off to wash his hands. Judy stepped away with him. I walked with Abby and Dominic into a dining room that could easily have hosted fifty people. Our places were all set at one end of the table. While we had a moment without Leonardo, I decided to see if Dominic's advice would match Mr. Tuttle's.

"Dominic, I have a question."

We stopped beside the table. "Okay."

"Do you think people only treat other people as well as they demand to be treated?"

Dominic rose in stature, and his eyes narrowed. "Who isn't treating you well?"

"Oh no, it's not me. I'm asking for a friend."

"A friend." Dominic repeated the word in a harsh tone.

Abby laid a hand on his arm. "Riley, what Dominic is trying to say is that we are here for you. If it's you or 'a friend' who's having issues with someone, don't feel that there's anything you can't tell us."

"I really am asking for a friend. She's having trouble with her moth-er-in-law and asked me for advice. I've never been married, so I wasn't sure what to say." I turned to Dominic. "What would you do if your mother wasn't nice to Abby?"

"It would never happen," Dominic said.

Abby looked up at her husband, then at me. "Family is compli-cated, Riley. Marriage is too. Solutions to situations like that aren't one size fits all. Rosella has never been unkind to me, but if she ever were, I don't think I would mention it to Dom."

Dominic frowned. "And why not?"

Abby smiled. "Because you're a fixer, and not every situation is best handled that way. Sometimes women have to talk things out. Your friend might need to sit down with her mother-in-law and ask her if there's a problem."

I grimaced. "I'm pretty sure they're beyond that. The problem my friend has is that she wants her husband to stand up for her, but he doesn't."

"Do you want me to talk to him?" Dominic asked.

My eyes rounded.

Abby laughed. "No, Dominic, I don't believe that's what Riley wants."

I imagined what Eugenia's husband's reaction would be if he had a visit from my brother. He'd probably piss himself. "Yeah, please don't do that."

"Then what *do* you want?" Dominic asked in a tone that I imagined intimidated most people.

"Some big brother advice." His demeanor softened almost instantly, and he became the version of Dominic that kept me coming back. Beneath all his gruff questions was a man who wanted his sister to be happy and safe. How could I not love him for that? "I'd like to help my friend, plus I may find myself in that situation one day and need to know if there's a good way to deal with it."

"Anyone who treated you like that wouldn't for long," Dominic said in a matter-of-fact tone. Threats came easily to him, but I understood what had made him that way. His mother had run from our father, leaving him and his sister to face Antonio and his fury alone. He was a survivor who tended to come ready to fight until he'd assessed a situation as a safe one.

Abby slipped under her husband's arm and hugged him. "The secret to any relationship is communication, respect, and honesty. Without those, even the best relationship begins to crumble. Dominic and I don't always agree on things, but we do our best to hear each other. That's not something that happens automatically. You have to work at it. When you love someone, you don't give up on them just because they don't hear you right the first time."

I liked that. I also kind of liked how Dominic would take my side even in an imaginary dispute. The Corisis were a powerful family, and they definitely had an edge to them, but I wished my mother could see this side of Dominic. If she did, it would be as hard for her to imagine him ever hurting any of us as it was for me. He was not his father. I'd tried to tell her that, but she never heard me.

Maybe it was time to try to tell her again.

Judy and Leonardo rejoined us, and the conversation naturally flowed to lighter topics. Although we were seated at a large, formal table and waited on by house staff, the atmosphere was relaxed.

Leonardo made a case for why he needed a pet lizard. Although his request wasn't granted, I did admire the amount of research he'd done on the various species. Abby was the wall of resistance that no amount of persuasion could break through. I watched Dominic's expression while his wife and son debated the pros and cons of a reptile in the house. He really was the softie his wife claimed he was. Without Abby, the household would have been chin deep in reptiles.

I'd learned enough about both Abby and Dominic to understand their differing approaches. From my experience, all parents wanted better for their children than they'd had, and they attempted to deliver that in their own way. Abby lost both of her parents early and then raised her younger sister on her own. She told me once that what she wished her childhood had had more of was structure. Dominic's childhood was an abusive one at the hands of our father. He swore he would never let anger into his home. What he wanted most was for his family to be happy, and that made it difficult when it came to refusing them anything.

When Leonardo sighed in defeat, Judy walked over and hugged her brother, telling him she knew of a store that had robotic reptiles. He perked up at that and asked if any of them were large enough to ride on.

"We'll find out," Dominic promised.

"Can I get one if they have one?" Leonardo asked.

"I'm sure Mom's okay with that. It's not alive or in the house," Dominic said.

Judy interjected, "We could get two and race them."

"A robotic lizard large enough to ride on? Isn't that a dinosaur?" I asked.

Leonardo said, "Actually, dinosaurs are more closely related to crocodiles or birds. Dinosaurs come from the reptile group Archosauromorpha. Reptiles come from a distantly related group,

Lepidosauromorpha. If you look at their skulls, you can see the difference."

"Right." I nodded, even though I'd never heard either of those terms before.

Judy returned to her seat. "Lizard or dinosaur, I hear the robotic ones are fast. We could keep them in the spare stalls in the barn. Imagine how fun they'd be to race! Riley, would you want one?"

I laughed. "I'm not in this."

Leonardo clapped his hands in excitement. "We'd need five to have a proper race."

"Let's start with two," Dominic suggested.

Abby wagged her finger at her children. "Hold on, are these the same robotic reptiles you asked about last month? The ones I thought were crazy expensive and would tear up the lawn?"

Judy and Leonardo exchanged a look, both expressions so innocent they were obviously guilty. "Maybe?" they said in unison.

Dominic kissed Abby's cheek. "Outside toys. Harmless. If we need a special track for them, we'll build a track."

Abby cocked an eyebrow at her children but didn't look upset. "Smooth, and effective, but I am not riding a robotic anything around the backyard."

Leonardo turned pleading eyes to his father. "Get five, Dad. Please. We need to race them."

"Five?" I asked.

Leonardo leaned toward me. "One for you. It's a *family* race."

"You're always saying we should try new things, Riley," Judy added.

Oh, they're good. I leaned over and hugged Leonardo, then Judy. Family. Yes. I went all happy and mushy on the inside. I wished I could bottle this moment and share it with Kal as well. So much about how the Corisis lived was completely foreign to me, but they were the same in all the ways that mattered. Kal and I had done our share of tag team begging when we were young. That was likely how I got a parakeet, even though my mother couldn't stand birds.

RIP, Cookie, you were a good friend.

Abby winked at Dominic. "They won this round, but I'm onto them now."

Dominic laughed and put an arm around her chair. "Good thing we have you to keep us in check. I've always had a problem with the word 'no.'"

Abby leaned over and said something in his ear that had him flushing. The exchange went over Leonardo's head. Judy rolled her eyes. I smiled. I loved that my brother had found a partner who brought him such happiness after all he'd been through. They complemented each other well. I hoped one day to find that for myself.

After dinner we moved to the family room to play board games. There was laughter, teasing, apologies, and just enough competitiveness to make it fun.

"Judy, thank you," I blurted out.

She gave me an odd look.

I leaned in and said, "For this." My eyes teared up. "All of this." It was scary to think how easy it would have been for our lives not to have connected.

She blinked back tears as well, then sniffed. "If you're trying to soften me up so I'll let you win, I should warn you that doesn't work with Corisis."

Leonardo chimed in. "Riley knows. She is one."

I had to wipe happy tears away from the corners of my eyes at that. My gaze met Dominic's across the table. His expression appeared strained. He wasn't good at expressing his feelings, but his love for me was right there in his eyes. And, like me, he was aware of how close we'd come to not being a family. If Judy and Gian hadn't made a silly bet that included finding more family for Dominic, I wouldn't be there.

But I was.

It wasn't perfect. I yearned for my brother and mother to be able to share this with me, but for now it was enough.

The evening ended with hugs and a promise that I'd return the following week. I smiled the whole drive to my Back Bay apartment. I almost had Mr. Tuttle drive me back to Lockton, but I was tired and wanted to see Eugenia again before I left. Spending time with family always left me feeling more optimistic. I was sure something I'd say would help her.

Edward hadn't heard his wife yet, but he would.

My mother and brother couldn't hear me yet, but they would as well.

I waved good night to Mr. Tuttle and greeted Fred with a huge smile. Life was good. Basking in the leftover good vibes from spending time with the Corisis, I made my way to the elevator.

I didn't notice Gavin until I was within a few feet of him. I almost didn't greet him. He appeared to be in a foul mood.

"You look like you had a great night." He closed the distance between us. My heart jumped in my chest. The way he looked at me had my body warming in the most delicious way. There was a coldness in his tone, though, that definitely didn't match the desire in his eyes.

"I did, actually. Thank you." *What is his problem? Oh yes, I forgot— he thinks I'm some wealthy man's plaything.*

He frowned as he studied my expression, then leaned closer until his mouth was just above mine. The instant heat between us was thrilling. I licked my tongue over my bottom lip. He said, "I believe that. What I don't believe is that you love him."

I could have cleared his confusion up right there, but he wasn't curious; he was judging. When he spoke, all I could hear was Edward's mother putting Eugenia down, and it made me want to smack him. "I actually do, but that's not any of your business." I thought about what Mr. Tuttle had said about needing to stand up, rather than lying down and getting run over. "Obviously I find you attractive, but I don't like you, Gavin Wenham. I've been nothing but nice to you, and yet you have a low opinion of me. That says more about you than it does about me. Maybe if we were in high school this little cat-and-mouse game would be fun, but I'm only interested in the real deal now."

"The real deal?" he scoffed. "You think you'll find that with whoever moved you in here?"

I raised and lowered one shoulder. "Doubtful, since he's *my brother*." I let that sink in for a moment, then turned and walked to my elevator, slipping away before he had a chance to say more.

CHAPTER SIX

—

GAVIN

Her brother?

I went back over all our interactions with that tidbit of information in mind and groaned. So much of what bothered me about her wasn't true.

Unless she's lying.

Why would she be?

Her words echoed in my head: *"I've been nothing but nice to you, and yet you have a low opinion of me. That says more about you than it does about me."*

She's not lying, I'm just an idiot.

This whole thing with my father has me off balance. That's the only rational explanation for why I'm chasing after some woman I don't know and acting jealous when I know nothing about her situation.

I watched her disappear into the elevator and mentally kicked myself for just standing there while she walked away. I was at a complete loss for what to say, and that was a new experience for me. I was raised to go after what I wanted. Sometimes that meant plowing through obstacles; other times winning required a longer-term strategy.

Women were entertaining companionship for me, as I'm sure I was for them. As long as no one was hurt, moving from one to the next was a guilt-free indulgence that could take the edge off like a good drink after a hard day at the office.

They weren't allowed to become a distraction. My father had married once and claimed it was the single worst mistake he'd ever made. From day one, my mother wasn't faithful to him. Fighting with her had brought him to his knees, and when she left him for her personal trainer, it had nearly ruined him. After insisting on a DNA test to prove that I was his, my father offered her a substantial cash payout to sign off on any parental rights to me. That she took the money told me everything I needed to know about her and was why I'd never bothered to contact her after she left.

Riley was the first woman I couldn't push out of my head, the first woman I wasn't sure I wanted to. Why? I didn't have an answer—it just was. If I were the type to chase a woman, I would have followed her and apologized. I'd already have been on my phone ordering enough flowers to fill her penthouse.

That wasn't me.

Would never be me.

I stood there in the middle of the foyer deciding what to do next. Work had always occupied most of my thoughts. Ongoing projects and strategies to move them forward were always ticking away in the back of my mind. I could have gone to my office in the building and called over to Wenham Global, but I didn't. I could have called a meeting with the staff of my apartment building, but I didn't want to.

What the hell did I want?

I could afford to do anything. Go anywhere.

Why did nothing seem appealing?

I walked toward the security desk. Keith sat up straighter as I approached and smacked Bill, who also came to seated attention. "Good evening, gentlemen."

"Good evening, sir," Keith said.

"Do you mind if I ask you both a personal question?" I asked.

Bill answered, "Anything, sir."

"Do you have hobbies? Things you do just for the fun of it?"

They exchanged a look, as if there might be a possibility they were in trouble. Keith cleared his throat. "Nothing that violates the terms of our employment here."

"What he said," Bill added.

I coughed back a laugh. It was good to know my employees. My father had taught me to remember their names and those of their family members, and to stay abreast of any major life changes our employees had. It was important for them to feel valued and heard, but it was not important for them to know anything about me. I'd always thought that in business, too much familiarity weakened a person's authority.

I paused as I saw a correlation between how my father ran his business and how he'd raised me. He'd always known where I was, who I was with, and what my interests were—but outside of work, I couldn't say I knew what he cared about. Interesting.

"Is there something in particular you're concerned about?" Keith asked.

This is insane. "No, sorry." I went to turn away, then turned back. "It's not a concern but a question. Let's just say you found yourself with an unexpected day off. What would you do with it?"

"Are we being fired?" Bill asked.

"No." I sighed. "I need to find a hobby."

The two men exchanged another look. An awkward silence followed. I understood why. No one wanted the glimpse behind the curtain to reveal uncertainty or weakness. I sought the right words to put a different spin on what I'd said.

Before I came up with anything, Bill smiled and said, "Don't ask Keith. He does whatever his girlfriend likes to do. How was that pottery class, Keith?"

"Fuck you," Keith said, then added quickly, "I didn't mean to say that, Mr. Wenham."

"No problem." Profanity was something all my employees knew to keep out of the establishment, but not because I found it offensive. The building was full of people who were used to the best of everything and the illusion of peace, even if life outside the door was batshit crazy. To lighten the mood, I smiled and asked, "How was that class?"

Keith shrugged. "I didn't mind it. Maya agreed to come to the gun range with me. I agreed to go to some stuff with her. She's a pretty good shot now, and I made a mug for my mother that she uses whenever we visit. It's called compromise. If you tried it, Bill, maybe you'd have a woman who sticks around longer than a week."

"Who needs more than a week with any of them?" Bill joked. "Right, Mr. Wenham?"

I nodded, because it was what I'd always believed. As if just to irritate me, my thoughts filled with images of Riley again and how she was currently only interested in "the real deal." What was that, even? Marriage? Kids? Promises couples made that neither person had any intention of keeping? If so, she was holding out for a fantasy.

With someone else, because that would never be me.

Keith made a show of brushing off one of his shoulders. "I'm going home to a meal cooked by a woman who wants to hear about my day and actually cares about how it went. What are you going home to, Bill?"

His jab at his friend stung, as it hit me as well. I opened my mouth to counter with the quality and ease of any meal I could have delivered to me with just a call down to the building's kitchen, but I kept that thought to myself. That wasn't the point Keith was making. He had someone who cared about him. I was tempted to tell him that time would prove what a bad investment any one woman would turn out to be, but I kept that to myself as well.

Bill waved a hand in Keith's face. "You used to be more fun, Keith. She has you so whipped you can't even hear how pathetic you sound."

"I'd name our first kid after you, but neither Bitter nor Drunk would have a nice ring to them."

"Shut the f—" Bill stopped just before swearing.

I took that as my cue that the conversation wasn't headed anywhere better. "Thank you, gentlemen. I have a few calls to make." I didn't, but it was as good an excuse as any.

"Mr. Wenham," Keith said.

"Yes?"

"I saw you and Miss Ragsdale talking. She's such a nice woman. I hope things work out for you two."

I frowned.

Bill elbowed Keith. "We see nothing. Know nothing."

When my attention riveted onto him, Bill hastened to add, "When it comes to personal things. You're invisible to us. But of course we watch everything that might be a security risk."

"Understood." I gave them each a long look. There was no harm in Keith wishing me well, nor Bill realizing his friend might have crossed a line. "I appreciate your concern as well as your discretion." I prepared to turn on my heel, then decided to leave them on a good note. I knew that statistically, happy employees were more likely to perform their jobs more diligently. "Keith, we do have a problem." Keith's eyes widened, and his Adam's apple bobbed as he swallowed hard. "Now I want a mug from you."

Keith laughed. "You got it. I'll get right on that."

"Good night."

"Good night," they both echoed.

I made my way to the elevators, pausing at Riley's before calling for my own. Yes, I was headed toward an empty penthouse, but that was by choice. My life wasn't muddled with the emotional needs of someone who would likely end up never being satisfied anyway. Rather than tying myself down to any one person, I kept myself open to limitless possibilities and decadent variety.

The lights of my penthouse automatically came on as I made my way through it. Everything was immaculate, just as it should be. There was not one damn thing wrong with my life the way it was.

I shed my jacket, tossed it across the back of my leather couch, and loosened my tie as I looked around. Women tended to describe it as a man's place. The furniture was dark. Wood, glass, metal, and stone. Straightforward. Uncomplicated. Like me.

I wondered how Riley had decorated her side. It irked me that I had no idea.

I stepped out of my shoes and carried them to the closet in my bedroom. My gaze went to the wall that separated my sleeping area from Riley's. The building was designed so that no sound would permeate the walls, but the layouts mirrored each other. I stripped off my shirt and tie and headed for the shower. Naked beneath the hot spray, I wondered if she was ending her day the same way.

Then, dressed in cotton pajama bottoms, I looked out the floor-to-ceiling window in my bedroom and wondered if she was looking at the same view. She might already be asleep. I checked the time on my phone. It wasn't very late. She might be reading or watching a show.

I'd always been good at remembering numbers. I considered texting her but shook my head. What would I write? Sorry if I acted like you were a prostitute when we first met, then decided you were some married man's mistress instead. Let's have dinner and see what wild thing I can accuse you of next.

Or not.

I turned off the lights in my room and sank onto my bed. Some days were best ended early.

I lay there looking at the faint outline of the ceiling details in the darkness. My thoughts wandered to my father and a hope that he hadn't done anything that day that I couldn't repair. I closed a door to that line of thought, since there was nothing I could do about it until I got an update from my people in the morning.

I realized Bill had never said if he had a hobby or not. I guessed that if he did, it would be gun related. I didn't own a weapon, never had the need for one. Target practice didn't sound like such a bad way to waste an hour, though.

Better than making pottery.

Not better than making love.

Love.

I nearly gagged on the word.

Fucking.

People who believed in love were the same who made wishes when they blew out candles. Who exactly did they think granted their requests? Why was it even a thing? Take a cake. Build a tiny forest of wax candles on it. Blow them out, and the god of wax forests will be so happy he will grant you any wish.

People are stupid, I thought. *Plain and simple. They put all their energy into wishing for shit rather than doing anything to actually make it happen.*

I grabbed my phone off the table beside my bed, tapped in Riley's number, and held my breath. She answered almost immediately. "Hello?" Her voice was husky, as if she was also already in bed.

"It's Gavin Wenham."

"Oh."

Just "oh." She didn't hang up, though, so I took that as a good sign. "About earlier . . ."

"Yes?"

"I misspoke."

"And?"

"And where you go as well as who you go with is none of my business."

"So, you called to remind me that I don't matter to you?"

"No. No, that's not what I'm saying."

"So I *do* matter to you?"

"I'm not saying that either."

She chuckled, and the sound was music in my ears. "I'll help you out. I think the words you're choking on are 'I'm sorry.'"

I'd expected her to be angry with me and wasn't sure what to do with this playful side of her. "I'm unfamiliar with that phrase. Is it what someone says when they repeatedly act like an idiot?"

"I believe it is."

I sighed. I did regret misjudging her. "Then I'm sorry."

"Apology accepted."

It felt too easy. "Since we both live here and will likely run into each other on a regular basis, I didn't want things to be awkward between us."

"They won't be. I don't hold grudges. We're good."

Neither of us said anything for long enough that it grew uncomfortable. "Well, then, good night."

"Good night."

I didn't end the call. "Riley."

"Yes?"

"I don't like the idea of you with another man."

Yeah, I went there. I hadn't planned to and wouldn't have been able to justify why I had, but it felt important for her to know.

When she didn't immediately say anything, Jared's advice came back to me: *"If you do see this woman again, try to come across like less of a creeper."* I groaned. What I really needed to learn to do around Riley was to shut up.

After a pause, she said, "My favorite flower is a pink carnation. Roses feel too flashy. Lilies always make me sad. Carnations are earthy and resilient. They usually outlast all the other flowers in a bouquet, but somehow they aren't appreciated as much. If what you're trying to say is that you like me, send me some."

"I'm not—" I stopped myself. I wasn't actually clear myself on what I was trying to say. "I'll keep that in mind." After another lull in the conversation, I said, "Good night, Riley."

"Gavin?"

"Yes?" I wasn't ready to hang up either.

"What would you do if a member of your family wasn't being nice to your wife?"

I answered with a knee-jerk response. "I can never imagine myself with a wife."

"Of course." I thought that was the end of it, but then she asked, "But if you did have one, would you defend her to your family, or would you expect her to defend herself?"

"Are you married?"

"No, but a friend of mine is, and she shared something with me that is still bothering me."

This time I gave the question some consideration. I might not have been the relationship type, but I was raised to treat everyone, women and men, with respect. "Is your friend in any danger?"

"No, just sad."

I tucked an arm beneath my head. "Hypothetically, I chose this woman, correct?"

"Of course."

"Why can't she speak up for herself?"

"She's too nice to."

"I can't see myself with that woman."

Riley made a frustrated sound. "Imagine you're a rich, weak, spoiled brat of a man who cares more about what his mother thinks than how his wife feels."

"Oh. Then I definitely wouldn't say anything."

She gasped. "You'd let your mother go around calling her your 'first wife' to her face?"

"If I were a rich, weak, spoiled brat? Probably."

"Forget it. You're not helping."

"What do you want me to say? I don't intend to ever get married, for the same reason your friend is wishing she hadn't. Marriage is an outdated practice that was fine when people didn't live as long as they do."

"Wow. You're a real romantic."

"I never claimed to be."

"Well, I know who not to turn to if I'm ever in any trouble. You'd just let anyone say anything to me."

"Highly unlikely."

"Would being pregnant change your opinion of the situation?"

"You're pregnant?" I liked that idea even less than imagining her with a rich lover.

She let out another irritated sound. "No, but if you knew I was, would that make you a better husband?"

What? "Are we still talking about your friend?"

"Yes. She doesn't want to tell her husband she's pregnant because she wants him to be a better person before she tells him he's going to be a father. Do you think knowing about the baby would even make a difference?"

"To clarify, you're *not* pregnant. Your *friend* is."

"Oh, my God. I'm not using the friend thing as a cover. I actually do know someone who asked me some tough questions today, and I was hoping to have a better answer for her by tomorrow."

Fair enough. "What did you tell her so far?"

"That I couldn't advise her, but that I care."

"I'd leave it at that."

"*You* would. Because you don't care. I know. You've already made that clear. Let her suffer, right? She deserves to for being stupid enough to get married. I'm sorry if I can't write people off that way. I want them to be happy. All of them. Even him. I was hoping I'd find someone who knew what she could say to him to wake him up."

I let out an audible breath. "I doubt that person exists. He sounds like an ass."

"No one is all bad. He could be a good father. He used to be wonderful to my friend." She sighed. "Sorry, this isn't your problem. Sometimes people just suck."

I always tended to have a jaded view of people, but it bothered me to hear that she was headed down that same path. If I were the type to spew inspirational quotes, I would have then. Instead, I said, "Carnations, huh?"

She sounded surprised as she said, "Pink. Never a yellow one. Yellow symbolizes rejection and disappointment."

"Pink."

"Oh, and do me a favor. If you ever ask me out and if I ever say yes—don't stand me up. I'm so done with that."

I laughed. "Pink carnations, and show up for our date."

"If we ever have one. You haven't asked, and I haven't agreed to anything."

"Understood. Good night, Riley."

"Good night, Gavin."

CHAPTER SEVEN

RILEY

Well, that was unexpected.
And kind of wonderful.

I turned onto my side in my bed and hugged a pillow. Sleep wouldn't come easily, not with my heart racing like it was.

Gavin was a tough one to figure out, as tough as I found sorting through how I felt about him. I went back and forth between thinking he was hot as hell and writing him off as someone I shouldn't waste my time on.

When Teagan returned from Europe, there would be a wedding, followed by babies. Gian's brothers all had children; he'd want them as well.

I didn't mind being single, but I'd always hoped she and I would find love at the same time, raise our families together. The rational side of me knew love wasn't something a person could rush, and I certainly didn't want to settle for being with someone just to have someone. Still, I thought back to the day Gian and Teagan had met. At my urging, she had jokingly asked the universe to send her Mr. Right, and BAM, he walked into her shop that morning. Her engagement supported my belief that making such requests out loud worked because they focused a person's intention. Once she put her wish out there, she made it happen.

I no longer had the luxury of test-driving men who may or may not be the one, not if I wanted to stay on the same page as Teagan. It was time to clarify what I wanted. I closed my eyes and said, "Dear Universe, please send me a man who wants what I do. I want a two-parent household, a man who treats me and our children well, and someone who is as loyal as I am. I need someone who will understand why I'll always want to live near my mother, why I worry about Kal, and why I don't hate the Corisis. Also, he can't be afraid of Dominic."

Wow, that's quite a list I have. Before opening my eyes, I added, "If he could also be good in bed, that would be great. I'm willing to work with him if necessary, but it sure would be nice to be with someone who knows what he's doing."

I rolled onto my back. If nothing else, I knew what I wanted.

So did Gavin, though. He'd called marriage an outdated practice, said he couldn't imagine himself with a wife. Dating him would only be an exercise in disappointment. Maybe not in the bedroom, but in all the other areas.

If he does ask me out, I need to remember what I want and say no. Spending time with him, regardless of how exciting it might be, will prevent me from being open to meeting the man who is right for me.

Sorry, Gavin. I wish we'd met sooner. We could have had some fun, but I have to focus on finding my own Mr. Right.

I rolled over again and buried my face in my pillow. Images of Gavin and me sharing a first kiss filled my head. All it took was imagining us together for my body to warm in anticipation.

Not good.

Fate was a beautiful thing to believe in, but I also believed a person was responsible for shaping it. My biological father had charged into my mother's life like Prince Charming, only to abuse and ultimately desert her. Lust had wooed my mother into choosing to be with a man who clearly wasn't for her. I didn't want that for myself.

Relationships are about a lot more than sex. Hear that, brain? Stop imagining Gavin tossing me over his shoulder and hauling me off to his bed, because he doesn't fit what I need.

To distract myself, I sent a quick text off to Eugenia to see if she wanted to meet for breakfast before I headed back to Lockton. She couldn't, but she did want to see me again later in the week when I returned. I promised to make that happen and reminded her I was there for her if she needed me. She might not want to talk again about Edward, but if she did, I felt more prepared to support her.

I let the variety of the advice I'd received circle around in my head as I looked for a common thread. Edward was being an ass. Was there anything that could wake him up to that fact? Gavin and Mr. Tuttle didn't seem to think so. Abby had sounded the most hopeful: communication, respect, and honesty. Don't give up if someone doesn't hear you right the first time.

My brother was a lucky man. I couldn't imagine that Dominic was an easy person to love, but Abby didn't give up on him. That was what I wanted for myself. I was far from perfect, in many ways still very much a work in progress, but I had to believe the right person would love me just the way I was.

So she wouldn't worry, I sent my mother a quick message that I was staying over in Boston. I didn't add where or with whom. I didn't want to lie to her anymore. It was definitely time for me to sit down with her for a heart-to-heart.

She asked if I'd be around the next day. I promised to drop in when I got back. We needed to talk.

I rolled over again, this time punching my pillow to fluff it. She wouldn't like hearing what I had to say, but I hoped she could put aside how she felt long enough to hear how I did. Past attempts to speak to her about the Corisis hadn't gone well, but just because she hadn't heard me the first time didn't mean she wouldn't this time.

I wondered if Gavin was already asleep or if thoughts of me were keeping him awake. Although I tried to shut them out, snippets from our conversation kept coming back to me.

He'd made his thoughts on marriage absolutely clear. He could never imagine himself with a wife.

Never.

I needed to stop thinking about him.

I tried to conjure up any of the other men I knew, but the only face I saw when I closed my eyes was Gavin's. I fell asleep thinking about him and woke the next morning irritated with myself for having frolicked with him in my dreams.

After a quick shower, I dressed for home. The jeans I wore were older, the shirt less expensive. It was best not to stand out in my neighborhood. If people thought I had money, it would change things. I wasn't ready to leave one life behind for another. I was hopeful that if I was careful, I wouldn't have to.

When my breakfast was delivered, it came with a small crystal vase that held one pink carnation. I circled the table like a lawyer readying to cross-examine a suspect.

I stopped, placed both hands on my hips, and said, "No. I've already made up my mind. A little flirting was fun, but we want different things."

The flower didn't respond.

I sat across from it and poured myself a glass of water. "I have too many things I'm doing wrong to knowingly get involved with a man who doesn't believe in marriage."

The carnation just sat there, all pink and cheerful. I buttered my toast and took a bite before saying, "It's better this way. I don't have time to waste, and he can move on to the next woman, who will probably be perfectly happy settling for whatever he's offering."

I choked, then gulped down some water to help clear it. And still the flower just sat there, mocking me. "I know what I want, and he's not it."

My phone vibrated with a message: What are you doing? Gavin.

Aloud, I joked, "Just having a heart-to-heart with the flower you sent." I slapped a hand to my forehead. *Snap out of it.* I typed back, Eating breakfast.

I have early morning meetings, but I'm free by noon. Spend the day with me.

I put my phone down and rose to my feet. The only answer that made any sense was no. I folded my arms across my chest and, knowing full well that he couldn't hear me, said, "I asked the universe to send me Mr. Right. He's probably waiting for me right now. If I say yes to you, I'll miss out on the one I'm actually meant for." I groaned, did another lap around the table, then grabbed my phone and typed, Thank you, but no.

I waited for him to type something else, but he didn't.

I told myself it was for the best, but when breakfast was cleared away, I kept the carnation. There was no reason for me to hurry home, and it was a beautiful day, so I decided to take a walk along the esplanade before heading back. I'd always found being near water helped clear my thoughts. And who knew—Mr. Right might be a jogger. Or a vendor. He might be working with a team of volunteers to clean the area.

Whoever he was, Gavin wasn't him.

CHAPTER EIGHT

GAVIN

She said no.

To be precise, she was more polite than that. "Thank you, but no."

Between frequent reminders to the top management of the Terraanum that their jobs were only as secure as the quality of their performance was reliable, my thoughts kept returning to Riley and her refusal.

Was it possible that I had misread our exchanges? I knew men got themselves into trouble all the time for thinking something was there that wasn't, but I was more levelheaded than that. Still, I'd asked, and she'd said no.

I needed to put Riley Ragsdale out of my head.

Easier said than done.

She haunted my thoughts right through the conclusion of my meetings as well as through my phone calls to my team at Wenham Global. My father had cleared the schedules of the top execs and asked each of them to write a list of what their priorities were—in and out of work. My team said he intended to meet with them individually to reevaluate how their dreams fit with the vision of the company. He wanted them all to find balance and happiness. He was out of his fucking mind.

You don't change the rules of the game in the middle of it. No one understood his new goals. Half of them thought it was a test. The other half were beginning to question if he'd had a breakdown.

Either way, there was a rising panic within the higher ranks of Wenham Global, which meant trouble. It was definitely not the time for me to be wasting energy wondering why Riley said no when my gut said she really wanted to say yes.

I sent her a damn carnation.

In the color she'd requested.

I didn't send flowers unless someone had died, and even then my secretary handled those rare circumstances. For Riley I'd made special arrangements for the kitchen to always include her favorite flower with her orders.

For my first attempt at wooing a woman, I considered it pretty damn romantic.

Be worried, Dad, be very worried. I don't know if I can save you, since I'm losing my mind as well.

After wrapping up my calls for the day, I returned to the bench by the water that was becoming my go-to place when things stopped making sense. I took out my phone and called my father. He hadn't answered my last call and didn't answer texts, but considering he'd given everyone the morning off, he had to know I'd be concerned.

"Gavin, how are you?" His relaxed tone almost indicated he was on vacation. He didn't take time off, though. I didn't either. He and I had a lot in common, which had always been a strength when it came to understanding him, but I was struggling to get inside his head lately.

"Same. Being back at the Terraanum has turned out to be a good thing. Amazing how quickly things can take a downward slide when you look away from them."

"Working was not what I gave you time off for."

"Yes, about that, Dad. It's time for me to come back."

"Have you met someone?"

Holy shit. Saying I hadn't would get me nowhere with him. I had to say something. "I have a hobby now. I watch the sailboats go by on the bay. It calms me."

"Good. That's a start. It's important for you to have things that bring you joy outside of the office."

"Couldn't agree more. This time away has been incredibly enlightening. I'll return feeling refreshed."

"Not without a fiancée."

"Unlike a hobby, finding a life partner takes time. I'm confident, though, that with my improved state of mind, it will happen naturally."

"Bullshit. You're telling me what you think I want to hear."

I was. Was it time for some hard truth? I hated to go there, but he wasn't leaving me another option. "Because you're not making sense lately. I'm giving you time to work through whatever you're struggling with, but don't put this on me. I'm not the one who is confused or who needs to change. If you need to talk to someone, I'll find you the best doctor money can buy. I'm doing my best to support you through this, but you're sinking, Dad, and it's not a pretty thing to watch. People are beginning to worry that you might not be competent to run Wenham Global."

"Is that what you think?"

"You could be in need of an intervention." I expected my father to dismiss my suggestion.

"What you're not seeing, Gavin, is that I just had my intervention. My eyes are open now, and everything is different. So much of what I thought mattered doesn't. I get it now." He sounded so serious it was unsettling. Any hope that time alone would have him snapping back to his old self was beginning to wane.

If the board did opt to remove him, I'd go to battle for him—but what the outcome of that battle would or should be was becoming less clear. Was any of this a sign of early-onset dementia? I didn't want to think so. I wasn't ready to parent my parent. "See, this is the kind of talk you need to keep out of the office."

"Or it should be at the heart of every meeting I have."

Oh God. "Have you considered taking time off, Dad? There is no shame in saying you need a moment to clear your head."

Steel returned to my father's voice. "Introduce me to the right fiancée, and I'll let you back into your old office. Seal the deal with her, and the company is yours."

One sailboat. Two sailboats. I took a deep breath. "Dad, I'll always have your back. Almost everything I know about running a successful business I learned from you. I'm not going anywhere, but you need to hear me. If you choose to boot me from Wenham Global, I'm not afraid to start over. I can't claim to understand your fixation with my finding a wife, but I assure you I will never introduce you to a woman I intend to marry, because I have no intention of ever getting married."

"Today."

"Never."

"Never is a long time."

"Yes, it is, but you of all people should understand my conviction."

My father sighed. "I did you a disservice, son. I see that now."

"You did fine. There's nothing wrong with the way I was raised."

My father was quiet at first, then said, "Gavin, none of us live forever."

I stiffened. Had my father gotten a prognosis I wasn't aware of? "What are you saying?"

He cleared his throat. "I'm saying I could have done better than I did—for you and for myself. I *should* have done better. I see that now. I refuse to believe it's too late to right that."

I thought about what Jared had said about how facing one's mortality could make a person second-guess themselves and now felt sympathy for my father. Still, he needed to reel his breakdown in. "Dad, you just lost two of your oldest friends. Everything you're feeling is normal, but—"

"Was I a friend to them? In the real sense of the word? I don't know anymore. I could tell you all about Winston's activities, but we never talked about how we felt about anything outside of business. I lost track of Rutger when he moved to Connecticut. He destroyed a thriving business to move closer to his wife's family. Who does that?"

I made a sound of encouragement, because I hoped this was what my father needed—to unload how the funerals had left him feeling. He'd spouted ultimatums upon returning, but he hadn't addressed how the losses had affected him.

"Winston's funeral was perfectly executed," he said. "Top notch. I would have expected nothing less from him. The list of attendees was impressive, and I'm not easy to impress."

"Oh, I know."

"No wife, though. No children. No one in attendance would miss him personally. Hell, they ended the service with a reading of his will. Why gather twice, right?"

"You always said he was a man who didn't like to have his time wasted."

"Mourning someone shouldn't be considered an inconvenience."

I rubbed a hand over my face. "Agreed."

"Rutger's service was at a tiny funeral home in a town I'd never heard of."

"Well, you did say he lost his fortune when his business went under."

"He tried to run it from Connecticut. I warned him it wouldn't work out, but he said he was putting his energy into what mattered most to him. For thirty years I believed he was a fool."

I hoped my father heard the warning when I said, "It's sadly easier than one would think to lose everything."

"Gavin, I wish you'd gone to his funeral with me. The line to enter the funeral home wrapped around the parking lot. I stayed for hours, and it opened my eyes. His wife stood there with their daughters and their husbands, strong, proud, still very much in love with him. I met his grandchildren. Some were in college, some were in diapers. Some of his friends knew my name because he'd told them how proud he was of me." My father's voice grew thick with emotion. "I hadn't spoken to him in over twenty years, but his wife said he often added me and you to his prayers."

"Sounds like you were a better friend to him than you thought."

"No, I wasn't. Maybe while we were in college. Certainly not after your mother left. I had no respect for the life he'd chosen. Winning was all that mattered to me, and in every way that mattered I thought I had—until I attended those two funerals. Winston died with enough money to buy and sell the town Rutger lived in, along with everyone in it. There were no tears at his funeral. Worse, there was no laughter. Rutger's family pooled their money together to pay for his funeral. None of them are breakout successes, but you could tell how much they loved each other. They sat around with photo albums, laughing, crying, sharing stories about him. I lost count of how many people told his wife he'd touched their lives. It was beautiful."

Okay, I could see how the very different funerals might have left my father shaken. "You've touched lives, Dad. Jared would be the first to say so."

"Maybe, but I didn't do enough. I closed myself off, let things that don't matter become all that mattered."

"I don't agree."

"I know, and that's where I failed you. I let my relationship with your mother taint how I saw all women—and I passed that down to you."

"You gifted me a healthy skepticism of people's motives. That's not a bad thing."

"Is it healthy to have no one in your life you trust? I don't think so. Not anymore. That's not what I want for myself, or for you."

Was this a case of my father being afraid he would die alone, or was he simply burning out? "You're not alone, Dad. And you're not at death's doorstep."

"Not today, but one day I will be, and I need to know that when it's my time, my funeral won't be like Winston's."

"Dad, you'll be dead. Do you really think you'll care?" I winced as I heard my own words.

My father was always blunt, sometimes painfully so. I could see he'd also gifted me that trait. "What I mean is—"

"I know exactly what you're saying, I would have said the same thing a month ago. I was wrong, though, and you are too. You weren't there. You didn't see how little Winston's money mattered in the end. Rutger was right. Family is what matters most."

Oh boy. "Of course it is, and you can live your life however you want to, but you might want to consider retiring earlier—before you destabilize Wenham Global. You've always told me that to lead, you need to maintain the respect of your employees. Your current behavior is putting your ability to do that at risk."

"I don't care, Gavin. My priorities have changed."

That was clear. "This isn't just about you, Dad. You have hundreds of employees who rely on Wenham Global for their salaries. What will they do if you tank the company?"

"That's not going to happen."

"I'm glad to hear you say that."

"Because you're going to find yourself a nice wife, settle down, and give me a slew of grandchildren to spoil while keeping the company going."

"If marriage equates to happiness, wouldn't you and my mother still be together?" As a rule we never spoke of her, but I thought a few slaps of reality might be what he needed to bring him back around.

He took a moment before answering. "Your mother was a lapse of judgment on my part. I wanted her because she was beautiful. She wanted me because I was rich. We were both too young to understand how quickly that would become not enough. You can do better."

"Before you retire? That's not realistic."

"I'll make you a deal."

It was the furthest we'd gotten, so I was at least ready to listen. "Shoot."

"Show me that you're open to the idea. Introduce me to a woman you could imagine spending the rest of your life with, even if you're not dating her. No engagement necessary. Just dinner. If I approve of her, I'll sign the company over to you and retire."

I wasn't looking to push him out. Retire? Seriously? My father? I couldn't see him actually wanting that. "I'll make you a counteroffer. One dinner, and you take a few months off and go on one of those vacations you've never allowed yourself. When you come back, we'll talk about what you want to do next."

"I don't need a vacation, but I accept that offer. One dinner at my home to which you bring a woman you could imagine yourself with, if you allowed yourself to go down that road."

"I can do that." Really, any of the women I'd been with could handle meeting my father. I did have standards.

"I'm serious about this, Gavin. Don't bring just any woman here. I'll know. If I'm not convinced you could be happy with her, the deal is over. We'll go back to a fiancée or nothing." In case I wasn't sure he was serious, he added, "I've already spoken to Jared about possibly buying out the company. He's considering it."

No, he's not. According to him. One of them is lying. Okay, maybe I do have trust issues. "You're putting me in a difficult situation, Dad. Sell the company to Jared, if that's what you want to do—just don't destroy it. Too many people are relying on you for you to just piss it away."

"You've always been hardheaded."

"Look who's talking."

"This is for your own good, Gavin. Call me when you meet her."

"So you don't want to hear from me ever again?" I joked.

My father hung up without laughing. He never did appreciate my humor.

I sat there for a long time, rehashing what I'd learned while watching boats come and go. At least I'd confirmed what was bothering my father. What my next move should be wasn't clear yet, but understanding the problem was progress.

The question wasn't whether or not I could find a woman I could imagine spending the rest of my life with. The question was, Could I find a woman my father could *imagine* me imagining spending the rest of my life with? It was an important distinction and made the otherwise impossible much more achievable.

My father thought Rutger had lived a better life. What was his wife like? I decided to call his widow, under the guise of offering my condolences, and spoke to her until I was satisfied I had a workable profile for who would satisfy my father.

Bea Rutger was all about family. She'd been a stay-at-home mother who volunteered in the school her children attended. She laughed easily, in general sounded optimistic, and was proud of the fact that she was considered outspoken. When she said she was okay with where she was in her life, because she'd been lucky enough to have had "the real deal," I got goose bumps.

I knew the woman my father wanted to imagine me with.

What I didn't know was how to get her to say yes instead of no.

CHAPTER NINE

RILEY

My walk ended with meeting Eugenia for lunch after she'd called to see if I was still in the area. At first I was worried, but nothing had changed on her side since the day before. She just wanted to see me. It was a welcome surprise, and I passed along the advice Abby had given me.

Communication, respect, honesty, and patience. Edward would come around.

"And if he doesn't?" she'd asked.

"You're stronger than you think." I decided to sprinkle in the advice of Mr. Tuttle. "As far as your mother-in-law, a friend said something recently that made a lot of sense to me. He said that if you lie down in a road long enough, a car will run you over. I'm paraphrasing, but essentially, you choose the road you're on, and you can't choose how the cars on that road behave, but you can stand up. It's time for you to stand up, Eugenia."

Our talk seemed to inspire her, and that left me feeling better about myself too. My steps lightened as I made my way back to my apartment building.

I paused when I spotted Gavin on the same bench he'd been on the day before. He was definitely a good-looking man, but he never appeared happy. I stopped and watched him for a moment. He seemed healthy. He obviously had money. Why was he so miserable?

And why did I care?

He rose to his feet and turned toward me as if sensing my presence. I flapped my arms once, embarrassed to have been caught staring at him, and started walking again.

"Riley," he called out.

Without being rude, I couldn't not engage. "Hi, Gavin." The closer he came, the more my heart raced and my body revved. *No. No. No. He's not the one, remember?*

He fell into step beside me. "I was hoping to run into you again."

"That's nice." I forced a smile. I wasn't upset with him; I was irritated with myself. What was it about the decision I'd made regarding him that my body was not getting? He was off the menu.

We paused outside the building. He leaned closer. "I'm wondering if I misread the situation."

I swallowed hard. God, it was difficult to concentrate when he looked down at me like I was already his. "Situation?"

"Should I not have sent the carnation?"

I flicked my tongue across my bottom lip and told myself there was nothing unique about how excited he could get me with just a look. "No, I thought it was sweet."

"Sweet." There was a dash of devil in his smile. "Okay. So, having one delivered each time you order something from the kitchen won't make things uncomfortable?"

"Not at all." I should have said it would. He shouldn't have been sending me flowers . . . any more than I should've been saving them. I shifted from one foot to the other and had briefly lost track of the conversation when I made the mistake of looking into his eyes. No man had ever looked at me the way he did, and I had to admit it was pretty freaking hot to be wanted by a man who didn't hide how he felt. *No, I'm not doing this.* "But I can't date you."

"Can't. Interesting." Outside of desire, his expression didn't give much else away.

"Don't take this the wrong way, but you're not what I'm looking for."

"I see."

"That doesn't mean you're not a wonderful man, because you probably are. I'm just not in a place right now where I'm looking for—"

"Wonderful?" He was teasing me.

I blushed. How honest should I be? I hardly knew him, but that wasn't how it felt. "Temporary."

"Right. You're looking for the real deal. I remember."

I forgot I'd said that. "Yes."

"You can imagine yourself married, a stay-at-home mom, volunteering at the school where your children go?"

I didn't know if that was all I wanted for myself, but it didn't sound bad either. "Possibly. I guess it depends on if our family requires a second income or not."

He glanced at the building behind him. "Do you believe that will be an issue, considering your brother's generosity?"

How dare he? I glared at him. "I agreed to the apartment, but I would never—" I stopped myself. "I don't have to explain myself to you."

"You're right." He pocketed his hands and briefly looked away. "My question wasn't intentionally offensive. I'm blunt by nature. It serves me better in the business world than in my private life."

My guard lowered at his show of vulnerability. "I'm dealing with some complicated family issues lately, so I might be a little defensive when it comes to anything regarding them."

Our eyes met again. *Wham,* my knees felt all wobbly, and I was tempted to use his body to steady mine. His voice went low and husky as he said, "The first time we met, I almost asked you to do something for me, but it felt inappropriate and still does now."

My mouth went dry as my thoughts filled with possible deliciously naughty requests. Naturally, I wouldn't agree to any of them, but was there any harm in hearing him out? "What kind of something?"

He looked around. "I can't talk about it here. Are you up for a walk by the water?"

I was up for mountain climbing barefoot if it meant he'd keep looking at me the way he was. Being the center of his attention was addictive, and regardless of all the reasons I'd told myself I should stay away from him, I nodded and said, "Sure."

We made our way toward the dock and the path that ran parallel to it. "This is one of those delicate matters that requires some discretion."

Holy crap, what was he into? "I understand."

We stopped at an area that was open to the bay. The wind blew my hair wildly as the sun warmed my face. Gavin had yet to give a hint as to this big question, and the longer I waited, the more X rated my imagination became. I hoped it wasn't beyond what I'd be interested in. Once, during sex, a man flipped me over and gave me what he thought was a sexy spanking. It hurt. I kicked him in the head by accident while trying to explain that to him. He broke up with me, saying I was too violent for him.

Me? He hit first.

I was just flailing.

I learned something, though. You know what didn't lead to orgasmic sex? Arguing over whether or not he deserved the black eye I gave him with my foot.

I glanced at Gavin's profile. He looked like he was battling with himself over how much he should share. "Gavin, I should tell you . . . I'm not really the type to walk on the wild side."

He gave me an odd look. "I'm sorry?"

"I don't like pain, I don't have any desire to be tied up, and being blindfolded freaks me out."

He blinked a few times without speaking.

"I do like sex." I could have stopped there, but I felt I needed to be clear. "I just don't like to be told what to do, and I'm not good at demeaning others. If that's what you're into, you have to find someone who is better at insulting people, because I've tried that, as well, and all I felt was guilty. And even if it's been a while since I've been with someone, casual sex isn't what I'm looking for right now." The silence that followed was painful, so I filled it by saying, "You looked like you were unsure, so I thought I'd help you by being clear."

"I appreciate that." There was laughter as well as heat in his gaze. "What I had originally considered asking you seems anticlimactic after hearing what you thought it was regarding."

"Oh." I had no idea what else to say.

He looked away, then back. "It was about my father."

My mouth rounded with horror. I had not seen that one coming. "You proposition women for *your father*?"

He barked out a laugh. "God, no. Where do you come up with this stuff?"

I shrugged, becoming defensive as embarrassment swept through me. "Hey, I don't know you. I have no idea what you're into."

"Good point. And my behavior since we met hasn't given you the best impression of me."

I agreed, but whenever we were close, none of that seemed to matter. It felt good to be with him, even when I told myself it shouldn't. "We all have bad days." I shot him a tentative smile. "You've had a few."

His gaze flew back to mine, his expression suddenly quite serious. "It's impossible to not like you."

"Is that a problem?"

"It's not. It's perfect, but it complicates things."

"You've lost me."

"I wasn't planning on being honest with you."

My eyebrows rose. "You don't have many friends, do you?"

His head snapped back. "Why would you say that?"

I waved my hand in his general direction. "Just a guess. I'm not judging. My best friend is horrible with people too. She's as paranoid as she is brilliant. A lot of smart people don't have great social skills."

He frowned down at me. "Are you suggesting I'm socially awkward?"

I grimaced. "It's not a bad thing. It actually makes me like you more. I thought you were just an arrogant asshole, but that's a cover, isn't it? You're actually an introvert."

"Definitely not."

"Do you like to hang out in large groups of people?"

"No."

"You're most comfortable when you work on projects alone?"

"It's more efficient that way, but listen, I'm not an introvert. I just don't like most people."

Teagan was the same. She'd learned to keep a side of herself hidden. I wondered what Gavin was hiding. "You mean you don't trust them."

"Same thing."

Not really. "I trust people until they give me a reason not to. I believe most people are good."

"That's a recipe for constant disappointment."

Wow. Who hurt this guy? "Or opportunity. Look at this conversation, for example. I'm willing to give you a chance to ask me something that might be offensive. Why? Because maybe it's not. Maybe you're about to ask me something wonderful that kicks off a real friendship between us."

"Cue the release of glitter and balloons."

My hands went to my hips. "You're being an ass again."

"Sorry. That was condescending."

"Yes, it was."

"Something happens to my brain around you." His frown deepened. "I don't normally walk around saying stupid shit to women."

I searched his face. He looked truly conflicted. I lowered my hands. From his tone, it didn't sound like he was about to ask me to be his dungeon mistress either. Not that I would have agreed to be one—or his. I was just really at a loss about what he wanted from me. "What were you going to ask me the first time we met?"

He made a sound akin to a growl. "To pretend to be in a relationship with me, but I don't require that anymore."

Weird. Intriguing. Mostly weird. "Why would you want someone to pretend to be with you?"

He sighed and looked back out over the water. "My father lost two of his old friends recently."

"I'm so sorry to hear that."

He nodded. "The experience has confused him a bit. He thinks my lack of desire to settle down and have children is proof that he failed me. Unfortunately, since I work for my family's company, he has leverage over me. Or thinks he does. At first he said returning to the company hinged on my finding a fiancée he approved of."

"So, you were going to ask me to pretend to be engaged to you?"

"Yes. Ergo, the NDA."

"Ergo"? On the sly I looked the word up on my phone. *Therefore. Hey, I just learned a new word.* I stuffed my phone back into the pocket of my jeans. "I would have said no. I really hate lying. I'll do it when I have to. I mean, currently I'm drowning in half truths, but that's a temporary state that I intend to rectify."

His expression tightened. "I have zero tolerance for lies."

"Says the man who was going to produce a fake fiancée for his father."

"Touché."

"*Ergo*, you're no better than I am."

He gave me an odd look. "It would seem so. Anyway, a fiancée is no longer necessary. My father's newest terms are that I must bring a woman to dinner at his home. She must be someone I could see myself spending the rest of my life with."

My eyes rounded. "And you think that might be me?" It was probably the nicest thing he'd ever said to me. He really did like me.

"No, but that's not important. What's important is for him to think I think you might be that woman."

I almost kicked him in the shin. Seriously. Did he not see how insulting he was? "When you sell the idea like that, I can't see why there aren't a slew of women vying for the privilege."

"I haven't asked anyone else."

"You technically haven't even asked me."

He rubbed the back of his neck. "Would you do it? Go to dinner at my father's house? No lies. No stories. All you have to do is show up."

"No." He looked surprised, so I added, "Why would you think I would want to?"

"You say you like to make people happy."

"I do, but—" *I get stupid around you. You're not the man for me, and I really need to stop spending time with you.*

"He's reeling from his recent loss. All he needs to get back to his old self is a spark of hope that he was a better father than he fears he was. You could give that to him just by sharing one meal with us."

The mental image of an old man mourning his friends while dealing with his jackass of a son pulled at my heartstrings. "Why me?"

In a matter-of-fact tone, Gavin described the two very different funerals his father attended. "The experience left my father feeling that he'd wasted his life on things that didn't matter. Rutger had children and grandchildren. According to my father, he also had a lot of friends and lived a better life all around. My father essentially wants that for himself. And me. He's confused. I spoke to Rutger's widow to see what she was like, because that's who my father is imagining me with, and she's essentially you."

Perfect. I laughed harshly as I digested the many layers of his explanation. "You're a real piece of work."

"I could have lied."

I folded my arms across my chest. "That's not a great defense."

"Because I've done nothing wrong. I'm offering you a chance to bring happiness to someone simply by being yourself. You're either interested in doing that or you're not."

I was normally a good read of people, but I couldn't figure Gavin out. I looked him right in the eye and asked, "Do you love your father?"

"Yes," he answered without missing a beat. And I believed him.

A horrible thought occurred to me, and I voiced it. "And all this . . . all our interactions . . . have they been about getting me to help you help him?"

A fire leaped back into his eyes. "No. I'd also love to fuck you, but if that complicates things, I'll settle for you just having dinner with me at my father's."

My mouth dropped open. He had to be joking. He wasn't. "I can't decide if I'm flattered or insulted."

"My request wasn't meant to do either. My father is struggling. Nothing good is headed our way if he continues on the path he's on. One dinner with you would get me back to the company. He agreed to take some time off. When he returns, I can hopefully talk some sense into him."

"It sounds to me like your father is already making sense. He wants you to be happy. What's wrong with that?"

I thought he would respond with a claim that he was happy, but instead he said, "Who the hell is happy? No one I know."

"I am."

"No, you're not."

"Yes, I am. I had a wonderful childhood. I couldn't have asked for a better mother or brother. And I just recently discovered I have another whole amazing side of my family. I couldn't be happier. Okay, I'll admit I'm struggling with not being entirely honest with everyone, but I'm going to fix that."

He put his hands up in mock surrender. "You don't have to prove anything to me. I don't—"

I poked him right in the chest. "Don't say you don't care. You say that a lot, and it really bothers me. If you really didn't care about anything, you wouldn't be looking for a way to cheer your father up.

Instead of trying to sell me on how indifferent you are, be brave enough to ask me to help you with your father."

His hand closed around mine, and time stilled as he simply held it there against his chest. Heat seared through me as that simple touch brought a sexual charge to the conversation. I went to pull my hand free, but he held it there. His eyes darkened with the same yearning I sensed in him the first day we met. "Help me with my father."

It was more of an order than a request, but I melted anyway. "Yes." That one word came out as a breathy whisper.

He smiled. "You said yes."

I did. "On one condition."

His eyes narrowed slightly. "And what would that be?"

"That you meet my mother first."

"Why?"

I swallowed hard. That was a good question. The condition had popped out of my mouth before I'd put much thought into it. Having him with me, though, would definitely help soften the blow of the conversation I knew I needed to have with her. "I'm a coward. I have something I need to tell her, but if I'm alone with her, the conversation will go very differently than if I have someone there. I need a buffer, and my best friend is out of town. So what do you say? I'll help you if you help me."

He nodded. The desire rising within me was reflected in his eyes. It would have been too easy to rise up onto my tiptoes and kiss him. Way too easy. Like, I'd already imagined doing it about a hundred times while attempting to focus on our conversation.

I pulled my hand free of his. "I'm still not sure I like you; ergo, no sex."

"What is it with 'ergo'?" When I didn't answer, he shook his head, then tilted it to one side. "I'm not quite sure what I think of you either."

I shook my head. "Such a charmer."

The devil was back in his eyes as he leaned down until his mouth was just above mine. "No one has complained so far."

I laughed. "Then you might want to consider surrounding yourself with more discerning women." I made a scissorlike move with my fingers. "We'll trim that ego right down for you."

He looked at me for a minute, then cupped my cheek with one hand, chuckled, and said, "Bring it on."

Then he kissed me.

And I forgot everything beyond him and how his touch brought me to life. I wound my arms around his neck. He encircled me, claimed me, invited me to open myself to him. I did, and he tasted as good as he felt. Everything about him—his scent, the feel of his muscles rippling beneath my hands, his hardening cock—all of him felt made just for me.

It didn't make sense.

It shouldn't be.

But it was, and for a moment I gave myself over to the pleasure of it.

CHAPTER TEN

GAVIN

After a few minutes I raised my head, breaking off our kiss, because fucking her right there on the public path was not an option, and I felt dangerously close to not caring. We stood there, both breathing raggedly. I wondered if I looked as shaken as I felt.

I was hyperaware of every place our bodies still touched. Each breath I took moved my chest deliciously against hers and kept the blood surging downward to my cock. No kiss should feel as good as hers did—or all kisses should. I couldn't decide, because there was literally no blood left in my brain.

All that mattered in that moment was that everything I was feeling was reflected in her face. Desire. Wonder. Fear. Thank God it wasn't just me losing my shit over one kiss.

The intensity of the moment was painful to sustain, so I joked, "Forget about my father and dinner. I choose this over saving the family company."

Her laughter moved her against me in a way that had me ready to give in and claim her mouth again. "Where's your conviction?"

"It left as soon as you started rubbing yourself against my cock."

Her cheeks flushed, but she didn't pull away. "Your poor father."

"He'd make the same damn choice." I kept my arms looped around her waist but eased the evidence of my excitement off her. If we were going to engage in any discourse at all, I needed some of my brain to function.

She searched my face. "Obviously there is something here."

Obviously. "So, what do we do about it?"

I didn't like the length of time she debated my question. Nor did I like how she lowered her arms and stepped away from me. "I've seen good relationships and I've seen bad ones."

"I'm not looking for—"

She raised a hand to my mouth to silence me. "I know. I get it. Some guys would lie and say they were. I appreciate that you're up front. But if you tell me again that you're not interested in having a relationship with me, I may knee you in the groin because my emotions are all over the place right now."

Fair enough. I took a step back. "There's no pressure here either way. We're adults. You say yes, I'm good to go. You say no, I'm fine with that too."

She rolled her eyes. "Can you hear yourself?"

I replayed my words in my head and didn't see a problem with them. "You just said you appreciate that I'm not dressing this up as something it isn't." The look she gave me had me going over our conversation again. Yes, I'd been blunt about wanting her, but there was no longer a question about whether the attraction was mutual. "Your issue isn't with me—it's with you." I smiled as the possibility made sense of what otherwise didn't. "You're tempted to have sex with me, even if that's all it is. I won't apologize for being irresistible."

Her mouth dropped open and she laughed, then ran a hand through her hair as if taking a moment to think something through before responding. "You're serious?"

"You have a better theory?"

She shifted her weight back and put a hand on one hip, slowly looking me over from head to toe. "You're good looking, and I'll admit we have chemistry, but I'd hold off on labeling yourself 'irresistible.'"

"To all women, sure, it would be a ridiculous claim. You, however, keep telling me what won't happen between us, but you keep circling back to me. I'm seeing a pattern." I was giving her shit, but I liked that she wasn't immediately defensive. Riley was a woman who was used to being found attractive, and it gave her an edge that was hot as hell. "And it's one I'm okay with."

She gave me another long look. "You are so lucky you're not a mind reader."

A grin spread across my face. "Actually you are, because your thoughts wandered to some scenarios I hadn't hinted at. To be clear, I enjoy sex as well. Under the right circumstances and with the right woman, I don't mind being told what to do or being blindfolded. I wouldn't tolerate being insulted, not even as part of a pleasure/pain game. I don't enjoy hurting anyone, although it's not guilt that holds me back. I simply prefer pleasure. It hasn't been that long at all since I've been with someone, but I'll admit that no one else has interested me since I met you. Casual sex is all I'm looking for—regardless of whether you're hoping for more. Your feelings are not my responsibility."

"Do women actually have sex with you after you talk to them that way?"

"All the time."

"Huh." She pursed her lips. "I don't like it."

"Being told the truth? Or that you still want to fuck me?"

Our eyes met and held. "Both. I want better for myself."

"Then maybe you shouldn't spend time with me, because we both know where this is headed."

She shook her head. "Because you're irresistible?"

I shrugged. "Prove me wrong if that's not the case."

Her Mona Lisa smile sent my heart racing. Would she hold out, or cave and drag me off to her bed? I had no idea, and not knowing was fucking exciting. I couldn't remember the last time I'd wanted a woman as much as I wanted her. Part of me hoped she took her time deciding.

I'd never been one who believed the thrill of the chase was worth it, but this was excruciatingly wonderful.

"When would you like to meet my mother?"

"When do you need me to?"

"This afternoon would be ideal. I'm heading home to Lockton, and the sooner I tell her the truth, the better."

"My schedule is unusually open at the moment."

She nodded and buried her hands in the front pockets of her jeans. "You should change first."

"Change?" I looked down at my expensive suit. "Gotcha."

"The neighborhood I grew up in has its issues, but there are a lot of good people who live there. Just don't let on to any of them that you're well off."

We'd met in Lockton. I was aware it had rough areas. If I thought she was worried about what I might think of her living there, I would have assured her that it didn't make a difference, but that wasn't the conversation we were having. "No one knows you have money."

"I don't have money. My brother does. What my mother won't be happy to hear is that I've been spending time with him. He and I have different mothers, and our father was not kind to any of the women he was with. My mother doesn't see a difference between my brother and the man who hurt her."

"Who is your brother?"

She hesitated, then said, "Dominic Corisi."

"No shit." Normally it would have sounded unbelievable, but when aligned with everything else I had learned about Riley, it made sense. I knew the Corisis by reputation alone—everyone did. Antonio Corisi had been a very successful, highly controversial businessman whose career had been plagued by scandal from his personal life. Although he was no longer alive, his ruthlessness in business was something still spoken of across many industries. Dominic was known for utilizing some of those same smash-and-grab techniques to catapult himself into a category of wealth few attained. He was arguably the richest man on the planet, with an influence that was felt globally.

She watched my reaction closely. "Does that change anything?"

"What would it change?"

"I don't know. People have all kinds of reactions to his name. They love or hate him. He's been nothing but good to me, and that's all I care about."

I could see how the Corisi name might raise hackles, but our paths had never crossed in business, and I had no feelings toward him one way or another. I was curious, though. "There's a story behind this that you want to share."

She tipped her head to the side. "That I want to share? Not that you want to hear?"

I smiled at that. "Anyone would be curious."

"But you're not just anyone, and neither am I. I'll tell you, but only if you admit you *want to* hear it."

There it was—the push/pull sizzle between us. God, it was invigorating. I leaned down and growled in her ear, "You can safely assume want on my end. The only part in question is your comfort level when it comes to . . ." I made her wait for the next word the same way she was making me wait. Anticipation, I was finding, was not a bad thing. *"Sharing."*

Her quick indrawn breath, the color that entered her cheeks, and the way her eyes darkened all told me she was just as turned on as I was. Talking wasn't the activity either of us was craving, but it was where we needed to go first.

Her voice was suddenly delightfully husky. "Go change your clothes and meet me in the foyer in an hour. My driver will take us back to Lockton."

It wasn't the offer it could have been, but it was still a welcome one. "Tell your driver I'll take you."

She wrinkled her nose. "Mr. Tuttle is kind of nonnegotiable, at least as far as Dominic is concerned. For safety purposes."

That made sense. If anyone knew of Riley's relationship to Dominic, she would be a tempting ransom target. "Mr. Tuttle it is." I winked at her and joked, "I hope he likes me."

She chuckled and shook her head. "He barely likes *me*, but you are *irresistible*, so who knows."

I smiled even as my thoughts took a more serious turn. I needed to meet this driver. I couldn't imagine Dominic tolerating anyone being less than respectful toward Riley, but perhaps he didn't know. Mr. Tuttle and I needed to spend some time together. If he stepped out of line, it would be his last day on the job, regardless of how Riley or her brother felt. I'd protect her.

My thoughts jolted me. In general, I believed in coming to any woman's defense. More men should. The feminist movement had made too many men into frustrated observers. It wasn't about thinking women couldn't defend themselves; it was about believing no one should be treated badly. Men simply tended to be better at using physical intimidation to shut a situation down.

Was that fair? No. Life wasn't fair.

Still, my instinct to keep Riley safe went beyond the norm for me. It felt—territorial. Uncomfortably so.

"The foyer in one hour," I said, because I needed to step away before I said something foolish.

We made our way to the building without saying much more. I was lost in my thoughts. She seemed to be the same. When we neared the elevators, I asked, "Who will you tell your mother I am?"

"Just a friend," she answered with insultingly little time to ponder it. "I'd like to think we're at least becoming that."

I frowned. I almost said that wasn't what I was looking for from her, but I held my tongue. I didn't have many friends, and I liked spending time with her. Wherever we were headed together, I could see friendship being a part of it.

She smiled up at me as if she knew exactly what I had been thinking and approved. I didn't like the idea that she might think she could train me. I also didn't like how I found myself smiling stupidly back as she disappeared into her elevator.

I was who I was. I never had been and never would be someone who put a woman's happiness above my own. Relationships were like kryptonite to successful men.

Nothing would change my mind about that.

CHAPTER ELEVEN

RILEY

Putting aside an hour to get ready had been a mistake. I only needed five minutes and had given myself too much time to second-guess my decision to take Gavin home to meet my mother.

The presence of anyone would temper how my mother would respond to the news I was about to deliver. Her lecture, if it happened at all, wouldn't be lengthy, and she wouldn't give in to the tears that would gut me. I called myself a coward, and maybe I was one, but I was becoming resentful of the guilt I'd been carrying, and that wasn't fair to either of us. Without Gavin, my mother would shut down the conversation at my first mention of the Corisis.

I wish you were here, Teagan. I would have taken you with me instead. Bringing Gavin is crazy, isn't it? He doesn't really care about me or what my mother has been through.

Maybe that's a good thing. He's a guilt-free wingman.

After a lifetime of being my mother's caretaker, I found myself in the uncomfortable position of needing to lay out boundaries. I refused to believe love came with all-or-nothing ultimatums. In my mother's mind, any communication with the Corisis was a betrayal that would put our family at risk. Although I could understand why, I didn't agree, and she needed to hear that.

Once she learned that I'd been spending time with Dominic and his family, I wouldn't just be dealing with what she felt now but also all the pent-up fear she'd carried with her for over twenty years. The conversation had the potential to go very badly. I was confident that Gavin could handle it. He wasn't as . . . sensitive . . . as the men I'd been with in the past.

There was something in his expression when we'd parted at the elevators, something I kept telling myself not to read into. Unless I was completely off base, he was becoming interested in me—and for more than sex.

My mother often said, "When a person tells you who they are—believe them."

I paused from brushing out my hair. If I did believe Gavin, then I was a fool for choosing to spend any further time with him, and I was definitely reading more into our exchanges than was there. According to him, we wanted very different things. Okay, that wasn't entirely true. We both wanted to have sex. I just wanted it to matter.

My resolve faded away, however, whenever I was standing within five feet of him. And when we touched? I was ready to shed my clothing right then and there. Yeah, it was bad.

Or good. Depending on how you looked at it.

I closed my eyes as an aching need washed over me. My mind wavered about him, but my body didn't have a doubt. There had to be other men capable of making me feel the same way.

What if there weren't? What if my decision to find Mr. Right robbed me of my chance to be with Mr. Best in Bed?

It wasn't like I was old. I could have a day, a week, a month of amazing sex, then look for a man who wasn't afraid to change a baby's diapers. A month? Would sex with Gavin be good that long? I let myself relive how exciting it had been writhing against him even while we were both fully clothed.

Irresistible.

The woman looking back at me in the mirror certainly thought he was. My eyes were dilated. My cheeks were flushed. I bit my bottom lip and remembered his kiss. His lips were firm and confident. His tongue was bold and talented. That man knew how to make a woman feel fucked from just a kiss. What else was he good at?

I fanned my face with one hand and laughed at myself. *This is such a bad idea. Teagan would agree. Eugenia would as well.*

Why couldn't the universe send me a nice family guy?

I don't require a drop-my-panties-hot hookup. Give me a sweet, reliable, commitment-ready man with a family like the Romanos, the family Gian had.

Gavin Wenham, we are not going to have sex.

Not today.

Not tomorrow.

Never.

You are not allowed to come into my life and confuse me about what I want.

Except for today, because I apparently thought spending the afternoon with you was a good idea.

And one more time when we have dinner with your father.

Then we're done.

I might allow myself one or two more of your kisses, but that's it.

I can't go further than that.

After retouching my makeup, I gathered up a small bag of my things and headed toward the elevator. My resolve held the entire ride down. It wavered as soon as the door opened to Gavin standing there waiting for me. All it took was stepping toward him to make me want to remove the distance between us and wrap my arms around his neck again. I clutched my bag tighter instead.

"Punctual. I like that." His gaze raked over me, leaving me flustered in a good way. His voice was deliciously deep.

I gave myself a mental shake and told myself to calm down. "I don't really care what you like." It was a bold-faced lie, but one I needed to shield myself with. "This isn't a date; it's a favor you're doing for me before I do one for you."

"Of course." His grin was all sex and put a spin on my words I hadn't intended. He stepped back, and we made our way across the foyer together. As we did, he dipped his head down near my ear and said, "For the record, I'm always interested in hearing what you like."

I shuddered with pleasure when he placed his hand on my lower back as if claiming the right to. "Be on your best behavior in front of my mother. The conversation we need to have is actually a very important one."

Gavin looked down at me. His expression was difficult to decipher. I wondered if he was already regretting his decision to come with me. "I'll follow your lead."

He sounded like he meant it. "Thank you," I said simply.

We stopped and greeted Fred, then we walked through the door he held open for us.

"Mr. Tuttle," I said as we approached my driver. "This is Gavin Wenham. He'll be accompanying me back to Lockton to see my mother."

Mr. Tuttle opened the rear door to the sedan. "Welcome, Mr. Wenham."

I slid into the vehicle. Gavin stopped before following me. Instead he held his hand out for Mr. Tuttle to shake. "I've heard good things about you, which is reassuring, because Miss Ragsdale is important to me."

My eyes widened. Had he just said that? Why?

Mr. Tuttle shook his hand. "I've heard nothing about you, but Miss Ragsdale's safety is my responsibility."

I leaned out so I could see their expressions. They didn't look angry, but nor was it a friendly introduction.

"Then I'm sure we'll have no issue," Gavin said.

"I'm sure we won't, sir," Mr. Tuttle said in a firm tone.

Gavin slid in beside me. I gave him a questioning look that he responded to with a shrug I wasn't sure how to translate.

After Mr. Tuttle pulled away from the building and into traffic, I leaned forward and said, "Mr. Tuttle, please drop us off where you normally do."

"Understood."

I sat back and met Gavin's gaze. "My mother doesn't know I have a driver, and my neighbors would ask too many questions if they saw him, so we keep it discreet."

He shifted closer, close enough for our thighs to touch and for me to find it difficult to concentrate. "We've got time before we get there. Tell me what you need me to know."

His tone was businesslike, and I grew disappointed. Yes, I knew he had trouble expressing his feelings, but couldn't he summon a little warmth? I sighed. Whatever. It was good for him to keep things real between us. Hopefully it would help stop me from making an impulsive mistake.

As if hearing my thoughts, he took one of my hands in his and brought it over to rest on his thigh. My heart started thudding wildly. The drive to my mother's, beneath the eagle eye of Mr. Tuttle, was not where things should heat up between us. I didn't pull my hand away, though. When he spoke, his voice was deeper, and my eyes flew to his. "I want to be what you need me to be today. Tell me what will help me be that."

Be careful what you wish for. A woman could easily fall for a man looking down at her the way he was looking at me. It was nearly impossible to keep my defenses up. "I do have a story for you, then. It's complicated and not pretty, but it's mine, and today I'm hoping to put a better spin on it."

Holding his hand, looking into his eyes, I told him about my life before Gian Romano found me. It was important to me that he understood I had already considered myself blessed. I had all the things that mattered: a loving family, a loyal best friend, a roof over my head, food on the table, and a strong work ethic. My brother and I would have paid off my mother's bills without Dominic. We would have saved up the money to pay for the operation she would soon have. Gian bringing Dominic into my life had just made the surgery possible sooner.

"This is where things get a little complicated."

"I'm listening."

He was, too. How could someone so wrong for me also be so right? I pushed that thought back. Some things just were. "When my mother met Antonio Corisi, he was still married to Dominic's mother, but she had run off to Italy to hide from him. Antonio was violent, not only with his wife but with Dominic and their other child, Nicole." I chose my words carefully because some of Dominic's story was mine, but I also didn't want to share things he wouldn't want people to know. "My mother said he came in and swept her off her feet, but once they were together, things quickly deteriorated."

"He hurt her," Gavin said in a tight voice.

I nodded. "Many times. She tried to leave him, but he would find her wherever she went. He's the reason she has back issues. His last beating was so harsh it broke several of her vertebrae. While she was in the hospital healing, she discovered she was pregnant with me and Kal."

Gavin's lips thinned, but he held his silence.

"My bio father's lawyer came to see her. He told her that he could keep her safe from Antonio if she kept her silence. He said if Antonio ever found out about me and Kal, he would take us. My mother lived in constant fear of that happening until the day my bio father died. My mother never wanted us to know about our father, and now I understand why."

"That's why you never knew Dominic was your brother."

"Exactly. I never would have known if Gian hadn't made a bet with Dominic's daughter that he could find more of Dominic's siblings faster than she could."

"Interesting bet." His tone was full of disgust.

"I felt the same until I heard about Sebastian's and Gian's relationship to Dominic. Sebastian Romano is also my brother, because Antonio slept with his mother as well. Neither knew about that for a long time."

"And Gian?"

"He's not technically related to me, but Dominic's mother got pregnant with him while she was hiding from Antonio. Dominic's relatives were popping up like popcorn for a while, so I guess I can see how it might feel fun to look for more."

"Fun." His tone implied he didn't agree.

I shrugged. "None of it was malicious, and it's been kind of an amazing experience to discover I had more family." I sighed. "I wish Kal and my mother felt the same. My mother made me promise I'd have nothing to do with the Corisis. She thinks they'll hurt me like my father hurt her."

His hand tightened on mine. "Are they like that?"

In a rush, I said, "No. Not at all. Dominic and Nicole were victims of his temper as well. They've both married, had children, and are adamant that anger has no place in a family."

I searched Gavin's face. His expression was shuttered and tight. "What's your goal today?"

"I'm done lying. Even if it upsets Mom and Kal, I need to be honest with them. Kal sees my choice to see the Corisis as me betraying our mother. I don't."

"What do you need from me?"

My heart thudding in my chest, I met his gaze. "I need a buffer. She'll be calmer because you're there. But know that even if she says awful things, she won't mean them. I don't think she will say anything out of anger, but I am preparing myself for the possibility. This will cut deep for her. If I'm prepared, though, her words won't hurt me, and I won't say things I also won't mean. This isn't a situation where there will be a winner and a loser. I'm on her side—and I always will be. I just also need her to be on mine. It'll take time for her to accept both that I lied and what I lied about, but that's okay. Loving someone means being patient with them as well."

Gavin nodded slowly. "That's what you were referring to when you said who you choose to spend your time with, who you choose to love, is something you refuse to feel guilty about."

He listens. "Yes, it's been bubbling inside me. I shouldn't have unleashed that on you."

His fingers laced with mine. "I was certain you were referring to a lover."

I gave his hand a squeeze. "So, you're not perfect. I don't require that in a friend."

A fire lit in his eyes, but he didn't say what I guessed he was still itching to. I didn't know why I'd brought it up again. Why was I pushing him to say what I didn't want him to? And why wasn't he saying it?

Mr. Tuttle parked around the corner from where my mother and I both lived. He opened the back door for us.

Gavin released my hand as he exited the car. I slid out and was about to join him, but I turned to Mr. Tuttle instead. "I don't know how much you heard or didn't hear, but please keep it in confidence."

Mr. Tuttle closed the door without admitting or denying that he might have been listening. I placed my hand on his arm. "Either way, wish me luck. I need to do this right."

Mr. Tuttle placed his hand over mine and said, "Your mother raised a wonderful daughter. You'll do fine."

I blinked back the tears that filled my eyes. Crying in front of my mother would not take our talk where it needed to go, but I was grateful for Mr. Tuttle's support. "Thank you. I might need you to take Gavin back afterward."

"I'll arrange my own transportation," Gavin interjected. "Thank you, Mr. Tuttle."

Mr. Tuttle nodded toward both of us, then moved to the spot where he always watched me make my way to my apartment building. Gavin seemed to notice and approve.

Side by side, Gavin and I walked away. Our hands brushed against each other's, and my breath caught in my throat. I thought he might take my hand in his again. Part of me wanted him to. Part of me didn't want that to be the impression we gave my mother. I already had more than enough to explain to her.

He didn't take my hand. I was a bundle of disappointment and relief as I led the way through the front door of our building. The hallway was small and lined with mailboxes. No security or marble where I lived, just musty old carpeting and a lingering scent of cigarette smoke. "My mother lives on the third floor," I said. "I live on the fourth."

When Gavin took a step in the direction of the elevator, I added, "We take the stairs. Much safer. That thing hasn't worked right since we moved in."

Gavin's tone was harsh. "Have you mentioned it to the owner?"

He reminded me of Dominic for a second, which helped me guess his irritation wasn't with me but with the building management. "Once or twice. But don't worry—I grew up in this building. Using the stairs hasn't killed us yet."

"Your mother deserves better."

I froze at that. He was right. Why had I never made that leap? I thought back to all the times my mother had told us to not make a fuss. That things would go better if we didn't complain. She was fine taking the stairs. The stairs were her exercise.

Was any of that true, or had she been afraid to raise her voice? Afraid if she did anything to stand out, Antonio would find us? Not much made me angry, but my temper rose as I saw our acceptance of our struggle through Gavin's eyes. I could have fought better for my mother. I should have. Until that moment I'd never realized I hadn't. It floored me.

I steadied myself with a hand on the wall. I'd always considered myself a good daughter, but now doubt washed over me. I'd accepted a penthouse apartment for myself when I could have taken less and done much more for my mother. I didn't like what that said about me.

"Riley?" As we stood there near the stairs, Gavin bent so his face was even with mine. "Are you okay?"

I waved a hand between us. "Yes. Sorry. I'm just realizing a few things."

He tipped my face up so my eyes met his. "What is going on in that head of yours?"

I pulled my chin free and fought to breathe normally. I was heading in to tell my mother she was wrong, but what if I was? What if what I thought was the way love should be was really just me being selfish? Was I about to make a huge mistake? "I need a minute."

He dropped his hand but remained close. "Is there something else going on? Something you're afraid to tell me?"

I brought a hand to my mouth, and tears welled in my eyes. "What if I'm wrong?"

"About?"

"Everything. I'm so sure I know what I'm doing, but what if I don't? What if lying is the kinder choice? What if I could help my mother without hurting her more but I'm just not thinking it through enough?"

"You've got this." He kissed me then, his lips moving gently over mine. It wasn't a kiss full of passionate promise. It was tender and reassuring and everything I needed in that moment. When he raised his head, I felt better and worse at the same time.

I fisted the front of his shirt in my hand. If I didn't know better, I'd have thought the man looking down at me was falling for me. But I did know better. "Don't do that. Don't pretend to care. You've been very clear about how you feel. Let's not confuse anything."

"Right," he said. I released his shirt as he stepped back. "But remember, the only plan that works is the one you believe in."

I wiped my hands beneath my eyes. "I did believe in it. I just wish I knew if there was a better way."

"There's always a better way, but nothing is achieved by the person who waits for the perfect solution."

Calm was returning. I met his gaze. "Why do I feel like you're feeding me advice from someone else?"

"My father often said both." Gavin's smile held some sadness. "He's always given me solid advice. Sadly, so far he's been unable to take any from me."

My heart opened a bit to him then. "He'll come around. Don't give up on him."

"I don't intend to."

I raised a hand to his cheek. We were very different people, but in some ways we were also very much the same. "I'm glad." I took a deep, steadying breath and dropped my hand. "Let's go deal with my parent, and then we'll take yours on."

He had that look in his eyes again, the one I had to keep telling myself I was imagining. "I'm ready if you are."

I smiled at the irony of his statement. "I'm far from ready, but things can't stay the way they are, so this is the plan I'll have to believe in."

Together we made our way up three flights of stairs to the door of my mother's apartment. I knocked once, then used my key to unlock the door as I always did. My last thought as I opened the door and saw the happy surprise on my mother's face as she realized I wasn't alone was that I should have told her I was bringing someone with me. I should have considered what she might read into it.

She rushed forward to greet us, hugging me first, then Gavin. The hug she gave him was an extra-long one he wasn't fast enough to evade and then seemed to not know what to do with as it dragged on.

I definitely should have explained that he and I were not a couple.

I'd forgotten how my mother hoped every man I introduced her to would be the one who would bring her grandchildren.

CHAPTER TWELVE

GAVIN

Okay, then. Riley's mother was a tiny woman, but her hold on me was fierce. I hadn't spent much time with my father's family over the years—a few weddings, some gatherings he sent me to in his place—but none of them were huggers. I'm not sure one would call the stranglehold Riley's mother had me in a hug. I glanced at Riley. She mouthed an apology to me.

What could I do? I hugged her mother back.

When her mother finally released me, she took my hands in hers. Have I mentioned I'm not big on touching most people? But short of shoving her away, there wasn't much I could do.

"What's your name?" she asked.

"Gavin Wenham."

"Gavin," she said, repeating my name. "Call me Fara. You have no idea what a relief it is to meet you. I should have guessed it was a man who was keeping my daughter so busy."

I met Riley's gaze again. I expected her to jump in with a correction. When she didn't, I returned my attention to the woman clutching my hands. "It's a pleasure to meet you, Fara." She was about my father's age but looked younger. Simply dressed, but well kept, and beautiful in a timeless way. She must have been truly stunning at Riley's age. I could see what had caught Antonio's attention. My hands tightened on hers. I'd never met the man, but knowing that the woman before me still struggled with health issues from the abuse he'd subjected her to lit a fury in me that had nowhere to go. I was glad he was dead, but I also wished he were still around so I could dole out some justice.

Riley and her mother had different eye colors and different hair, but their features were the same. I looked at Riley again. It saddened me to think I wouldn't be around to see her beauty bloom and mature. The odd thought left me feeling a little sad.

"Mom." Riley stepped forward. "We need to talk."

Her mother released my hands and turned away, talking over her shoulder. I noted a curvature in her back and a stiffness to her gait. "I have some fresh soup that's still warm and some fresh bread. I'm sure we can eat and talk at the same time. It's not every day you bring a man home for me to meet."

Riley sighed and closed the door behind her. In a low tone, she muttered, "Stop looking so perfect. I should have told her we aren't together. I didn't think this through. You don't have to charm her—you just have to be here."

I blocked Riley's advance toward the kitchen. "So if she touches me again I should smack her away?"

She sighed again. "No. That's not what I'm saying. Just don't be—don't be"—she waved a hand in my general direction—"so likable."

I straightened and placed a hand on my chest. "I'll try to tone it down, but when it comes to women, I can't help that they're all drawn to me."

"Ew, that's my mother."

I hadn't meant it the way it came across. I rushed to add, "I meant in a purely platonic, likable way." The answering humor in her eyes told me she was giving me shit, and I smiled. I hadn't gone into that day with expectations of much, but I found myself becoming emotionally invested in the outcome of the talk. I knew Riley was worried, and earlier I'd glimpsed the confusion that lay behind her easy smiles. I was still reeling from how much seeing that side of her had made me want to reassure her that she wasn't alone.

We were nothing to each other, but that wasn't how it felt as I took the seat her mother ushered me to at a small wooden kitchen table. Riley remained standing, at first telling her neither of us was hungry, then helping deliver bowls of soup to the table. A large plate of what smelled like fresh homemade bread followed. I started to rise to help them but was told by both to stay where I was, so I did. Riley handed me a glass of water from the tap, a large spoon that didn't match the others, and a piece of paper towel torn off from a roll. It was a very different setting from the one I'd grown up in, but there was also an allure to it. It felt . . . genuine.

Riley had said she was close to her mother, and that was obvious in the way they worked seamlessly together. This was how they lived, not a show for my benefit. I watched the two make a joke when they accidentally bumped into each other. The space was small but overflowing with love.

I stood again when they both joined me at the table, and Riley gave me an odd look. I shrugged and sat back down. I was raised to stand when a woman joined the table. So shoot me.

I reached for a slice of bread but stopped before touching it when Riley shook her head. Her mother closed her eyes for a moment. Riley leaned toward me and said, "She's saying grace in her head. She doesn't want to make you feel like you should, but it's important to her." She must have seen the question in my eyes because she added, "If you weren't here, I would have been saying it as well."

Outside of movies, I really had no idea what "saying grace" entailed. "Don't let me stop you."

She blushed. "We're not showy. It's really just a thank-you. I already said mine silently."

Fara opened her eyes, smiled at me, and passed me the plate of bread I'd reached for earlier. I didn't feel uncomfortable, and that surprised me. Like Riley, Fara had a warm strength about her.

I looked around the kitchen. Nothing in it was new, but it was clean and bright. I thought about what Riley had said about having had a good childhood that no one needed to "rescue" her from. I understood now why she hadn't felt a need to yank her mother out of her life here. There was struggle to their lifestyle, but there was struggle in every lifestyle. If wealth equated to happiness, I wouldn't have known so many rich drug addicts. Riley had grown up with love, and that was what gave her the confidence I'd sensed in her. I knew a lot of lonely people who would have traded everything to have a place that felt as safe as Fara's kitchen.

My father, for one.

"So, Gavin," Fara said as she scooped a spoon into her soup. "How did you and Riley meet?"

I decided the truth was the best path. Riley could add in any corrections she felt necessary. "I was attempting to order a coffee, and she was standing there, blocking the line."

Fara laughed. "She always was a daydreamer. Riley, that's one way to catch a man's attention." She wagged a finger at her daughter. "Normally I'd be hurt that Riley kept you a secret, Gavin, but I think it's a good sign. She wanted to make sure before she brought you home."

Riley cleared her throat. "Mom—"

Fara placed her spoon beside her soup and caressed her daughter's cheek. "I'm not upset, Riley. You're an adult. You don't have to tell me everything. I love it when you do, but I understand that you also need a life of your own."

After meeting my gaze briefly, Riley sat up straighter and said, "Gavin and I—" She stopped, seemed to second-guess what she'd been about to say, and started over. "Mom, we need to talk."

Her mother looked from Riley to me, then back. "So this isn't just a social visit?"

"No, it isn't." Riley closed her eyes briefly, then leaned forward and took her mother's hand in hers. "I have something that I should have told you right away, but I was afraid to. I didn't want to disappoint you, and I'm afraid you'll see this as me having done just that."

Fara's expression turned to one of pure love. "Honey, don't ever worry about that. Whatever it is, we're in this together. All of us." Her eyes flew to mine, and I almost shook my head in denial, but I was just the buffer. I sat there and did my best to be just that. "Family is much more important than whatever life could throw our way."

Riley nodded. "I'm so glad you said that, because this is about family and about how ours can't stay the same, not even if we're comfortable with how it is. It's natural for families to grow—evolve."

Fara gasped, and both of her hands flew to her chest. "You're pregnant."

Riley froze, appearing completely sideswiped by her mother's assumption as well as her joy. Fara was on her feet again, hugging Riley, then hugging me.

"Mom," Riley said with panic evident in her tone. "You need to sit down and listen to me."

Fara floated back to her seat with a beaming smile full of such joy that my heart hurt, because I knew it wouldn't remain. "I know. I know. This is a serious conversation, and babies never come when people expect them, but even if you're afraid now, Riley, you'll feel differently as soon as you hold that baby in your arms."

"Mom—"

"Gavin," Fara spoke over her daughter, "before you start worrying about what I think of you, I want to be clear that I'll be on your side as long as you are good to my daughter and the child you two are bringing into this world. Of course I'd prefer if you marry, but how people treat each other is more important than any document they sign. Do you love my daughter, Gavin?"

"I—I—" I was not a man who was normally at a loss for what to say, but the truth wasn't an option, and lying wasn't either.

"I'm sorry, I'm making you uncomfortable. Gavin, what I should have said was, there is a place in my heart for you already. You take your time and figure everything out together, but know that I'm here for you if you need me."

The kindness in Fara's eyes did something funny to me. I nearly stood up. If I had, I knew I would have hugged Riley's mother as tightly as she'd hugged me when we'd first met.

I looked down at my glass and pushed it away. What the hell was wrong with me? These women were making me nuts.

"Mom, I'm not pregnant. I've been spending time with the Corisis and the Romanos. That's what I'm here to tell you. No baby. No relationship news. All the times I've gone to Boston have been to see Dominic and to spend time with his family. Sebastian and the rest of the Romanos have come up to see me there."

Fara took a moment to absorb Riley's declaration. My gut twisted as all joy left her expression and she brought a shaking hand to her forehead. "I'm sorry—I thought—"

Riley was at her mother's side, crouched down beside her. "I know, and that was my fault. I did this all wrong. I promised you I wouldn't make contact with Dominic, but it was a promise I couldn't keep. He's my brother, Mom, no different than Kal."

"Very different than Kal." Her mother rose to her feet. The devastation in her eyes was painful to bear witness to. She looked at me. "That makes you . . ."

"A friend." And it was true. As crazy as it would have sounded had I tried to explain it to anyone, I cared about these two women. Riley was no longer just a woman I wanted to fuck. And her mother wasn't some stranger I hoped wasn't prone to hysterics. I cared about them and about how this would work out. I had no idea what the hell that meant as far as where any of this was going, but I didn't regret agreeing to be there.

Riley put her hand on her mother's arm. "I brought him because I thought having someone else here was the only way you would listen to me. I know all the reasons you don't want me to see the Corisis, but I need you to hear the reasons I want you to."

"You don't have to tell me how charming that family can be. When they want something, they'll stop at nothing to win it. And they wanted *you*." Her mother's expression was tight. "Enjoy the good times, Riley, because when it turns ugly, and it will, I won't be able to protect you."

I frowned and rose to my feet. Why would things turn ugly between Riley and the Corisis? Was this nothing more than the fear Riley had said her mother still had regarding that family? Or was it based on more? Either way, her mother's level of distress was rising.

Riley blinked and wiped tears from the corners of her eyes. "Dominic is not his father. He's a good man, Mom. The Corisis are a wonderful family. If you came with me to meet them, you'd see that. His wife—"

Fara began to sob, and I took a step toward her in support. Riley put her arm around her mother, murmuring to her the way a parent would comfort a child. "It's going to be okay, Mom. Antonio is gone. He can't hurt you anymore. We don't have to hide."

I hadn't known true hate until that moment. Dead or alive, I hated the man who had hurt this family.

Riley continued to speak softly to her mother. Had someone asked me what I would have done in that situation, I would have said my presence wasn't needed and that my best course of action would have been to leave. That wasn't how it felt at all, though. Nothing could have dragged me from that room.

There was no reason to believe that Dominic Corisi had ill intentions regarding his sister, but if I discovered he did, his wealth wouldn't be enough to protect him from my wrath. This family had been through enough, and no one would hurt them again. Not while I was around.

Riley looked up from her mother and shot me an apologetic look. She seemed sad, and I wondered if she thought she'd failed. I didn't see it that way. Riley was making a stand for something she believed in, but her loyalty to her mother was unwavering. Fara was hurt and afraid, but her love for her daughter was rock solid. They would survive this.

My own mother had chosen money over me. My father loved me, but his was a conditional, performance-based love. This was something different.

Over her mother's head, Riley mouthed, "You can go if you want."

I shook my head. I was right where I wanted to be.

Crazy.

Unexpected.

Scary.

But no way in hell was I leaving.

CHAPTER THIRTEEN

RILEY

He's not running out the door.

Why isn't he running?

I continued to rub my mother's back gently, torn between caring for her and wondering what Gavin was waiting for. There was no way to reel this back to the outcome I'd hoped for. My mother didn't normally get so emotional in front of people she didn't know, but then again, it wasn't every day she had the prospect of a grandchild ripped away and replaced by the one thing she feared the most. The Corisis were back in her life, and once again she didn't have a choice in the matter.

My heart was breaking for her, but I still couldn't imagine cutting Dominic, Abby, their kids, or any of the Romanos out of my life. I didn't love that way.

My mother was trembling beneath my touch from a fear I didn't know how to lessen. "Mom, no one will ever hurt you again."

She raised her eyes to mine. "It's not me I worry about. The only way anyone could ever hurt me is if they hurt my children."

"I understand your fear, Mom—"

She shook her head. "No, you don't, and I pray you never do. If I thought Dominic was a good person, don't you think I would've encouraged you to get to know him? He's *not good*. Money does something to people. They begin to think they can do whatever they want to—that they're above the law."

"Not all—" Gavin started to speak, then stopped. I shot him a look, and he shrugged. "I'm just saying there might be some good people with money."

Really? This isn't about you. I rolled my eyes.

He fell silent again.

My mother took a deep breath and sat back down. "It's your life, Riley. You're too old for me to tell you what you can and can't do. Just be careful."

I sat in the chair beside her and leaned close. "Come with me to meet them, Mom. If you get to know them, you'll see that they're survivors just like you. Dominic suffered at Antonio's hands as well."

Tears entered my mother's eyes again. She was quiet for a few long minutes before she said, "I would do anything for you, Riley, but I can't do that. Please don't ask me to. He looks too much like his father."

I sat back. "I look like Antonio as well." I held up a handful of my hair. "I have his hair, his eyes. Is the sight of me difficult?" She looked down. I knew she didn't mean it to, but her response stung. I sucked in a deep breath. The emotions welling within me had no place in the conversation we were having. She was in pain. Piling more on would be cruel. I took one of her hands in mine again. "Mom, do you know why I am fighting so hard for Dominic?"

She met my gaze again and shook her head helplessly.

I gave her hand a shake. "It's all your fault. You taught me to be a strong woman who stands up for what she believes in. You taught me that family is what matters the most and that perfection is not necessary. The Corisis are not like us. They're rich, but that doesn't make them bad people. Yes, they have flaws, but so do we, Mom. I'm impulsive. Kal sounds like an ass half the time. You always overcook your meatballs."

My mother made a sound that might have been a surprised laugh. "I do not."

"Little round golf balls—that's what Kal and I call them, but we eat them anyway because we love you."

116

Wiping the tears from her cheeks, my mother smiled. "Gavin, my daughter is making that up."

"I reserve judgment until I've tried them myself," Gavin said.

Gavin.

I'd almost forgotten he was there. The men I'd been with before him would have hightailed it out of there. Gavin looked perfectly content to remain in quiet support. It was completely unexpected.

And more than a little wonderful.

I smiled at him.

He smiled back.

For a moment the rest fell away, and it was just us and the attraction that flamed so easily to life. It was neither the time nor the place for that, so I stomped my reaction to him down the best I could. He retook his seat at the table and complimented my mother's soup after he'd tried it. She relaxed and told him the tweaks she'd made to a common recipe. For the next half hour or so, we talked about nothing of importance while we finished our soup.

My mother didn't ask probing questions. Gavin didn't divulge more than one would during polite conversation. It was comfortable, but we were being careful to keep it that way. My mother's opinion of the Corisis and of my decision to let them into my life hadn't changed, but I wasn't lying to her anymore, and that was a huge weight off my conscience.

When we stood to leave, my mother told me to bring Gavin around to see her again soon. I almost told her there was no chance of that happening, but I'd disappointed her enough for one visit. "Absolutely," I said as I kissed her cheek and gave her a parting hug.

When my mother turned to Gavin, she hesitated and looked uncertain. It must have been confusing. She'd first seen him as my boyfriend, then as a new family member, even if it was just via an imaginary child we'd created. Since we hadn't spoken about him, all she had to go on regarding him was what we'd told her, and that was that he was a friend.

I'm not sure he believes we're even that, Mom.

I'm sorry. I shouldn't have brought him. I know how easily you get attached to people. I'll come back and make you feel better about all this. I'm not sure how yet, but I will.

She gave him an awkward parting nod.

I thought that would be it, but Gavin smiled at her with more charm than I thought he had in him and held his arms out. "Is that any way to say goodbye to a man you greeted with a stranglehold a pro wrestler would be proud of?"

My mother smiled and stepped forward to hug him. As she did, she said, "Next time you come, I'll make spaghetti."

He straightened after she released him and winked. "With golf ball meatballs."

Her laugh was a welcome sound to my ears, and I nearly burst into grateful tears. Gavin hadn't just stayed; he'd made sure my mother was smiling as we left.

When we closed the door to her apartment, Gavin and I stood in the hallway next to the stairs. I was emotionally exhausted, and anything except sending Gavin away had a good chance of leading to somewhere I wasn't ready to go.

The problem was, I also didn't want to be alone.

He could have made it easier for me. If he'd leaned in and tried to take advantage of the situation, I would have reacted by panicking and retreating. But no, the asshole chose to stand there just waiting for me to give him a sign of what I wanted.

I would have helped him out, but I was confused.

My brain was telling me one thing.

My heart another.

And my body? It was convinced one good fuck would leave us both feeling better.

I made the mistake of looking up into Gavin's eyes. It didn't take more than that for my list of reasons to send him away to feel foolish.

We were both adults. I wasn't naive enough to believe that every relationship ended with forever. Seriously, I might have enjoyed my previous relationships more if I hadn't wasted time and energy on trying to figure out where they were going. When Teagan met Gian, I told her to let go and let herself enjoy him.

Advice was easier to give than take.

"Thank you for today," I said, because I wasn't ready to share any of my lustful thoughts.

"I'm glad I came."

Really? Men will say anything for sex. "You were kinder than I expected you to be."

He frowned. "That's a backhanded compliment."

I winced. "You know what I meant."

"No. Explain it to me."

I folded my arms across my chest. "You're the one who keeps saying you don't care about anyone."

One of his eyebrows arched. "I said I don't do relationships. That doesn't make me a monster. Your mother has been through a lot. Of course I was kind."

I conceded that point with a tip of my head. "All I'm trying to say is that I'm grateful."

"You're welcome." There was an awkwardness to the silence that followed. We both looked away, then back. When our eyes met again, he said, "I suppose I should head back to Boston."

I cleared my throat. "I suppose you should."

"You okay?"

I nodded, then looked away. I didn't feel okay. All I knew was that I didn't want Gavin to leave, but I also didn't want him to stay. "Would you like to come up?"

He didn't say anything at first, but he moved closer. His hand slid up one of my arms, then tipped my chin up so my eyes met his. The kiss he gave me was light and reassuring. When he raised his head, he said,

"I don't know who you've been with, but if they ever left you feeling that you weren't in control of what happened, then you were with the wrong type. If you want me to stay for a while, I will. If not, that's fine as well. But just to be clear, that doesn't mean I don't care; it means I do."

I swayed on my feet and fell for him just a little then. This was a man I could be real with. "I don't want to be alone, but—"

He stepped back. "As wonderful as this hallway is, show me your damn apartment."

A smile pulled at my lips. "Just when I thought you were so nice."

"I never claimed to be that."

Still smiling, I turned and started walking up the stairs. "Don't judge me if there are socks I might have kicked off while on the couch. The perks of living alone."

From behind me he said, "Totally going to be judging. I hope you didn't leave a dish out as well. That would definitely be a deal breaker."

We shared a laugh.

At the door of my apartment, as I dug for my key in my purse, I thought about how quickly Gavin had gone from a complete stranger to someone I trusted enough to let into my life.

My apartment. I quickly corrected myself.

He'd come with me to see my mother. I was about to let him into my apartment. None of that was an all-access ticket to my life.

I glanced at him over my shoulder. Even if we had sex, there was a good chance it would mean nothing. My cheeks flushed when our eyes met, and I turned quickly to finish unlocking the door.

Being with someone who had no intention of sticking around shouldn't have felt as right as being with Gavin did. By nature I was optimistic when it came to how things would turn out, but he'd been very clear.

If I get my heart broken, this one is on me.
He didn't say maybe . . . he said never.

CHAPTER FOURTEEN

GAVIN

In my experience, situations often arose that were novel and unexpected. Success required maintaining a clear head. I normally avoided emotionally messy situations, but my desire to stay with Riley outweighed everything else. She was vulnerable and confused. I'd leave as soon as I knew she was okay.

Her apartment was an upbeat, slightly more modern version of her mother's. The furniture was comfortable but worn. She had a virtual reality headset in one corner and a pile of clear storage bins in another, with what appeared to be an assortment of clothing inside sorted by size.

She followed my gaze to the bins and said, "Don't mind the mess. Through working with brides, I've come across a lot of people who wear outfits once, then discard them. I started asking if I could rehome those outfits. I never know exactly what will come in, or when, but they have it cleaned before they donate it, and when I have enough, I redistribute the items to local families, shelters, churches. We've had a few dresses come in that were so nice we were able to raffle them off to raise money for a food kitchen."

My breath caught in my throat. Riley was in an entirely different league of humanity than I was. And she was worried that I might judge her for the clutter? "What kind of work do you do with brides?"

She turned toward me and met my gaze. "Don't mock it. I also work at a printshop, but this pays better."

"The bridal industry is a very lucrative one. I simply didn't realize you worked."

"Of course I work." She stopped and nodded. "Oh, because of Dominic. One, I haven't known him that long, and two—his money is *his* money. I've always worked, and I can't imagine not."

The more I got to know Riley, the more I found to like about her. It was unnerving. "I'm the same. So, are you a wedding planner?"

"Not exactly."

I stepped closer as I imagined the possibilities. "You design dresses." She seemed like the creative type.

She shook her head. "I'm a bridesmaid for hire."

"A what?"

"Women hire me to be a member of their bridal party."

"Seriously?" *No.*

Riley walked over to a wall that was covered with photos. "Seriously. It's a job I just kind of fell into but discovered I'm good at. These are the photos the brides sent me after their weddings. They tend to stay in touch, which helps as far as the clothing collection goes."

I took a moment to study the photos. What struck me first was how genuinely happy Riley looked in each of them. She might have been paid to be there, but no one would have guessed it by looking at her. The fact that she was stunning in whatever they dressed her in did not help my ability to concentrate on the topic at hand. What struck me next was the number of grooms I recognized in the photos. They were all from wealthy Boston families. Riley had an impressive client list, and if they did stay in touch with her—a network of influence many would envy. Add in that she was related to both the Corisis and the Romanos, and Riley was everything my father told me *not* to bring home to him. *Normal,* he said. Not someone he'd think I'd see as a useful connection.

Pulling myself back to the conversation at hand, I asked, "Why the hell would anyone pay someone to be in their wedding?"

She shrugged. "Sometimes to even out numbers. Sometimes to run interference." She touched one of the photos. "Some just need to know they have someone in their corner."

"That's Edward Thinsley," I said. "I was invited to that wedding, but chose not to attend." I didn't say more in case Riley didn't see him in the same light I did.

"It was a beautiful wedding. They were so in love." She sighed in a way that implied that hadn't been a permanent state.

"Eugenia's the pregnant friend you wanted advice for."

"Yes." Riley's expression turned pained. "Please keep that to yourself. She hasn't told anyone and trusted me with that secret."

"I've known Edward for years. His mother keeps him on a short leash. I can't imagine him standing up to her."

"People change."

"Not usually."

"Everyone is capable of growth and improvement."

"Capable—sure. Likely to choose either? Doubtful."

Riley's hands went to her hips. "So that's it? There's no hope for anyone ever doing better than they currently are? We should just give up on everyone?"

God, she was hot when she was worked up. "I didn't say that."

She waved her hands and lowered them. "I'm sorry. You're speaking your truth; I'm venting mine."

I stepped closer and tucked a wayward lock of hair behind her ear. "I'm not good at this."

Her eyes raised to mine. "What?"

The urge to kiss her was so strong my hand shook, but I held back. She and I had some things in common, but in other ways we were very different animals. She was a nurturer, raised by a nurturer. I believed in loyalty, but my father and I had never sat around talking about how we felt. When I failed, he didn't come to my side and try to make me feel better about it. The secret to feeling better, according to him, was not failing again.

Be the brightest, fastest, strongest . . . or why bother? It was why I played rugby rather than football in college. To me, life was a contact sport in which extra padding gave a person a false sense of security. Having less protection kept a person focused and better able to pivot and bring an opponent down with a show of agility rather than brute force.

As I looked down into her eyes, I wanted to be someone she could trust, someone she'd turn to for—I stopped myself there and made an impatient sound deep in my throat. "I want to say something to make you feel better, but I've got nothing."

A smile spread across her lips. "You just did. Thank you."

I frowned. "I didn't actually say anything."

"Yes, you did." God, I could get addicted to her smile. "You're a funny man, Gavin Wenham. How is something this simple a mystery to you? Were you raised by wolves?"

"Something like that." I tensed. "My father raised me on his own."

"I didn't know."

"No reason you should."

Riley searched my face. "What happened? To your mother, I mean. If it's okay to ask."

Had anyone else asked, I would have shut them down, but there was real concern in Riley's eyes. "I have no idea, nor do I care to find out. After discovering fidelity was not to her liking, she accepted a cash payout to sign off her parental rights to me. I have zero memories of her. Wouldn't recognize her in a crowd."

She touched my arm. "I'm sorry. That must be hard."

"Ancient history. I can't miss what I never had."

"Yes, you can." Her hand made its way up to rest on my chest. "My father was a horrible man that you'd think I'd be grateful I never met, but that doesn't mean there isn't a little hole in my heart where he was meant to be."

"No place in my heart for someone who never gave a shit about me."

She nodded. "Your mother is why you don't believe in relationships."

"No, I don't believe in relationships because people have romanticized something that has no place in modern society. Trying to hold on to old practices is a waste of time and energy. People used to memorize the phone numbers of their friends and family. No one does that anymore. Why? Because we don't have to. There's nothing a person gets from making a commitment to another person that they couldn't get à la carte."

She tapped a finger on my chest. "À la carte. An interesting insight into how you date."

Could she feel how my heart was racing? It took so little from her to bring me to the brink of pulling her into my arms and taking this where we both wanted it to go. "You think your way is better?"

"I wouldn't expect you to agree, but yes." She smiled as if she'd amused herself. "You know those carnival games where you're hopeful you're skilled enough to win the prize, but you also know the odds are stacked against you? You keep trying, but even when a toss looks promising, it ends up being a near miss. Still, you want that big bear, so you dig deeper in your pocket and cough up enough money and courage for another try."

"You pay your dates?" I knew that wasn't what she was trying to say, but I did enjoy the way her mouth pursed in frustration.

"Jerk. I was trying to say that I know the process of finding a real partner involves disappointments, but I refuse to give up."

I wasn't ready to debate her on this topic, so I joked. "So, *bottom line*, you suck at carnival games."

She looked skyward as if asking for help from above. "No, bottom line, I refuse to settle for less than that big bear."

That much I knew. I countered with, "Have you considered that the prize you're trying so hard for is never worth the bother of carrying it out of the fair? It's filled with that crunchy cheap stuff that invariably ends up all over the floor."

She shook her head. "You can try, but you'll never change how I feel about carnival games. Or relationships. Looks like we will just have to agree to disagree. You can stay single, and I'll ride off into the sunset with some wonderful, non-commitment-phobic man."

It was the only outcome that made any sense to imagine, but I didn't enjoy picturing it. That might have been why there was some bite to my next words. "You claim to be happy here. Where would you ride off to?"

She held my gaze. "Into the sunset to make love in private for a few hours, then rush home because the babysitter promised her mom she'd be home by midnight."

I barked out a laugh, then gathered her to my chest and tucked her beneath my chin and simply held her. She looped her arms around my waist and rested her cheek on my chest. "I never know what you'll say."

She mumbled, "I really have to teach you to give better compliments."

I kissed the top of her head, then released her. "I like you, Riley, but you and I are too different for this to be a good idea."

"You're afraid I'll fall for you, aren't you? And you don't want to break my heart."

Did I come across as that arrogant? It wasn't how I felt, but she'd summed up my concern. "Like I said, I like you."

She leaned back so she could see my face. "Right. All of your concern is for me. It's not that you're afraid to spend too much time around me because you might discover I'm worth breaking your pattern for."

More than the perfection of her features, there was a confidence to Riley that would have made her stand out in any room. It was heady to be around. If there was ever a woman capable of taking me down the same foolish path my father had ventured, it was this one. "You should be afraid I might be that to you."

"Oh, Gavin." She gave my chest a pat. "Do you really think someone my age doesn't already have a list of men she wishes she hadn't slept with? I'd just add your name to it."

I didn't like that. "Long list, is it?"

Looking unfazed by my souring mood, she tilted her head to the side. "I do believe you like me. You're here because you were worried about me—and maybe because you're hoping I'll sleep with you. But you have a difficult time saying nice things to me. Why is that?"

"I'm comfortable being a dick?" It wasn't at all what I expected to come out of my mouth, but I'd said it. The things I said always rang wrong when I was with her. I wasn't nearly as indifferent as I played off being. "I have a question as well. If you don't like what I have to say, why keep pushing me to say it again?"

"Because I like you too." She gave me another long look. "I respect that you're honest with me. I might not agree with what you say, but whatever this is between us—that honesty makes it feel real. More real than with men who told me whatever they thought I wanted to hear."

Was that what I was being? How could I tell her what I was feeling when I had no idea myself? "On that note, I should go." I was losing myself in those beautiful eyes of hers. "I'd like nothing more than to explore whatever this is or isn't, but not tonight." I would have kissed her then, but I knew if I did, I wouldn't leave, and that night wasn't the right time for either of us. I needed to get my head straight, and she needed to digest the conversation she'd just had with her mother.

"You're certainly sure of yourself. In your mind, if it weren't for your resolve, we'd already be having sex?" I loved the challenge in her tone.

"Wouldn't we be?"

"Maybe." Her smile was cheeky and nearly my undoing.

I needed to get some space between us. "I'll let myself out."

"You do that."

127

"But I'll call you."

"I'm okay either way. Don't strain yourself."

I took a step away, then stopped, turned back, and hauled her to me for a deep, lustful kiss. It was wild, hungry, and so fucking good I almost lost control. She kissed me back with matching passion. I dug my hands into her hair. She clutched my back. Any other night I would have stayed.

Not this way. Not while she was upset about her mother.

I broke off the kiss and swore.

She brought a hand to her mouth, looking surprised, turned on, and totally fuckable.

I turned on my heel and grumbled all the way to the door. This wasn't like me. I didn't lose control or act impulsively.

"Talk to you soon, Gavin," she said in a husky tone.

Without responding, I closed the door behind me with more force than I'd meant to. I stood in her hallway for several minutes before finally walking away.

My father was eager for me to get married, to buy into all the crap he'd turned his back on when my mother left. I thought about how he regretted passing his view of people—especially women—on to me. I hadn't realized how much he had until recently.

As I waited for the car I'd called to arrive, I glanced up at the window of Riley's apartment. There was movement in it. Had she been watching and moved away when I looked?

Was she wishing I'd change my mind and return?

I was already kicking myself for not doing so.

When my resolve wavered, I told myself that my father had likely felt the same way for my mother. *Look how that turned out.*

But I'm not him.

And Riley is nothing like my mother.

I turned away from Riley's window.

Sure, she was intelligent, funny, socially responsible, loyal, and sexy as hell—but that didn't mean I needed to get sloppy and stupid every time she smiled at me. I scrolled through my phone again, through woman after woman I'd known intimately. None tempted me.

Not one damn one.

My car arrived. I slid into the back seat and glared at the empty window.

This is not happening. You hear me, Riley Ragsdale? I am not doing this.

CHAPTER FIFTEEN

RILEY

I woke the next morning to the buzzing of my phone. It had to be my mother. No one else would call me so early. I rolled over without opening my eyes and said, "Morning, Mom."

"It's Teagan."

My eyes flew open, and a huge smile spread across my face. "Are you back?"

"No, but we're in the air now. Best trip of my life. I have so much to tell you."

I adjusted my position so I could sit partially up while resting against the back of the bed. "I have time now. I want to hear everything."

"That's right, your boss is out of town. That is, if you still work for me."

"I might be able to squeeze time with you into my busy schedule. I'm not even working with a bride right now. It's weird. I've worked two or three jobs for so long that I'm not sure what to do with sudden time off. Usually a new bride would have called me already."

She laughed. "Perfect! I can hire you to be in my wedding."

I rolled my eyes. "Jerk. I'm serious. I went from being in demand to not. Isn't that weird? Word of mouth used to be enough to keep them coming to me. I guess I'll have to get proactive."

"You will always have a job at the printshop for as long as you need one, but I have a feeling a world of opportunity is opening up to you now. What happened to your plan to return to school?"

I ran a hand through my bed hair. "I don't know. I was undeclared the first time. I don't want to do that again. And then there's the money."

"That's not a problem anymore, is it? If you feel strange about taking money from Dominic, the Romanos would help you out as well. Sebastian was talking about that the other day. You're not just a Corisi, you know. As his sister, you're a Romano as well."

In the background, Gian said, "You sure are. The Romano/Corisi/Ragsdale family tree is a complicated one, but I consider you my sister, even though we don't share a biological parent, Riley. If there is one thing all of this has taught me, it's that family is about so much more than sharing the same genes. We're here for you—whatever you need. We've got you."

I swallowed a lump in my throat. Knowing his own journey, I knew he understood how confusing these family revelations could be and how they could shake someone's sense of identity. He'd also been up front with me regarding how his relationship with Dominic had been strained until he started standing up to him.

I couldn't imagine telling Dominic off, but I could see a potentially awkward conversation between us happening one day. We needed to find a happy balance of him feeling that he could show me he cared and me retaining pride in who I was and my ability to do things for myself.

"I agree, Gian, and I know you understand when I say all of these new relationships are a work in progress. I'm still very much stumbling through building them. I appreciate the support everyone has offered, but I want to get to know all of you without money being put in the mix." The Romanos were on my mother's no-contact list as well. Hearing about Dominic had been the biggest pill for her to swallow, but Sebastian looked an awful lot like Antonio too. I groaned. "I shouldn't have taken the penthouse in Boston, Teagan. I feel icky about it. I understand that Dominic wants to take care of me, but I just want him to be my brother."

"I can understand that. Have you—how is your mother?"

"I told her. At least about Dominic."

"Whoa. When? How? How did she handle it?"

"Yesterday, and about as you'd expect. We haven't spoken since, but I'll bring her lunch today and see if we can get past this. Neither of us changed our minds during the conversation, but at least I'm not lying to her anymore. I hated that."

"I'm so sorry I wasn't there. I know how hard that must have been for you. You should have called me."

"I didn't want to take away from your trip, and I'm glad I didn't. Now, spill. Don't leave a single detail out about Montalcino and everyone you met."

For the next hour Teagan did just that. I loved every part of the fairy tale she was living. Gian's grandmother sounded like one hot shit. Teagan listed off the names of Gian's cousins faster than I was able to remember them, but it didn't matter. I was just happy that she was happy.

Every once in a while, Gian chimed in to add to the stories she was telling. There was a time when, because of his mother's relationship with Dominic's father, Gian wasn't welcomed by his old-country family. That was ancient history, because I had never heard either of them sound happier and more in love.

The big bear—they'd played the game and won it. No one could convince me that a love like they had wasn't worth the effort or possible disappointments that preceded it.

I thought about Eugenia and her marriage. I would have asked Teagan for advice on the matter, but I wasn't confused anymore. Love didn't come with a guarantee, and it was only as strong as the people in it. I thought about Dominic and Abby. They didn't hide that they'd had their issues over the years, but they'd always chosen each other over whatever faced them.

The Romanos were the same. If I hadn't known the twists and turns of their family tree, I wouldn't have guessed at the complexity of it. Gian was adopted, Sebastian was from a man Camilla had been with before her husband, and yet there was no difference in how Camilla and Basil loved each of their four sons. Their love had been tested and had grown stronger because of it. That was the kind of love I wanted for myself.

What kind of love did Eugenia and Edward have? Only they knew. If they let his mother divide them, they probably wouldn't last. If they chose to stand and fight for what they had, to pull together and be each other's rock, then they just might remember why they gave vows to each other.

Edward, Eugenia doesn't owe you her love—you need to deserve it.

I thought about Gavin and what he'd said on the matter of family and taking sides. His stance wasn't clear to me. Would he stand up for me? I believed he would. He spoke like he wouldn't, but I couldn't imagine him sitting back and doing nothing while anyone was being mistreated.

Is that why Gavin hadn't attended Edward's wedding? Was being spineless a pattern for Edward and not a temporary lapse a few harsh words could wake him from? I only knew Edward from our interactions during the wedding planning. If Gavin had known him for years, he would have much more to base his opinion on.

"Are you still there?" Teagan asked.

"Yes, sorry. Still here."

"No, I'm sorry. I went on and on. It really was a magical trip."

"Shut up, I loved hearing about it. And guess what? I'm a good enough friend that if you want to pretend we didn't have this conversation yet and you want to tell me all about your trip again, let's grab breakfast together tomorrow morning."

Teagan laughed. "And this is why you're my best friend. I love you."

"I love you too. And I'm serious. I'm sure you have photos. Hearing about the trip will be even more fun when I can put faces to names."

"You're on." She lowered her voice. "Hey, how did your date go with that guy you met? Steve?"

"He stood me up."

"What?" Teagan's shock boosted my morale a bit.

"I know, right? That's three in a row. They all seem interested enough to ask me out, but they don't show."

Gian chimed in. "You're not, by any chance, telling Dominic about them, are you?"

"No, why?"

Gian made a sound in his throat. "He can be a little overprotective."

"You think he's scaring off my dates?" I asked it as a joke, but neither of them laughed. I hadn't thought of that. "I don't talk to Dominic about stuff like that, though. There's no way he would know." *Unless.* Mr. Tuttle wasn't *Mr. Tattle*, was he? I couldn't see him doing that.

"There's one way to know for sure," Gian said. "Ask him."

"Wouldn't he just lie?"

"That's not Dominic's style. Ask him flat out. He's over the top and definitely has problems with boundaries, but he won't lie to you."

I tried to picture how that conversation would go and couldn't. "We're not in a place yet where I could talk to him like that."

In a gentle tone, Teagan said, "Then maybe that's exactly why you have to have that conversation. Gian used to worry more about offending Dominic than he does now. And they're closer than ever. Sometimes trying to be nice to someone stops things from being real with them."

Her words struck home to me, since I'd just said essentially that to Gavin. "I'll bring it up to him. But not yet. I want to patch things up with Mom first. One fire at a time."

"You've got this, Riley," Teagan said.

Gian added, "You can always tell me to shut up, but I feel like I've walked the same path you're heading down. You feel torn between two families. There's a constant sense of guilt that you begin to resent. You don't want to hide anything from your family, but it's easier to say nothing."

"Yes. All that—yes!"

"Be patient and forgiving with yourself as well as everyone involved. Even good people need time to find their footing in new situations. If your mother isn't ready to let Dominic into her life, don't push her. Over time her fears will fall away. Trust me, we just spent time with some family who used to consider Dominic the devil. They love him now. These things don't happen overnight."

I blinked back tears. If I tried to draw my family tree, I'm not sure I could anymore, but that was beginning to matter less and less to me. "Okay, I have a question. When you and Teagan marry, Gian, can I officially call Teagan my sister? Because that's what all this is about for me."

They both laughed. Teagan said, "You've been calling me your sister for close to a decade."

"Oh yeah," I joked. "Then I guess this is really all about the souvenir you two surely thought to bring back for me. What did you get me? A T-shirt? A Colosseum pencil sharpener?"

"I told you we needed to get her something," Gian said to Teagan. "How about a bottle of a wine that will be sold exclusively through my store?"

"Oh no," I teased. "One of you is coughing up at least a key chain for me, or the three of us are heading back there sometime so I can get my own."

Teagan's voice rose an octave. "I would love that. Oh my God, Gian, what do you think? Could we go back with Riley soon?"

"Absolutely, but she stays with Nona, and we get the guesthouse."

I wasn't entirely sure what that meant, but I was okay with it.

Teagan continued, "Who knows, Riley, you just might come home with an Italian of your own."

"I may have met someone," I confessed and wrinkled my nose. "I brought him with me to see Mom yesterday, and she liked him."

"You did? Wait, how is this the first I'm hearing about him?"

"Technically we haven't been on a date yet, but this guy is different. Not sure if that's a good or bad thing, but I'm not telling the Corisis about him yet, that's for sure. You hear me, Gian? You know nothing. If this one stands me up, I'll really be sad."

"I'm a vault," Gian promised.

"Don't even think you're ending this call before telling us all about him."

"Okay, but hear me out. My first impression of him isn't my current one." I settled deeper into my pillows. "His name is Gavin Wenham, and when we first met, I thought he was trying to hire me for the night . . ."

CHAPTER SIXTEEN
GAVIN

I didn't call Riley the next day, because calling a woman the day after seeing her would set a precedent I'd never been willing to make. Essentially it would be the same as walking into a car dealership and announcing that you need to leave with one of their vehicles that day.

We could be friends. We could be lovers. There wasn't room in my life for more.

I didn't call her the day after that because I'd had difficulty sleeping. Why? Because I felt bad that I hadn't called her. I couldn't shake the feeling that I should have at least checked in to see if she'd spoken to her mother the next day and, if so, how it had gone.

All night long I tossed and turned, thinking about what would happen between us if I were anyone but myself. So, to prove something to myself, I didn't call her the next day either. That whole day went to shit as well. I couldn't concentrate during my meetings with various staff members. Worst thing I did? I rode the elevator down to the lobby and forgot to get out. The doors closed, and I was sent back up.

Only because we'd made eye contact just before the elevator doors closed, I made a point to tell Bill and Keith that I'd realized last minute that I'd forgotten something up in my penthouse. There was no way in hell I was about to admit the truth.

Riley was literally killing my mojo. Definitive proof that women like her were a danger to men like me.

Unfortunately, avoiding her for another whole day had not lessened her allure. It was time to address the problem head on. I had no choice but to see her again and let familiarity do what it was good at: breed contempt. There had to be something about her I didn't like. All I had to do was find out what it was and focus on that.

I walked out onto the balcony of my penthouse. Would she be irritated with me for not calling her? I hoped so. I had little tolerance for clingy women.

She picked up on the third ring. "Gavin. Perfect timing."

She didn't sound annoyed. A lesser man would have made an excuse for not calling, which was just as bad as actually calling. Instead, I said, "Always."

"Cute." She chuckled. "I am sliding off my shoes, pouring myself a glass of the best wine I've ever tasted, and there's a good chance if we talk long enough, you'll end up in the tub with me. Thank God my phone is waterproof."

Wait. What?

The sound of a cork being pulled from a bottle ricocheted through me. What the hell was I doing in Boston when I could be there with her? I took a deep calming breath, but that did nothing to stop my cock from coming to full attention. Shit.

I opened my mouth to say something witty but discovered my brain was not ready to cooperate by providing anything intelligent to say. "How are you?" was all I eventually got out.

"I am beat, but what a great day it was. My friend Teagan returned from Italy with her fiancé, Gian. I met them at his parents' house. It was so wonderful. The Romanos flew me down to Connecticut in a helicopter. I'd never been in one before, so that was an experience all by itself." She paused and made a happy sound. "This really *is* good wine." The next time she spoke, there was a slight echo, then the sound of water rushing. "I'm sorry, what was I saying?"

I had no idea. My mind was filling with images of her stripping down and submerging herself in bubbles. Or no bubbles. Having a clear view of her beneath the water was actually a better fantasy. I loosened my tie. "Something about the Romanos?"

"Oh yes. They're the kind of people you instantly feel like you've always known. Their home is always bursting at the seams with their children and grandchildren. It's loud, crazy, and like walking into a movie of how I've always imagined a family could be. They all sit around at this long table and eat meals for hours, passing wine around, laughing over stories they embarrass each other by telling. I love them so much."

Well, damn, there went my theory that she was the type to wait by the phone for my call. She didn't sound as if she'd given me a thought at all. "Sounds like you had a great time."

"I did. Hang on."

Holy shit, that was definitely the sound of the water being turned off and her clothing hitting the floor. Splash. Splash. Audible sigh of satisfaction. I could have come in my pants just listening. Did she have any idea what she was doing to me? My voice was strangled when I said, "Take your time."

"I probably should have waited until we ended our call before I hopped in the tub, but you can't see me anyway, so does it matter?"

Oh, it matters. It so fucking matters. "I—I—"

She's broken me. I can't even speak anymore.

"The thing is, I flew home in the helicopter alone, and I didn't say anything, but it was a little unnerving landing at night. I kept my composure, even though on the inside I was a wreck. I made it home, so now I'm just going to decompress."

"That's—" Holy shit, how long was the drive to her place? Not that I was actually going to race over there like some overeager teenager, but if I did, would the water still be warm?

I wasn't much of a drinker, but I walked inside and poured myself a double shot of scotch. I was speaking to a woman who happened to be in a tub, not watching porn. There was no reason I couldn't maintain some control over the situation as well as my reaction to it.

"You're killing me," I admitted in a guttural tone.

She gasped, then said, "It *is* kind of sexy to be talking to you while I'm bathing."

A little. "I'm not coming over." Then I groaned. Really? Why did I say that?

Her response was a chuckle. "You weren't invited."

Touché. I didn't have a comeback for that. She tangled me up with such ease. With some women this scene would have led to a whole lot of sex talk and us both bringing ourselves to orgasm. I had a feeling that was not where this was headed, though.

She asked, "So, how is your week going?"

Like shit. Until now. "Not bad. Long."

"Oh, I had a nice talk with my mother. She's essentially pretending we didn't have the conversation about the Corisis, but she asked about you. I told her we were just friends, but she said she doubted that stage would last long."

What the hell? Rather than continue to torture myself, I might as well get to the point. "Are you busy tomorrow?"

"I don't believe so."

"Come to Boston."

"To meet your father? Okay. You lived up to your side; I should live up to mine."

"No, not to see my father."

"Hold on, you sound so serious. Is something wrong?"

"No. Not wrong. I don't know. I just want to see you."

"Are you asking me out on a date?"

I slapped a hand to my forehead. "Yes. That's what I'm doing. Come if you want to. Don't if you're not interested."

"Oh, I see. So, you're asking me to go on a date, but you don't care if I show up?"

"Of course I care if you show up."

"Then leave off the rest. You're complicating something that should be easy. Most men just say they like me, and we choose a place to meet. It's just a date, Gavin. You can relax. There's absolutely no expectation of commitment until at least our third meal."

"What?"

She laughed. "I'm sorry. That was mean of me. I would love to see you tomorrow."

I should have kept my next comment to myself, but I said, "I don't like this."

"This?"

"I can't get you out of my thoughts. I get all goofy around you. I don't want to be this person."

She was quiet for a moment, then said, "Relationships are scary. If it makes you feel any better, I keep telling myself you're not my type, but I've talked about you so much these past few days that even the Romanos want to meet you."

That did make me feel slightly better. And it freaked me out a little. Mostly it freaked me out that it made me feel better. I cleared my throat. "About tomorrow. Do you like boats?"

"I love them! And it's supposed to be a beautiful day. What time would you like to meet up?"

"Eleven?"

"Sounds perfect. I'm going to hang up now. I don't know what tomorrow will lead to, but I'm going to shave my legs anyway."

I laughed and swallowed hard. "Thank you. I appreciate that."

"See you tomorrow."

CHAPTER SEVENTEEN

RILEY

I checked myself in the full-length mirror in my bedroom. I couldn't remember the last time I'd been so nervous before a date. I changed my outfit several times before settling on jeans and a nice shirt. We were going on a boat, after all. People didn't dress up to get windblown and work a sail, did they?

I grabbed my phone and typed to Gavin, I'm about to leave my house. If there's any reason why you think we might need to call off today, could you save me the trip and tell me now? I sent the message and waited.

It did seem like a needy question, but under the circumstances I felt it was something that had to be asked. I'd been disappointed by the men who had ghosted me, but if Gavin did the same . . . well, it would hit me hard. Even if he didn't necessarily want anything long term, I believed he cared about me, at least enough to not leave me standing somewhere waiting for him.

His answer came a moment later: Why would I call it off?

Confession: the day we met was the third time in a little over a month I'd been stood up by men who had asked me out.

That explains what you said to me.

What had I said? I groaned as I remembered smelling him, then announcing I wasn't interested because I already knew it would end with him standing me up. I'm not normally paranoid about things, but there's definitely a pattern. It's okay if you have a reason you can't make it today. Just tell me.

I'll be there. Call me as soon as you arrive and we'll meet by the elevators.

He sure sounded like he would be there. I dressed casually. Is that okay?

Is any of it difficult to take off?

I laughed. You're bad. And funny, which works at settling my nerves.

Get your ass to Boston, Riley. I have a nice day planned for us.

Leaving in two.

I sent a quick message to Mr. Tuttle to tell him I was on my way down, then pocketed my phone and rushed to collect my purse and keys. Mr. Tuttle met me at the corner of my block and held the door open for me as I slid into the back seat of the car.

"Mr. Tuttle?"

"Yes?"

It probably wasn't the best time to ask, but it had been on my mind a lot recently. "Does your job require you to report anything to my brother?"

I didn't like that he neither answered me nor looked me in the eye. I sat back and let out a sigh. "Is it a detailed report?"

Mr. Tuttle flexed his shoulders, and he finally met my gaze in the rearview mirror. "I'm highly trained in hand-to-hand combat as well as hostage negotiation. As a sharpshooter, I could remove a threat at a thousand yards. I would take a bullet for you, but you frequently put me in difficult situations." Some of my confusion must have shown on my face, because he added, "The less you tell me, the less I have to deny knowing."

I mulled that over and wished I hadn't asked. My mother saw the Corisis as people who used their wealth to control all those around them. Dominic had said I needed a driver to keep me safe, but was that true? Or was Mr. Tuttle Dominic's way of keeping track of everything I was doing?

That sounded sinister, and I tried to shake the thought from my head. If Dominic really was like that, then the Romanos would want nothing to do with him—and they adored him. "Did you tell him about the men I met? The ones who stood me up?"

"I didn't have to. Nothing happens in the realm of your brother that he doesn't know about."

That sent another shiver down my back. "He's a good man, though, isn't he?"

Mr. Tuttle was silent for a long moment, then said, "I like my job. It pays well. Money isn't everything, though. I wouldn't be here if I didn't think you were worth taking a bullet for."

I wasn't entirely sure that made me feel better. "I would never want you to do that, Mr. Tuttle." I also didn't like the idea that it was a possibility. "I should warn you: if it ever comes to that, you'd have to wrestle me to the ground, because I'd take a bullet for you as well."

He shook his head. "I believe you. Let me make it clear now, though, that if we ever find ourselves in a dangerous situation, drop to the ground yourself. Requiring me to split my attention between the threat and the possibility of you doing something foolish is what will get me killed."

I chuckled awkwardly, a little from nerves and a little in embarrassment. "Mr. Tuttle, you know what I like about you? You don't sugarcoat anything. I like that I always know where I stand with you."

"No one likes to be lied to. Not me. Not you. Not your brother." He met my gaze in the mirror again. "So, I'll turn up the music while you call your friend, because I know you are dying to tell her about your plans for the day."

I frowned at that. "Shouldn't you want to know where I'm headed? You know, so you could protect me there as well?"

"Do you honestly believe I'm the only one watching you?" Without waiting for me to respond, he turned on the radio.

I hugged my arms around myself. Dominic had *people* watching me? Not just one person? The hair on the back of my neck stood on end even as I told myself Dominic was only trying to keep me safe. My mother had said it was impossible to get away from Antonio. No matter how she'd tried to hide from him, he'd always found her. It was all about control.

Would I see an ugly side of my brother if I ever said no to him? I got goose bumps at that. No, Dominic wasn't vindictive. Kal was refusing to even meet with him, and he'd done nothing but continue to ask about him.

Was Dominic's patience based on my lies about how Kal felt toward him? What would happen when he discovered the truth?

Was I being paranoid? Or waking up to who my brother really was? The scariest part was not knowing.

I was excited to see Gavin again, but my conversation with Mr. Tuttle had cast a cloud over the day. Normally I would've been on the phone with Teagan telling her all about the date I was going on, but even though Mr. Tuttle had essentially said he wouldn't listen in, I still felt exposed and vulnerable.

Would someone be watching me while I was on my date with Gavin? The idea of that made my skin crawl.

I was beginning to believe Dominic was the reason the other men hadn't shown up. What would be his purpose in stopping me from being with anyone? And would he try to do the same with Gavin?

The buildings we passed as we entered the city were a blur through the windows of the car as I imagined what Gavin would say if Dominic told him not to see me. I couldn't imagine that conversation going well. There was a lot I didn't yet know about Gavin, but my gut told me he wasn't easy to intimidate.

I rubbed my hands over my face. *If Gavin doesn't show up today, my mother might be right—Dominic might not be who I think he is, and this could all be some kind of sick game to him. A game where the ones who get hurt the most will once again be the Ragsdales.*

No, I didn't want to believe it.

I considered calling Dominic then and asking him how much of what I was thinking was true, but there was nothing to stop him from simply lying to me. I'd let his actions speak for him.

CHAPTER EIGHTEEN

GAVIN

Feeling restless, I made my way down to the waterfront to confirm that the dinghy was there and ready. The captain had confirmed his arrival via text, but the fresh air walk was good for my state of mind. Even though there was still plenty of time before Riley arrived, I wanted everything to be perfect.

Originally I had planned to take Riley out to eat at an exclusive chef's table, but Jared had called about something completely unrelated and offered me the use of his yacht, staff and all, for the day. In my world, working high-end deals often meant networking and maintaining connections with a wide variety of wealthy people. Since they could already afford whatever they wanted, it was about providing them with unique experiences that made them feel special. If there was a way to create an experience their family could enjoy as well, then the deal was practically sealed. Jared's crew was a combination of experienced whale-watching tour guides, luxury-yacht staff, and top chefs he courted and rotated from all around New England. These private whale-watching tours were by invitation only and were coveted by many.

I found it amusing how people who could afford to do the same trip with their own yachts dropped the mention of having gone on Jared's to one-up each other.

Oh, you went whale-watching near Boston? On the Resolution? *Oh no. You haven't? You should try it sometime—it's amazing.*

The "you should try it" was the not-so-subtle challenge to be on the level of the braggart. Jared had offered me a trip many times in the past, but I'd always been too busy to take him up on it. *I guess I can finally claim the badge of honor.*

The dinghy was docked and ready. I could have driven Riley across town to the wharf where Jared normally had his yacht tied, but Jared liked to showcase the drive-in hidden garage in the back of his yacht. He said the success of the experience was in the details.

The experience was what I wanted for Riley. It wasn't about impressing her as much as wanting to make her smile. She was a local; she'd probably seen whales before. But had she seen them with a glass of champagne in one hand and some of the area's finest seafood in the other, served up by a North End chef? It sounded like the perfect backdrop for our first date.

I groaned. First date? That made it sound like I had many planned. That wasn't where this was going, was it?

I stood there looking out over the water, asking myself how the idea of seeing the same person on a regular basis no longer bothered me. It was time to admit the truth to myself—I wanted to get to know Riley. And not just for one night.

This wasn't about getting her out of my system.

What would anything else look like? I had no idea. This was uncharted territory for me.

"Mr. Wenham, thank you for making this meeting an easy one."

My head snapped around. She was a stunning redhead, tall, possibly in her late thirties. I had no idea who she was. "I wasn't aware we had a meeting. Your name is?"

"Unimportant. I'm here to offer you an opportunity."

I shook my head. "Sorry. I'm taken." Was I? Who knew. All I was sure of was that I wasn't looking to start anything new until I figured out what Riley and I had.

She laughed. "Already? That's fast. You just met her."

My eyes narrowed. "What is this about?"

Her expression sobered, and her eyes turned cunning. "You're meeting Riley Ragsdale today, aren't you?"

"If I am, why would it be of any interest to you?"

"Let's just say I represent someone who cares very deeply for her. He's generously offered to compensate you if you break things off with Riley before they go any further."

"Is this some kind of fucking joke?"

"No joke. If you don't mind my being indelicate, I'm in a position to make things happen for you that might not otherwise be possible. The situation with your father's company, for example, is teetering. You're about to have a fight on your hands, even if he gives you the reins soon. I could smooth that over. All it would take from the person I represent is a word, and that storm dissipates."

Anger rose in me, but I kept it contained. How did this woman know anything about what was going on at my family's company? And the board's waning confidence in my father? I was handling it. "Let me get this straight—you're bribing me to end things with Riley?"

Her smile was cold. "'Bribing' is such an ugly term. I prefer to call it 'encouraging' you. But like I said, we're prepared to be generous. So if there's something else you need, put it on the table. We'll at least entertain it."

"Who do you represent?" I had a pretty good idea, but I wanted confirmation.

"Maybe you don't want your father's company. Maybe what you wish you had was capital to start your own. Name your price. You might be surprised how well compensated you could be."

What the fuck is this? I remembered Riley saying she'd been stood up several times recently. Was this why? The high-handedness had Dominic Corisi written all over it. It had to be him. "Fifty million." I said the amount purely to see her reaction.

She didn't blink. "Higher than expected, but I'll run the number by him."

"No." Only years of learning to control my temper to keep the upper hand allowed me to retain my composure. I folded my arms across my chest. "You tell the person you represent that Riley will be here in less than an hour. If he wants to discuss that matter with me, he can damn well talk to me himself."

The redhead's eyebrows rose. "One moment." She stepped away and took out her phone, then returned and held it out to me. "Here you go."

I held her phone up to my ear. "Yes?"

"Fifty million? You do understand this isn't a blackmail situation? I'm giving you an opportunity to not only back out of this unscathed, but also be compensated for your discretion."

"My discretion depends on my opinion of the situation. Who am I speaking to?"

"Dominic Corisi." He said his name like it was enough to sway my decision.

"Well, Dominic, we have a problem. I've planned a nice first date for your sister and me. I don't want to cancel it. So my countersuggestion is that you stay out of my family's business and we pretend we never had this conversation."

"You don't want me as an enemy, Wenham."

If my father had taught me anything, it was to face down opposition. "Take it there if you need to, *Corisi*, but that won't change the fact that I intend to enjoy a nice day out with your sister. There's nothing you could offer me or threaten me with that would change that."

"Prepared to test that theory?" He growled the question.

It wasn't just the idea that I could be bought off that was offensive. That would have been bad enough. However, layered on top was how disappointing it was to witness Dominic living down to Riley's mother's opinion of him rather than up to Riley's. "Absolutely, Corisi, but before you do, I have a question for you."

"And that is?"

"Do you actually want to have a relationship with Riley?"

The fury in Dominic's voice was clear. "Are you threatening me?"

I wasn't, but not because I was afraid of him. I knew opponents came in all different sizes, but they all had vulnerabilities. If he came for me, he'd discover no one was untouchable, not even him. My anger, though, was being slowly replaced with a desire to fix this for Riley's sake. I didn't want him to be who her mother thought he was. Sometimes people didn't see things clearly until it was explained to them. "No, I'm saying if you do love your sister, this is the opposite of what you should be doing. Intimidation. Paying people to stay away from her. If she finds out, you'll lose her."

"*If* I love my sister? Push me, and you'll see exactly how far I'll go to protect her."

"I don't believe that'll be necessary, because you're smarter than that. I've met Riley's mother. I've seen how afraid she still is, not only of your father, but that you will ultimately hurt Riley, because in her mind you're no different than he was. Riley thinks you're better than that. She doesn't believe you're like him at all. One of them is right. Acting like this will ultimately hurt Riley, and you're the only one who can stop that from happening."

Dominic's response was silence.

I added, "I like your sister. Plain and simple. I have no idea if what we'll have will be a friendship or something more, but I can promise you this—push me, and you'll see exactly how far *I'll* go to protect her. Do things have to go there? No, but it's entirely up to you." With that, I ended the call and handed the phone back to the redhead.

She smiled. "You did good, Wenham. I approve of you. I'm sure he does too." She turned and walked away without saying another word, leaving me with more questions than answers.

Was Riley's mother right about Dominic, or was Riley? His next move would be telling.

What kind of men had Riley agreed to go out with if they'd let Dominic pay or scare them off? Men with the same sense of loyalty my mother had. None.

I thought about what Riley had said to her mother regarding how Dominic was also a victim of Antonio's cruelty. Had this really been an attempt on his part to protect Riley? If so, I couldn't hate him for that. It was better than not caring about her, but it was still too much.

There was also the issue of how much the redhead seemed to know about Wenham Global. I didn't like the idea that she might have inside knowledge.

As I headed back to the apartment building, I smiled, and my step became lighter. Work could wait. Dominic and whatever test he might have in store for me next could wait as well. I checked my watch. It was still a little before eleven.

My phone buzzed with a message from Riley: Here. On my way down the elevator.

Walking back to the building now.

She met me just outside the front door of the building and started walking toward me as soon as she spotted me. My pace increased. Hers did as well.

As natural as if we'd done it a hundred times, I lifted her into my arms and swung her around, lowering her only to claim her lips for a deep kiss. Her arms wound around my neck, her mouth opened eagerly beneath mine, and the moan she made wiped all coherent thought right out of my head.

I had to remind myself we were in public. The desire that flared between us was hot and heady. She moved herself back and forth against my cock in a rhythm that had me groaning with pleasure as well. Holy hell, the way she made me feel shook me to the core. I'd never felt so alive.

Whatever this was, it was powerful.

Heady.

Overwhelming in the most incredible way.

When I finally raised my head, we took a moment to simply look into each other's eyes. Her expression reflected how I felt—crazy turned on and loving it.

In a breathy voice, she said, "You're here."

"I am." I looped my arms around her waist and held her close. The conversation with Dominic echoed in my head. I didn't know the men he'd run off, but they were fools. "I'm looking forward to today."

She bounced in excitement against me. "Me too. I haven't spent much time on boats, but I love them."

"And whales?"

"Who doesn't love whales?"

"Seafood?"

"My favorite food after pizza."

"Then let's go." I took her hand in mine and started guiding her along the path that led to the dinghy.

She trotted along, smiling. "You planned all that?"

I frowned. "It wasn't a big deal to put together."

Her happy smile implied she didn't believe me. "I went up to my apartment before calling you. Guess what was in there?"

"You tell me." I knew, but I was enjoying her excitement.

"Dozens of pink carnations. Enough that I'm a little worried about you. Flowers. Dinner on a boat. Whale-watching. For a man who doesn't do relationships, you're putting a lot of effort into this."

She was right, but it wasn't something I was ready to admit. "Carnations are cheap enough."

"Oh, I see. You simply took advantage of a deal where if you buy dozens, it's cheaper than getting one?"

"See, this is why I don't do nice shit." There was no bite to my tone. She was giving me crap; all I was doing was giving it right back to her. I may not be a man who sends flowers, but I'd wanted to make her smile.

Her hand tightened on my hand. "I love them, thank you."

Approval from her shouldn't have felt as good as it did. Making her happy had an addictive quality—the more I did it, the more I wanted to. "I'm glad. Let's go—the boat won't come to us."

"And I'm excited about the whale watch. I'm sure it's going to be amazing."

I stopped and looked down at her. The smile she beamed up at me had me thinking I was crazy to be walking away from our bedrooms rather than toward one of them. "I wish I could find something about you I don't like."

"That's the sweetest thing anyone has ever said to me."

"Bullshit."

"I'm grading on a scale. A lot of people say more than they mean, and none of it holds up over time. You say it as it is. It's refreshing."

Refreshing? She really did have poor taste in men. Since I wasn't enjoying the idea of her with anyone else, even if those relationships hadn't worked out, I asked, "Do you want to see a whale or not?"

"Yes, sir." She laughed and increased her pace. I glanced down at her, which was a mistake, because she was definitely laughing at me. And damn, if I wasn't fine with being the source of her amusement. It was simply good to see her smiling.

We arrived at the dock where the dinghy was tied up. The man standing beside it introduced himself as the yacht's first mate and explained to us that he would be taking us out to where Jared's yacht, the *Resolution*, was anchored.

Riley sat next to me in the back while the first mate untied the dinghy and started up the engine. "Yacht?"

I shrugged. "It belongs to a friend of mine."

The speed at which we raced across the bay made talking difficult, but it did send Riley sliding across the seat against me. I put my arm around her to steady her.

"This is so fun," she said, laughing from the sheer joy of the speed.

Fun had never been a priority for me. Sure, I did things that I enjoyed, but laugh-out-loud, smile-until-my-face-hurts fun? No, I couldn't say I'd had much of that. I liked how Riley let go and enjoyed herself.

To be honest, I envied her a little for being able to. I also wondered if she wouldn't be a lot happier with someone . . . less like me. Liking her didn't make me someone who would be good for her.

I stopped myself there. Hold on—when had I started thinking in those terms? Exactly where did I think this was going?

"Oh, my God, is that the one we're going on?" Riley exclaimed.

"That's it." We slowed our speed as we approached.

"It's huge."

"It's a two-hundred-fifty-footer."

"Wait, is that a garage on the side?"

"It's a float-in tender that I suppose does lead to a garage of sorts." When Jared had described it to me, I hadn't been that interested. However, seeing it through Riley's eyes gave me a different perspective. How had I lost all sense of wonder? Once gone, was it gone forever?

"A boat with its own garage. No way, we're going straight in like this?" As we prepared to, she grabbed my arm. "I'm sorry, I have a fear of anything like car washes. Kal once opened our car door during one, and it scarred me for life."

I laughed at that and hugged her closer. "I'm pretty certain this will be nothing like that."

The dinghy effortlessly slid through the opening on the side of the boat, and Riley relaxed against my side. A panel closed behind the dinghy, which was secured by another deckhand. We stepped onto a deck that was walled on one side and open to the stern of the yacht on the other.

A steward greeted us with flutes of champagne. Riley took a sip of hers, but only one. As we followed him to the main part of the boat, I watched Riley. Her eyes were wide and she was excited, but I sensed something was bothering her. "What do you think of the boat?" I asked.

She waved a hand at the full bar that was the backdrop to an ornate lounge. "It's like a floating hotel—so shiny clean I'm afraid to touch anything."

That surprised me. It was easy to forget that this lifestyle wasn't something she'd grown up with. "And the champagne?"

She lowered her voice. "Does champagne go bad? I usually like it, but this one is bitter."

I sipped mine. If I had to guess, it was a $10,000 bottle of Jared's favorite brand, and it *was* bitter, just as it was meant to be. Interesting. If I thought about it, it wasn't a flavor I enjoyed either. I took her glass and returned it to the steward, along with mine. "Thank you, but we'd like . . . Riley, what would you prefer? Something sweet?"

"Oh yes. Actually, a ginger ale would be great."

"Make that two," I said.

The steward smiled politely. "Absolutely." He excused himself to retrieve our drink of choice.

Once alone, Riley asked, "It wasn't bad, was it?"

I smiled. "No, just expensive."

She wrinkled her nose at me. "Now I feel foolish."

"Don't." A snippet of my conversation with her brother returned, as did his offer to buy me off. "You didn't like it. The cost of it is irrelevant. How much you value something should never be determined by the price tag someone else attaches to it."

"I agree." She searched my face. Although she didn't say it, I could see that she was remembering what I'd told her about my mother. I hated the sympathy in her eyes but liked that she saw me—the real me.

Feeling conflicted was something I was getting used to when it came to her.

The steward interrupted us with our drinks. When he stepped away again, she raised her glass. "Cheers," she said, then hesitated. "Wait, isn't it bad luck to toast with a nonalcoholic drink? I read an article on it last week." She whipped out her phone and did a quick search, then waved the blog article at me. "See. Seven years of bad sex if you toast wrong. Even if you're not superstitious, is it worth the risk?"

I barked out a laugh. "Absolutely not."

"I already started the toast." She pocketed her phone again. "Does taking a drink now cinch it? How do I untoast?"

I couldn't tell if she was joking, half-serious, or truly worried, but for some reason the idea of untoasting for the sake of good sex struck me as truly funny. I laughed again and put my glass to the side. "Come here. I'm an expert at these delicate matters. Untoasting takes skill, but it can be done."

She moved closer, laughter dancing in her eyes as she did. "An expert? Really?"

"Put your glass next to mine."

She did.

Hands on her hips, I eased her against my growing excitement. "The next part is crucial to get right."

"Then you'd better know what you're doing." She smiled up at me. "Because the quality of the next seven years of my sex life is hanging in the balance."

She was joking, and I had been, too, as far as knowing how to avoid the curse, but as I looked down into her eyes, my solution felt more like a promise than a joke. "Say the word 'cheers' again."

"Cheers."

"Now kiss me the way you'd like it to be for those seven years."

Without another word, she pulled my head down and claimed my mouth. Fire shot through me. Her tongue was playfully bold, devilishly talented. She writhed against me, every inch of her bringing every inch of me to a feverish boil.

I'd told myself nothing would happen on Jared's boat, that the boat was for enjoying getting to know her, and my place later would be where I'd get to know her body. Being with her was too good to rush. Any resolve I'd had to wait melted away as she stroked my body with hers.

There was no boat.

No staff.

Just us and pleasure.

When she broke off the kiss, I shuddered. Nothing, not even our previous intimacy, had prepared me for how intensely I'd felt connected to her. I didn't want it to end, but could anything that good last? Suddenly my father's devastation after my mother left made sense.

Riley and I stood there, looking into each other's eyes, breathing raggedly. She seemed as shaken as I felt, but I might have needed to believe that. She was the first to speak. "Did it work?"

I looked at her a moment longer before answering. My voice sounded a little strangled when I said, "That should do it."

She chuckled. "Thank you for saving my sex life."

Thank you. I winked. "There are additional steps that should be taken to ensure the success of the method, but we can delve into those when we return to shore."

"I have a few ideas we could try out as well." She blushed, and my heart began to thud wildly again. She was the perfect combination of sweet and bold. "That is, if you're open to suggestions."

"Always."

She let out a shaky breath. "Gavin?"

"Yes?" Whatever her question was, I told myself, I would be as honest as I could be. Where was this headed? No way to know. Was this the norm for me? Hell, no. Had I changed my stance on relationships?

No. Yes. Maybe. I wanted to be honest with her, but I was still sorting myself out.

"When do we get to see the whales?"

A slow laugh started deep in my chest, then rumbled out as I pulled her close, tucking her beneath my chin. If there was a single thing wrong in the world, I couldn't think of it right then. The sun was shining brightly on the deck just outside the lounge. The waters were calm. And Riley was in my arms. Life was good. "The schedule is lunch, whales, tour the shoreline, return home."

She tipped her head back. "Thank you for making today so special."

I frowned. I hadn't, not really. Yes, I'd gotten the flowers, but the tour was Jared's design. I was unsettled by how much better I wished I'd done. The boat tour was good, but it highlighted how little I knew about Riley's interests.

I stepped away from her because I needed to clear my thoughts. "Let's head out on deck." As the yacht made its way toward a nearby preserve on the bay, we moved to a lookout area at the bow. "According to Jared, he chose the marine sanctuary we're headed into not just for the whales, but also for the possibility of seals, dolphins, or sea turtles."

"What are you most excited about?" she asked.

I hadn't given it too much thought. "The humpbacks, I suppose. We've all seen movies where they come out of the water near a boat. I doubt that happens much in reality, but I do hope we spot one."

"You should make a wish, say what you want out loud, see what happens. The universe might surprise you."

I turned my head toward Riley. "If I believed in such things, I wouldn't waste my one wish on seeing a whale."

She tucked a wayward lock of hair back behind her ear. "See, that's the thing about wishes—you don't get just one. And wishes are never wasted. They also should be shared. I never understood why we tell children a wish won't come true if you say it aloud. It's the exact opposite.

If you really want something, you have to be brave enough to say you want it, and only then will it come to you."

"And just who is granting all these wishes?"

"You are." There was a confidence in her eyes that made me want to believe her. "It's a self-fulfilling prophecy. If you don't believe something can happen, it won't. If you allow yourself to believe it can, allow yourself to wish for it, chances are you'll make all the right decisions and put in the effort to make it happen. Ergo, you grant your own wishes."

"Ergo, you really like that word."

"I'd never heard it before you said it, so it kind of reminds me of you. It's different from my norm, and so are you."

I'm "ergo" to her. I kind of liked that. "If you replaced 'wish' with 'goal,' you'd sound a lot like my father. He believes clear goals and tenacity are the secrets to success."

"Are you and your father close?"

"Depends on what your definition of close is. He raised me on his own and has always been very involved in my life."

"But?"

"No but. That's it."

"Do you have the same sense of humor?"

I tried and failed to remember a time my father and I had laughed over anything together. "We don't have that kind of relationship."

Her eyes rounded. "The kind where you *laugh*?"

"My father has little tolerance for foolishness."

She turned away from the view to look at me. "He must have been so sad after your mother left."

The anger that usually rose within me at the mention of my mother didn't come. Riley wasn't asking out of idle curiosity; she wanted to know me. I wanted her to. "He did take it hard."

"I wonder who he was before that. Do you remember?"

"No."

"Your father never fell in love again?"

"One trip down that road was enough. He says my mother was the single biggest mistake he made in his life."

"It couldn't have been."

"It was."

"No, it wasn't—because if he'd never met your mother, you wouldn't be here, and you're not a mistake." She pursed her lips. "I'm not either. When I first asked myself about how my mother could have been with Antonio Corisi, I used to feel like I wasn't the miracle she always claimed Kal and I were. How could we be, when we came out of something bad? But I've decided life is more complicated than that. It's not about one snapshot but the whole photo album. And it's a story that we keep adding to, growing, evolving. I refuse to let one photo shape who I am or how I see others. My biological father was a horrible man, but that doesn't mean all men are like him. For example, would you ever hurt me?"

"Never." In my mind, men who hurt women or children were the lowest form of life.

"So, you're not like my father."

"Absolutely not."

"I'm not like your mother." She raised and lowered a shoulder. "A lot of women aren't. So, maybe it's safe to wish for more than you've allowed yourself to."

Although I'd thought something similar myself, I hadn't made the leap to wanting more. It was an uncomfortable challenge and one I wasn't ready to take. *Not ready.* That implied it was something I was working toward being ready for. It was unsettling to realize there'd been a monumental shift in how I viewed what was happening between us. "Why don't I start with the whale?"

"Sure." She looked me in the eye. "But you have to voice the wish out loud."

It was crazy. Nonsense, really. I said, "I hope I see a whale today."

161

She poked a finger into my chest. "Not good enough. You have to say it like you mean it."

"I want to see a whale today," I said in a louder tone. It felt ridiculous but important at the same time.

"Don't tell me; tell the universe. There's no one but me here to hear you. Yell it. Let it out."

Maybe it was to entertain her. Maybe there had been something in that one sip of champagne, but I leaned over the railing and yelled, "Show me a damn whale!"

She smiled. "Didn't that feel good?"

"It did, actually. I can't remember the last time I yelled anything." I looked out over the waves. Nothing. I muttered, "The things men will do for sex."

Her eyebrows shot up. "Did you just say what I think you said?"

I laughed. "I'll have to remember that you have exceptional hearing." I held out my hand to her. She took it. "What I should have said is that apparently the universe doesn't listen to me, so perhaps you should yell to it."

She shook her head. "No need. We'll see a whale today. A big one. When you yell at the universe, it tends to yell back."

A steward came out and said we were nearing our destination and asked if we would like lunch served where we could overlook the water. Riley and I moved to a higher section of the boat and took our seats at a table. The yacht cut its engines and, apart from a few tourist boats in the distance, it was peaceful.

Plates of seafood arrived almost instantly, along with glasses of water and fresh ginger ale. The captain joined us. He was an older gentleman with a beard as white as his starched uniform. After introductions were made, I asked, "So, what are the chances that we'll see a whale today?"

The captain looked past us, out over the water. "It's a good season for spotting one, but the ocean is a very big place. Nothing is ever guaranteed. There are things you can look for, though, even if you don't see one on the surface."

"What kinds of things?" Riley asked, the pitch of her voice rising with her excitement.

"Although we haven't dropped anchor, we have turned off the engines because there are all sorts of marine life here. You might see a seal. Where you see seals, you'll likely see a shark. Last week we were surrounded by a school of dolphins."

"What did you do?" Riley asked.

"Nothing. This is a sanctuary. We're here to observe only. We have laws against going too close, especially when it comes to the whales." He placed a radio on the table. "So as not to disturb your meal, we will announce the sightings of any marine animals that come near. The volume is here. Feel free to press this button to call for us to come up if you'd like us to help you sight them. Or turn off the volume completely. Happy sighting."

I thanked the captain. Alone again with Riley, I reached my hand across the table to take hers in mine. Snippets of the conversation I'd had with my father about what was important in life circled in my head. "Do you have a hobby?"

"A hobby?"

"Something you do for fun."

She laughed. "I know what a hobby is. It was just a question that came out of nowhere."

"Isn't this what people do on dates? Ask questions to get to know each other?" It was more than that—I wanted to know her.

Her fingers laced with mine. "I love that you say that like you've never been on one. Yes, that's what people do. I don't really have a hobby. I've always worked more than one job. My mother did the best she could, but she often couldn't work. Things took a turn financially and physically for her after her last surgery. Kal and I were both in college before that. We dropped out to take care of her, pay off her bills so she could fix what the last surgery didn't. That's what family does. When one falls, we all stop to pick them up."

"Yes," I said, even though I was absorbing the difference between her philosophy on family and the one I'd been raised with.

She paused between bites of shrimp. "Life is so weird, isn't it? Kal and I were always so close. We shared the role of caring for our mother, and that gave us a common goal. I thought we were unshakeable. We barely speak now, and it's hard, especially because I know why. He doesn't want to hear about the Corisis, and I can't lie to him. When you grow up with someone, they know you better than anyone else."

"I guess." I had no experience with that since I'd never had a sibling.

"But part of life is change, right? Nothing stays the same, no matter how much we want it to." She took another bite, then said, "I'm not sure I'd want it to. I'm glad Gian found me. I wouldn't want to go back to not knowing the Corisis or the Romanos. It can't be wrong to let them into my life. I don't see how having more family could be a bad thing." She met my gaze. "Have you ever met Dominic?"

I wouldn't lie to her, but nor was it necessary to say something that might cost her a chance at having the relationship with him she seemed to crave. "I've spoken with him."

"Do you think I'm right about him or that my mother is?"

I took a moment to weigh her question. "I don't know him well enough to say, but my guess is he's somewhere in the middle between who he wants to be and who his life has made him." I expelled a breath. "No different than the rest of us."

I understood that feeling well. I'd always tended to be goal oriented. Emotions were messy distractions I had no time for. When it came to trusting people—I didn't. Was that who I was? Who I had to remain?

She chewed her bottom lip. "I need to have a conversation with him about boundaries. I don't want to hurt Dominic's feelings, but he can be a little—controlling. He sees it as keeping me safe, but it's too much."

"I can imagine." I was only half joking. In a more serious tone, I added, "It does sound like it's time for you to tell him how you feel."

"My mother thinks I'll see the ugly side of him when I do that." She closed her eyes briefly. "What if I'm wrong, and he hurts me or my mom and Kal?" She opened her eyes, and I hated the torment I saw there that I couldn't do much about.

"That'll never happen."

"You don't know that."

"I do." I'd never let it happen.

"You're right. He's been nothing but good to me. I have no reason outside of my mother's fear to doubt him. I'm just going to talk to him like I would talk to Kal. If he's upset, I'll help him see there's no reason to be. No different than you yelling for the whale, right? I have to believe it's possible for it to happen."

A little different than the whale.

The radio on the table announced a pod of dolphins off the starboard bow, and Riley rushed over for a closer look. I followed her, assuring myself that not telling her the nature of Dominic's talk with me was for the best.

He'd said he wanted to protect her.

If he couldn't—or did anything to the opposite—I would.

CHAPTER NINETEEN

RILEY

I was more interested in Gavin's reaction to the dolphins than in the dolphins themselves. Yes, it was exciting to see them so close to the boat, but the smile that came and went and came and went on his face touched my heart. He was like a child in a candy store who had been warned against touching anything in it. He'd see something so wonderful and forget to keep his guard up and grin at me; then, as if he'd remembered the rules, his features would become much more controlled.

His father had a lot to answer for. Was he even aware of how much of his own pain he'd laid at the door of his son? Maybe it wasn't such a good idea to introduce me to Gavin's father. I wasn't sure I'd be able to keep that thought to myself.

I understood Gavin's hard line against relationships now. Never was a long time, but it made sense that he wouldn't crave what he didn't know. I would have said I couldn't imagine the kind of mother who would walk away from her child for money, but Dominic's mother had deserted her children twice. Trying to find justification for the thought process of a person like that was an act of futility. Some people simply didn't have a good moral compass.

Maybe, like Gavin had said, his mother and my father were lost somewhere between who they wanted to be and who their experiences had made them. My mother was a very loving woman, and I doubted she ever imagined herself as a fearful person. I wondered if Gavin's father saw himself as the bitter man he sounded like.

Gavin knew Dominic. Well, had spoken with him at least. I wondered what had brought them together and what that conversation had been like. It was no secret that Dominic had a reputation for being intimidating, but I couldn't imagine Gavin fearing him.

Catching me watching him, Gavin wrapped an arm around my waist and nuzzled my neck. "You're missing the dolphins."

"I'm not missing anything," I said, turning in his arms so my back was against the railing. I placed both of my hands on his chest.

With a hand on the railing on either side of me, Gavin dipped his head to kiss me. It was a gentle caress, a slow exploration. His tongue flicked across my lower lip. I opened my mouth, wanting more of him. When he lifted his head, he said, "You have a frightening ability to make me forget where I am. Are we still on the yacht? I'd rather be in the elevator heading back up to my place."

I shivered with anticipation of our day going that way. There probably was a bedroom on the yacht, but I didn't want our first time to be on his friend's bed, any more than he seemed to. Just to have something to say, I asked, "What floor do you live on?"

"Same as you."

"Really? The other penthouse? I heard it belonged to the owner of the building." *Oh.* "You own the whole place."

"Yes."

"Wow. It's a beautiful building."

He frowned. "Why do I hear a 'but' in that?"

I hesitated. The setting was a romantic one. I was in his arms. It was neither the time nor the place to critique the atmosphere of an apartment building he owned.

Caressing the line of my jaw, he said, "Now I *know* there's a problem. Just say it. I value the opinion of all the tenants, owners as well as renters." He kissed my lips briefly. "Whatever's wrong I'll have fixed immediately."

I wrinkled my nose at him. "It's just not that friendly a place."

"The staff?"

"Oh no, the staff is amazing. Top notch. I'm talking about the other tenants. There's no sense of community."

"Does there have to be?"

It was a valid question. "Everyone in my building in Lockton knows everyone else. We watch out for each other."

"I can't imagine that at the Terraanum. That's not what people are looking for when they buy into it."

"Everyone wants to belong. I'm just saying that when I moved in, I tried to meet people, and the only shared space was the bar."

He looked genuinely curious. "What kind of shared space do you imagine?"

Since we were discussing it . . . "It's just a suggestion, but that area at the side of the building that is all cement could be a park or a playground or both."

"A playground?"

"There are children in the building."

"I suppose there are."

"You wouldn't see them because there's nowhere for them to be except the lobby. It might be nice to give them a place to get to know each other."

"Anything else?"

"A few benches? A couple of trees? You could put a sidewalk along the service road for people who like to walk without heading out into traffic."

"You've put a lot of thought into this."

"Well, I do live there. I just think if you give people a place to meet up, they will. And if people get to know each other, they're more likely to feel like they belong."

"And that's important to you."

"It's important to everyone. If you don't feel like you're a part of something, why would you care about it?"

Gavin nodded. "It's an interesting viewpoint. I'll look into the matter."

I chuckled. "You said that like a true businessman."

"I *am* a businessman. I'll crunch numbers, see if the potential benefit is worth the cost."

"It's hard to put a price on happiness."

"I don't yet know that my tenants are dissatisfied."

I laid my hand over his heart. "*Your* happiness. It's your building. Do you know the people in it?"

"Each and every one of them—stats as well as preferred name when addressed."

Interesting. "Is that something your father taught you to do?"

He nodded again. "Biggest insult you can give someone is to forget their name. Easiest compliment? Remembering it."

There were so many layers to Gavin, and the more of them I peeled away, the more I wished I could go back in time and hug the lonely child he must have been. "I like people to know more than my name. I like them to know *me*."

"Holy shit."

"It's not that shocking. You let people into your life, and they tend to let you into theirs. It's about making connections."

"No—holy shit, look at those whales. They're coming this way." He turned me in his arms so I was facing the water.

The first mate appeared at our side. He warned us to be careful, not to lean over too much, since a whale could create a wave that could rock even a yacht. "It looks like a mom with her calf. See how the calf keeps partially coming out of the water and slapping its pectoral fin? It's learning to breach."

"Breach? Like, jump?" Gavin asked.

169

"Why do they do that?" I added my question to Gavin's spontaneously.

The first mate turned to watch the whales as well. "It's believed to be a form of communication. The sound of a slap on the water travels a long way. Humpbacks usually travel alone or with a small group, but there's a lot we don't know about how they coordinate their migrations. If we're lucky, the mama just might show her little one how breaching is done."

As if curious about the yacht, the calf swam closer to us. As it did, it broke the top of the water, arched, and slid easily back under the waves. A moment later it did the same—closer still. I took Gavin's hand in mine. "Oh, my God, that's so beautiful. He's so close." I looked to the first mate. "He won't hit the boat, will he?"

"He shouldn't. We're big. If a whale accidentally lands on something, it's usually because it was so small the whale didn't see it. They know we're here, and like any good mama, the female has probably already told her little one to be careful."

The calf broke the water again, so close it felt as if, had we been on the bottom level, we could have leaned over and touched it. In a dry tone, Gavin said, "He doesn't appear to be listening to her."

"She'll correct him if he goes too far," the first mate said. "We have our motor off and are by far not the first boat she's likely seen. Right now she doesn't equate us with a threat."

The calf circled the yacht, slapping the water playfully as if interacting with us. When the mama rolled and slapped at the water's surface, it seemed to be a call for her calf to return. In response, the calf flanked the boat again, breaching out of the water almost completely before disappearing beneath the water again. Another water slap. Another partial breach, even higher.

"Oh, he's naughty." I laughed at his antics.

Behind me, Gavin was laughing as well. "Do we know it's a male?"

The first mate responded, "If you're really interested, next time it breaches, take a quick photo of beneath the tail, and I can tell you. The difference is—"

"That's okay," Gavin said. "Boy it is."

I turned and met Gavin's gaze, and we both laughed again. A splash in the water brought my attention back to the whales. The female dove fully beneath the water.

The first mate said, "I suggest you hold on to the railing."

Gavin moved so his arms were tighter around me as we both held on to the railing. With a force that was slightly terrifying, the nose of the mama whale broke through the water, and her entire body rose above the height of the yacht for a slow-motion moment that I held my breath for. She arched away, spinning backward as she did, before splashing through the water's surface with a force that sent the yacht rocking.

The calf broke the surface as well, in a much wilder, crazier imitation of his mother's spin. As she led him away, he breached the water again and again, wilder and higher each time, as if he was excited to have achieved a new skill and couldn't wait to show it off to his friends.

I leaned back against Gavin's chest and glanced up at him.

"You're crying," he said.

Without looking away, I wiped the tears from my cheeks that I hadn't realized were there. They were the kind of tears a person sheds when they've witnessed something so beautiful they lack the words to fully describe it. "I'm going to remember this day for the rest of my life."

His eyes darkened as he looked down at me, and in a gruff tone he said, "Me too."

CHAPTER TWENTY

GAVIN

I could love this woman.

The truth of that revelation rocked me onto my heels.

I didn't yet, but there was no longer a question in my mind that what we had wasn't something I'd found before or would ever find again. She connected not only with the man I was, but also with a side of myself I hadn't known existed.

The scene at her mother's house came back to me as I looked down at Riley. I believed everything Riley had said about belonging and connecting with people because I'd met the woman who'd taught her the importance of both. Family. Loyalty. Sacrifice. Fara Ragsdale didn't lecture about the importance of them; her life was an example of valuing them. Sprinkle on a generous amount of optimism, and one got Riley—a woman I couldn't imagine ever choosing material possessions or comfort over people.

"I told you," she said with a smile.

I had no idea what she was referencing, since in that moment there was nothing for me beyond her and that beautiful smile of hers. "What did you tell me?"

"If you're brave enough to ask for something, there's a much greater chance of it happening."

I wiggled my eyebrows.

She slapped my chest. "I wasn't referring to that."

"So I shouldn't yell out what I want next?"

Her smile widened. "There are some situations where whispering works better."

I bent my head so my mouth was beside her ear. "The only tour I want is one of your body. What do you say we tell the captain to take us back? I want to taste you until you're begging to come, and when you do, I want to flip you over and start all over again. I want you wild in my bed, on my couch, against every fucking wall in my penthouse. I want to bury myself in you, come while your lips are wrapped around my cock, and be certain we couldn't possibly fuck again, then find the energy to. That's what I want."

When I raised my head, Riley's cheeks were flushed, and the desire raging within me was burning in her eyes. "Captain," she said in a husky tone meant just for me, "please turn this boat around; we're heading back." The engine of the yacht restarted. Her mouth rounded. "Do you think he heard me?"

I kissed her then, chuckling as I did. "Possibly, or he's been around enough couples who can't keep their hands off each other and has learned to cut those trips short."

She cupped my face with her hands. "I love it when you laugh."

I didn't have an immediate answer to that. But after a moment, I said, "Being with you brings that side of me out."

"It's a good side."

"We're very different people."

"Is that a bad thing?"

"I'm beginning to think it isn't."

She smiled, tipped her head back, and yelled, "I want to go back to shore. Right now."

When she met my gaze again, she joked, "Clarity is important when making a wish."

I laughed. "Wish? That sounded more like a demand."

She shrugged. "I know what I want."

So do I. I leaned away from Riley and also yelled in the general direction of the crew: "Take us back to shore!" Although I yelled the demand, I was smiling. Even though the crew wasn't in view, they had to have heard us. I didn't doubt for a moment that the yacht would take us directly back.

Unable not to, I bent to kiss her again. She met me halfway and wrapped her arms around my neck. Had we been alone, clothing would have been falling away, but we kept it contained to hot and heavy kisses. Not since high school had I felt so close to not being in control.

The sound of a helicopter approaching turned our attention toward the sky. It came to a hover about a hundred feet from the yacht. The captain appeared at the door of the lounge. "Sir, did you call for a helicopter? It's requesting permission to land on our pad."

"I didn't." Weird.

The captain spoke into his radio, then walked toward us with it held out. "The pilot would like to speak to Miss Ragsdale."

She stepped away and took the radio with a look of confusion on her face. "Yes?"

"I heard you might want a ride back to shore."

"Mr. Tuttle?" She waved at the helicopter, then turned to me with a bemused look. "It's my driver . . . in the helicopter."

"That's odd." I looked around the deck and caught a glimpse of a familiar face. The redhead from earlier that day was dressed in a steward uniform. She winked, wagged her fingers at me, then turned away. *Boundaries, Dominic. Looks like we need to have another talk.*

Riley asked, "What are you doing here, Mr. Tuttle?"

"First dates can be tricky," her driver responded.

"So, you followed me?"

"It wasn't that difficult. Like I said, you're never alone. Would you like a ride back?"

"Oh." Riley looked to me. "Do we want to fly back?"

I didn't ask how Dominic could have planted someone on my friend's boat. I was sure I didn't want to know. As long as no one was sent overboard, it didn't matter. "Why not? If Mr. Tuttle is here, flying back is faster."

Riley told Mr. Tuttle to land, then handed the radio to the captain. "I wasn't raised with money, but this isn't normal, right? Helicopters don't just appear like you're hailing a cab."

"No, this is over the top by anyone's standards."

She frowned. "It's kind of sweet that Dominic's worried about me. I guess? If it turned out that you weren't nice . . ."

"True. Being on a boat with someone could be an uncomfortable situation with the wrong person. You're more trusting than you probably should be, considering who your brother is."

"My mother would lose her mind if I told her Dominic had people watching me. This is what scares her."

I sighed. "I can see that, but you need to have a conversation with him before you'll know how to frame this. I can't speak to his motivation, but you'll know as soon as you talk to him about it. If you want me to, I'll be there beside you when you do."

"You'd do that?"

"Absolutely. I can understand how he might have seen today. If I weren't who I am, today might have been dangerous for you, and he wanted to protect you. If that wasn't his motivation and he isn't who you think he is, I don't want you to face that alone either."

She hugged me then—a full-body hug of gratitude. "I'll think about it, but it means a lot that you offered." She looked at the helicopter landing on the back of the yacht and said, "We might as well fly back. It'll be faster, like you said."

I agreed, because unlike my plans for later, faster, in this case, was better.

CHAPTER TWENTY-ONE

RILEY

We were in the air a short time later. The cabin, off white with wood trim, was impressively luxurious and modern, just like everything my brother owned. No headsets were even necessary since the rear of the helicopter was self-contained. Being in the air, however, was not what had my heart racing.

Gavin and I were heading back to either his place or mine. If I told him I wasn't ready, I had no doubt he'd respect that. Rushed wasn't how I felt at all, though. I'd never wanted to be with a man more, and that was equally scary.

When our eyes met, the air sizzled with heated promise. It was difficult to think of anything to say, when both of us knew what would happen as soon as we were alone. I joked, "I don't think we're using the ride home for the purpose Dominic intended."

Humor filled Gavin's eyes. "No, I doubt he'd approve."

I searched his face. "He doesn't have to. I love him, but my life is my own."

"As it should be." Gavin held his hand out for me to take. I laced my fingers through his.

"Today was amazing."

"I have a feeling it's about to get even better."

My cheeks warmed, but I didn't look away. "That's strange—I have the same feeling."

He leaned over and gave me a leisurely kiss that ignited a need within me that wiped everything else away. I wanted much more than was possible where we were, but I also wanted that moment to last forever. Anticipation was its own form of sweet torture.

The flight back might have been long or short, bumpy or smooth; I had no idea. All my senses, my entire being, was focused on the man beside me and how good kissing him felt.

Too soon, we arrived at a small helipad that jutted out into the water near the Terraanum. We thanked Mr. Tuttle, then ran, hand in hand, toward the building. I'd never felt freer or more in . . . I stopped myself there. I'd almost said "love," and that scared me.

I didn't have time to overthink it, though, because just outside the building, Gavin pulled me to a swinging stop that landed me in his arms. This was a different kiss—wild, hot, impatient. Just like my feelings as I kissed him back without restraint.

Our passion bordered on being too uncontrolled to be unleashed in public, but there was no holding it back. Nothing I'd felt with men before him had prepared me for how much I wanted him. I'd never quite understood people who had sex in less-than-ideal locations, but I understood it then. Where we were didn't matter. All I cared about was how good he felt against me, around me, inside my mouth, teasing me. My body was vibrating with hunger for more.

When he lifted his head, I sighed at the loss. "Where will you be more comfortable?" he asked. "My place or yours?"

"Either," I said, then added, "Yours." I wanted to know all of him—his body, his mind, what his place looked like, what else he was wishing for. All of him.

He placed his forehead on mine and groaned. "This is fast. If it's too fast, I'm okay with waiting as long as you need me to."

It wasn't a line; he meant it, and I fell a little bit more for him because of it. "You're a nicer person than I am. After all this, if you don't put out, I just might kick your ass."

He laughed and raised his head. "That settles it, then. My place, but only because you scare me a little bit."

Sure I did. He wasn't intimidated by me at all, but I loved this playful side of him. "Then what are you waiting for? Get going."

With another laugh, he released me, retaining one of my hands in his. We walked that way through the front doors of the building.

"Mr. Wenham?" a male voice called out as we made our way across the lobby.

Gavin turned in time to greet a young man in a staff uniform who came trotting up. "Kenyon. This is Miss Ragsdale."

"Nice to meet you, Miss Ragsdale."

"Nice to meet you too. Call me Riley."

Kenyon nodded to me, then, looking both embarrassed and excited, turned back to Gavin. "I haven't had a chance to thank you. Human resources worked with me not only to receive your grant, but they're helping me apply for more I may be eligible for."

"That's great," Gavin said. "Kenyon is studying dentistry at Tufts. I also hear he can make a mean martini now."

Kenyon smiled with so much pride I had to rethink my belief that Gavin didn't do much as far as community building. He clearly did. He obviously took the time to make connections with people. The young man before us was evidence of that.

Feeling a well of affection toward Gavin, I squeezed his hand. He must have read the move as impatience because he shot me an "I'm sorry, but what can I do?" look. Before I had a chance to correct his misconception, Kenyon began speaking again.

"I hope this isn't a bad time, but if I could just ask you for a quick favor." He took out his phone. "My mother made me promise to call her the next time I saw you. She wants to tell you something."

Gavin looked from Kenyon to me and back. "Why don't you come to my office tomorrow—"

Kenyon made a pained face. "Oh, I already started calling her." His mother's voice called out his name. Kenyon started to tell his mother that he hadn't meant to call her, but when Gavin held out his hand for the phone, Kenyon handed it to him.

"Hello, Ms. Sanders. This is Gavin Wenham."

I couldn't hear her response, but I loved how unguarded his expression was. After listening to her for a moment, he said, "You're welcome. My father always said the two most valuable things a person can't take from you are your education and your dignity. Your son handles himself well and is a reliable worker. We're happy to have him, and you have a lot to be proud of."

Once again, Gavin listened before responding. "He told me that a moment ago. Our HR department has a solid reputation for going above and beyond. I'm pleased to hear that is still true." Gavin laughed. "I will." After ending the call, he held the phone out to Kenyon and said, "Your mother asked me to remind you to pick up rib tips for dinner tonight and to tell you she loves you."

Looking flustered, Kenyon pocketed his phone. "I will. Thanks, Mr. Wenham. And thank you for talking to my mom. I know that meant a lot to her."

"Anytime," he said.

Kenyon seemed to realize then that I was still there and that he might have interrupted something. He said, "Thanks again," then bolted away.

Gavin smiled as he watched him go. "I like him. I bet he goes far in life."

I searched his face and said, "I wish I could find something about you I don't like."

His attention turned back to me. "That's the sweetest thing anyone has ever said to me."

He was teasing me, but rather than calling bullshit as he had done, I kept it real. "I believe that. I get the feeling you don't let many people see this side of you."

He leaned closer. "Which side is that?"

"The caring one. You don't come across as someone who would be so invested in the education of his employees." When he opened his mouth to say something, I guessed that it would be a denial of what he'd done and added, "Before you dismiss it as good business sense, his area of study will likely mean he'll stop working for you as soon as he graduates."

"True, but employees who feel valued tend to work harder and raise the morale of their fellow employees."

"Why don't you want me to think you're nice?"

He looked down into my eyes for a long moment. "Because I'm not—at least not by the definition you likely have of the term. I don't waste much time asking myself how people feel. I do what has to be done, don't go out of my way to be an asshole, and keep my focus on what's productive."

"That's not what I see when I look at you."

He moved closer still, running his hands down my arms. "What do you see?"

"I see a man who has worked hard to please his father, so hard that he's lost track of what makes him happy. I see someone who doesn't let people close, not because he doesn't like them but because he considers liking them too much of a weakness."

His expression tightened; then he looked around as if just then becoming aware that we were still in the middle of the lobby. "Let's continue this somewhere less public."

I glanced around as well and realized there were more than a few eyes on us. "Good idea."

We made our way to his elevator and stepped inside. I knew what we were headed upstairs to do. He did as well. Funny how the ease of the passion we'd enjoyed during the flight back had given way to an awkwardness that had us standing side by side in the elevator without touching.

The elevator opened to a masculine mirror of my penthouse—familiar yet different at the same time. We made our way into the living room and stood there.

He cleared his throat. "Would you like a tour?"

I smiled. "Not really. It looks like a flipped layout of my side."

"It is."

We nodded in unison.

"Would you like a drink?"

"I'm fine."

We nodded again.

The silence dragged on as we simply stood there looking at each other. Finally, with a forced laugh, I said, "I'm actually a little nervous. Isn't that weird?"

His nostrils flared. "I am as well."

"Really? You? I have a hard time believing that."

He stepped closer and traced the line of my jaw. "Believe it. My heart is racing and my hands are sweaty."

"What do you think is different?"

He swallowed visibly. "This feels important. Too important to get wrong."

My heart melted at that, and all hesitation left me. With a cheeky smile, I whipped my shirt up over my head and tossed it on the floor. "How was that? Right or wrong?"

"Oh, so right." He shed his own shirt.

I kicked off my shoes. He did the same.

My bra was next. He cupped each of my freed breasts with his hands and bent to kiss them. When he raised his head, I reached out and undid the fastening of his pants. He stepped out of them as well as his underwear, then helped me with the rest of mine.

Once again we stood facing each other but this time completely nude. My gaze was riveted to his, and even our breathing felt in sync. "I'm not nervous anymore."

He cupped one of my breasts and circled its nipple with his thumb. "I'm not either. The secret might be that we should both always be naked."

I stepped closer, grazing my nipples across his chest. "Shut up and kiss me."

He kissed me, and I was transported to that glorious place where desire and pleasure beat back everything else. His lips caressed mine, gently at first, then more powerfully. His hands were the same. They ran over my bare back and ass as if savoring a gift, but as his need rose to meet mine, his touch became more demanding.

I arched against him, loving the feel of his huge, hard cock jutting against me. I dug my hands into his hair and writhed my body against his. Every place our bodies touched brought pleasure; every place they didn't—pure torture. I wanted to feel every inch of him. He kissed his way down my neck to my breasts.

There was an expertness to his technique, but also the feeling that he was barely holding back. I encircled his cock with my hands and stroked him as he teased my nipples with his tongue.

He lifted me, and I wrapped my legs around his waist as naturally as if we'd done this a hundred times before. We were still figuring out everything else, but this was where no time was needed for us to know we fit.

We kissed as he walked. I held on and gave myself over to wherever we were going. He was an addiction I welcomed. The more he took, the more I wanted to give him. The more he touched, the more I wanted to be touched. Somewhere along the hallway, he stopped and propped me up against the wall. Taking his time, he kissed every inch of me, grazing over my sex with his tongue before continuing down my inner thigh with kisses.

Then he turned me around to face the wall, put my hands out on either side of me, and told me to spread my legs. Had I been capable of speech then, I might have asked him what I was under arrest for, but he was overwhelming my senses.

He pushed my hair aside and kissed my neck, trailing kisses down my back, all while his hands teased my nipples to full excitement. When he bent to nibble on one of my hips, one of his hands parted my folds, and he dipped a finger inside my sex. I was not only ready for him but also ready for whatever he offered up next.

He pumped that finger in and out of me while kissing my lower back. With his tongue, he traced the curve of my ass and slipped a second finger inside me. In and out, slow and easy, until I was clenching his fingers and jutting against them.

He picked me up again, carried me into his room, and laid me across his bed. I was shaking with anticipation. He didn't make me wait. He rolled onto the bed, scooping me as he went, and rolled me on top of him. Our mouths met hungrily. Our hands were greedy in their exploration.

"Sit up," he commanded, and I adjusted my position. His hands went to my breasts, caressing, teasing deliciously. I moved my wet sex back and forth over him, impatient to feel him inside me.

His hands slid down my sides, across my hips, then farther down to the inside of my thighs. When he lifted me, I lost my balance a little and clung to the headboard of the bed to steady myself. He lowered me over his face, and I gasped at the first thrust of his tongue.

I liked oral sex. Who didn't? But this was something else. This wasn't a gentle flicking tease or a building rhythm. This was a full tongue fuck that left me breathless and wild. He brought a hand around to circle my clit, but it was the magic of his tongue that held me spellbound. It was so big, so strong. Never had I felt anything dance within me with such skill.

I gripped the headboard tight as waves of rapture washed over me. I might have called his name. I don't know. I was yelling something, mostly for him not to stop. The orgasm that rocked through me was mind-blowing.

I was still floating down from that high when he shifted his position and tumbled me back onto the bed, this time moving so he was above me. The sound of a foil wrapper being opened was all the warning I had before he spread my legs aside and thrust himself deep within me. Deep, oh so deep. I widened my legs to welcome more of him.

With a hand under my ass, he lifted my bottom so he could have better leverage. He thrust deeply into me, withdrew, then thrust again. Powerful and sure. Hard and unforgiving. He took what I offered in a way that made me want to give more. An urgency built within us. I felt his in the way he began to pound into me harder and faster. I gripped the bedsheets at my sides as a second orgasm rose within me. I wasn't riding this one out alone, though. He was there, meeting every wave of pleasure with another thrust, deeper and deeper, wilder and wilder, until I didn't think I could take anymore. It was too good, too intense, and continued to get better even when I was sure it couldn't. When I finally climaxed, he gave himself over to his own pleasure and joined me with a few powerful thrusts.

Afterward, he removed the condom, wrapped his arms around me, and kissed my forehead. I cuddled against him, loving how completely he enveloped me.

"Gavin?" I asked against his chest.

"Yes?" He ran a hand through my hair.

"That wasn't half-bad."

I felt his laugh before I heard it. He gave my naked ass a light swat. "Thankfully, this is just the beginning."

CHAPTER TWENTY-TWO

GAVIN

I woke in the morning to discover Riley still cuddled into my chest. Normally I didn't allow lovers to stay over, but she could stay as long as she pleased.

There's a calmness that settles over a man when he's not only had a good number of orgasms but also has come while his woman's mouth was wrapped around his cock. The world might be a much more peaceful place if every man's day started that way.

I kissed the top of Riley's head and acknowledged that what we'd shared was more than just good sex. Although I'd spent the night exploring her body, there was still so much about her I wanted to know.

She stirred in my arms and opened an eye. "Why are you awake?"

I smiled. "Why are you?"

"Go back to sleep." She raised a lazy hand to caress my cheek, then covered my eyes briefly. "You are not allowed to watch me while I sleep."

"I do what I want," I joked as her hand fell away. There wasn't a man alive who could hold this woman and prefer to sleep.

She searched my face. "Everything okay?"

I kissed her lips gently. "More than okay."

She smiled, her eyelids lowering as she did. "That was some first date we had."

"It sure was. I don't normally let anyone sleep over."

She rolled over, away from me, jutting her naked ass against my stomach. "If this is where you ask me to leave, I suggest *you* go."

I wasn't asking her to, but . . . "We're at my place."

"How about we make a deal? The next time we have sex, we'll do it at my place so you can leave when you want. For now, close your eyes and pretend I'm not here."

As if that were possible. I did like that she imagined a next time for us. I wanted the same. I wrapped myself around her back. "I'm not asking you to leave."

She wiggled her ass against me. "Then stop talking."

I chuckled. She really was a combination of sweet and bold. I could imagine that despite her financial situation, her looks had made some things easier for her. When it came to people in general, she was caring, nurturing, often uncertain. When it came to men, she was used to getting her own way. I'd bet she'd left a lot of broken hearts in her wake without even realizing it.

I nuzzled her neck, then sighed and settled my head above hers on the pillow. The plan had been to bring her to meet my father and pretend she mattered to me. The more she began to matter to me, the less I wanted to introduce her to my father.

I liked who I was when I was with Riley. She was bringing life back to a side of me I hadn't realized I'd lost. Not only did she make me laugh; she made the sun shine brighter, food taste better . . . all the clichéd indicators that she wasn't just any woman.

No one before her had challenged my beliefs about relationships. I didn't know what was possible between us, but I wanted to believe something was.

Wanting to believe was more than I'd ever given a woman.

I thought about what she'd said about my father and how he must have been so sad after my mother left him. Nothing we'd spoken about was anything I hadn't always known, but looking at my father through her eyes made me wonder if he hadn't always been the man I knew him to be. Had there ever been a softer side to him? A more hopeful one? Who would he have been if things had worked out with my mother?

What would it take not to follow in his footsteps?

Riley and I both had one parent who had stuck by us and one parent who'd disappointed us. Both of us had witnessed how a person could be forever scarred by someone they'd loved and lost. Riley's mother had been injured physically and then stuck with a fear she couldn't shake. My father had been humbled and devastated emotionally.

The difference between us? Riley refused to succumb to her mother's fears. She genuinely believed in happy endings and sprinkled her optimism on people like a fairy tossing magical glitter. And me? I'd become my father—closed off, numb to more than I'd realized.

Before Riley, I hadn't thought there was a thing wrong with my life. As I held her in my arms and thought about how many women I'd slept with who had deserved more than I'd offered them, I wanted more. Riley deserved to be with the man she thought I was. Could I be that man? I didn't know, but I was willing to try.

Riley was sound asleep, snoring lightly, when I came to a decision. I wanted this—her. I smiled against her hair as I remembered her advice about how important it was for a person to voice what they wanted. It made sense. Only once a person clarified their goals could they truly go after them. Clarity followed by focused action was the secret to success.

What did I want? I closed my eyes and let the answer come to me. When it did, I opened my eyes and yelled, "I want this woman in my life today, tomorrow, forever!"

Riley bolted straight up into a seated position facing me, breathing heavily. "What happened?"

Feeling a little silly, I sat up as well and rubbed a hand along her back. "Happened?"

She blinked a few times, as if trying to focus her vision. Her hand went to her chest. "Sorry, I thought you'd yelled something."

I neither acknowledged nor denied that claim. I simply held her gaze.

Her breasts heaved as she took a calming breath. "It was probably a dream. Funny, I don't think I was having a nightmare, but I must have been."

I pulled her into my arms and smiled over her head, feeling a little guilty but not enough to confess. "Should I turn on the light?" The room was dimly lit enough for me to see her features, but the lamp beside the bed was off.

"Don't be an ass." She sighed. "You really didn't yell?"

I couldn't lie to her. "I may have."

She tipped her face back. "I knew it. Why?"

"I made a wish."

Her eyes rounded. "A wish? What for?"

I kissed her lips lightly. "I'll tell you someday."

She framed my face with her hands. "It has a better chance of coming true if you share it."

I kissed her again. "I will, but on my own time, when I'm ready."

She moved so she was once again lying on her side. I mirrored her position and tugged the bedsheets back over us. A smile curled her lips. "You're a funny man, Gavin Wenham."

I wrapped my arms around her and pulled her closer, settling her head on my chest. "I think the word you meant to say was 'hot.'"

She chuckled. "You're both, and I like it. I'm never quite sure what you're thinking."

I should have been fully sated, but my cock had other ideas. My hands did as well. I ran them over her back and down to cup her firm ass. "So you have no idea what I'm thinking right now?"

She smiled and feigned wide-eyed innocence. "No idea."

I hauled her up so she was on top of me. With my hands on her hips, I lifted her pelvis just high enough so I could slip my cock between her legs and move it back and forth against her wet sex. "Now?"

She stretched to nip my bottom lip. "No clue. Give me another hint."

I sat her on my thighs, quickly sheathed myself in a condom, then brought her back to just above my erection. This time as I held her, I lifted myself so the tip of my cock slid between her folds and entered her. I withdrew and repeated the move, making sure my path took my cock across her clit again and again. She bent to claim my mouth with a hot, deep kiss.

I lowered her so I could enter her deeper and loved how her muscles clenched around my cock. We found a slow rhythm that had us both breathing heavily and grinding against each other. She sat up and took control, riding me as hard as I'd pounded into her the night before. She threw her head back, brought her hands up to squeeze her own nipples, and drove me deeper and deeper into her until we both came and she collapsed onto my chest.

Once again tucked against my side, she mumbled, "Was that what you wished for?"

I put a hand beneath her chin, raised her mouth to mine, and let the deep kiss I gave her be my answer. I still had a lot to figure out, but if that was the form the universe chose to answer my request—I was okay with it.

CHAPTER TWENTY-THREE

RILEY

A week later, Gavin and I were walking the Freedom Trail in Boston. The last seven days had flown by in a whirlwind of sex, laughter, and day trips. I hadn't gone home to Lockton. He managed work over the phone but spent the rest of his time with me. It was a magical bubble where everything felt possible and being together mattered more than anything else.

"Tell me about your mother," I said on impulse. I couldn't shake the feeling there was more to the story than he'd shared.

"There's not much to tell. I don't remember her at all."

"That's so sad."

"I don't see it that way. I was never alone. I had nannies. A different one every year, but they were all quite nice."

"Why wouldn't you keep the same one?"

"My father didn't believe it was healthy to get attached to someone who was paid to care for me. It makes sense."

"No, it doesn't. I don't care what he said; I bet you got attached. That's a lot of loss."

He shrugged. "I don't remember it being difficult. Maybe the first few. After that, I didn't care."

Because you learned not to.

Your father made sure of that.

"That's why you make it very clear with the women you date that you're not promising them a future. You keep the rules clear so you don't get hurt."

I expected him to deny it, but he didn't. "I'd rather not see myself in that light."

I slipped under his arm and hugged him. "If it helps, I consider myself independent and fearless, but I haven't spoken to Teagan, my mother, or Dominic this week. They keep calling, but I haven't picked up. How can I be *fearless* if I'm hiding?"

He tightened his arm around me. "I'm hiding right along with you, so I'm not exactly the badass I think I am."

We exchanged a look. I'd heard him on the phone with people from both the Terraanum and Wenham Global. What was he hiding from? "From your father?"

He didn't answer at first, and I didn't push him. When something was bothering me, I often needed a little space to think it through. I sensed he was the same. Gavin was slowly opening up and sharing more with me, but it didn't come easily to him.

"Maybe." His smile turned sad. "More than anything else, I don't want you to get hurt."

"What are you afraid of?" As soon as the question was out, I regretted my choice of words. I'd meant to say, "What are you afraid will *happen?*" Men didn't like the implication that things scared them.

"I don't know," Gavin said, answering more honestly than I'd expected him to. "I love my father."

"But?"

He sighed. "This week with you has been amazing, but this isn't who I am."

Part of me was tempted to panic as I asked myself if we were having the "It's not you, it's me" breakup talk. I took a deep breath and told myself that if others could hear me incorrectly, I could hear them incorrectly as well. It wouldn't help either of us for me to react before I understood what he was saying. "So, who are you?"

His pace slowed as he seemed to mull the question. "A man who wants to be with you but has no idea what that looks like." We paused and simply looked into each other's eyes. He was conflicted, which should have sent me running, but it didn't. "Or if I'd be any good at it. When I built the Terraanum, I was overcome with the feeling that I was doing something I was meant to do. I liked creating it from the ground up. It was concrete and . . . *mine.*"

"You'd found your passion."

He frowned. "I suppose, but that sounds—"

"Beautiful," I supplied.

"I was going to say it sounds like I don't enjoy working for my father. That's not correct either." His slight smile was grateful; then his expression turned serious again. "Wenham Global is my father's legacy . . . my family's legacy. I honor that. When my father said he needed me to focus on my role at our family company, I did, and the Terraanum fell by the wayside."

I was beginning to understand. "And you're concerned that the same might happen with us?"

He could have denied it. Many would have. "I don't know. I don't want it to. My relationship with my father has always hinged on my willingness to match my priorities to his."

"That's so sad."

"It wasn't." *Until you.* He didn't say the last part, but I saw the sentiment in his eyes. "I don't want what we have to be affected in any way by the expectations of my father."

I let that sink in for a moment. "He wants you to settle down and take over the company. Which part are you worried will happen?"

He took one of my hands in his. "My father doesn't know what he wants right now. He's not himself."

"And you? Do you know what you want?" I held my breath.

It had the potential to be a wildly romantic moment, where he might proclaim that he did. Instead he tucked my hand into the crook of his arm, and we started walking again before he answered. "Sometimes I think I do. Other times I wonder if I'm the right man for you."

I could have rushed to assure him that he was, but it was too real of a moment for me to be less than fully honest. "There's only one way to find out."

He glanced down at me and arched an eyebrow.

I continued, "We have to stop hiding. You've met my mother. I'd like you to meet everyone else who is important to me." When he nodded, I added, "And I'd like to meet those who are important to you." I gave his hand a squeeze. "No matter how things turn out, Gavin, I'll never regret being with you."

He turned and kissed me. It was full of such tenderness that tears filled my eyes. When he raised his head, he said, "How do you want to do this?"

His tone was businesslike, which was my cue that he was feeling uncertain. My heart melted. Like two people lost in a pitch-black room, we were stumbling around, but he trusted me to lead him out. I didn't have the heart to tell him I was just as lost when it came to taking a relationship to the next level. That's where things usually fell apart for me. "I don't think we should start with Dominic."

His smile was reflected in his eyes. "I agree." We began walking again.

"You'll love my friend Teagan and her fiancé."

"Your friend who owns the printshop?"

"Yes, she's amazing. More amazing than I'm allowed to tell anyone, but you'll have to take my word for it. Gian Romano is not only her fiancé but also my cousin, although not by blood." I'd attempted to describe the family tree to Gavin already, but I wouldn't have blamed him for not getting it.

"His mother was your biological father's wife, who had Gian with someone else while she was on the run from him. Gian was adopted by his mother's sister, Camilla, who had three other children, two from her husband and one from your biological father. Which is why Sebastian is your brother, but Gian isn't."

"You're good!" My smile was huge. If that wasn't evidence of a man listening, I didn't know what was. It gave me confidence that he and I could work everything else out. "I was worried when I first met the Romanos that they wouldn't see me as one of them, but they have a loving definition of family that isn't bound by blood. Their house is always chaotic and full of children running around, and I love it." *Exactly the kind of home I've always wanted.* "I have an idea."

He looked down at me, waiting for me to go on.

"Do you trust me?"

"Yes," he responded without hesitation, and my heart soared.

"The Romanos are wealthy, but they're also down to earth. Basil says he was just as happy when he had one store, his family, and some good table wine. My mother would like them."

"Okay."

"Your father would too. At least, I hope he would. He'd respect their success, and they have that family-first vibe you say your father wants for you. My mother might be too nervous to go alone, but if I tell her we are celebrating Teagan and Gian getting engaged, nothing would keep her away. She could meet your father on neutral ground, so she'd be less likely to be intimidated. The moment she meets the Romanos, I know she'll love them. They just kind of pull you in and make you feel like you're one of them." I smiled. "And the Romanos would get to meet you."

He searched my face. "And we get to see how well our lives fit together."

My smile wavered. I didn't see it as a test, but perhaps it was. "We do."

He gave me another long look. "What my father thinks of you is of no consequence, and I would never let him speak to you with anything less than respect."

I believed the second part. "I do care what my family and friends think of you, but I feel the same about respect." I leaned closer and went up onto my toes. "Plus, you can't bullshit me. I know you care what your father thinks." I gave his hand a squeeze. "And that's okay. And I know you're nothing like Edward Thinsley."

He held my gaze a moment longer. "Do you mind if I tell my father about your mother's history with Antonio? My father has an edge to him—not in an abusive way, but he can be direct and curt. If I gave him a heads-up, he would temper that around her."

"I think it's okay to tell him. My mother will be nervous, even if it all goes smoothly. She doesn't get out much, but that's something I'd like to change." I brought a hand up to his cheek. "I didn't take you for the protective type."

He covered my hand with his. "No one deserves to be treated the way she was, and I'll do what it takes to make sure no one mistreats her again."

How could I not fall in love with a man like that? I blinked a few times quickly and lowered my hand before the intensity of the moment overwhelmed us both. "I'll call the Romanos and set this up. They'll be excited."

"You really told them about me?"

"I did."

We started walking hand in hand again. Out of the blue, he said, "You should ask your brother too."

"I can, but I doubt he'll come." I made a pained face. "He's traveling for work. He was offered a huge international opportunity. I miss him, but I'm proud of him for believing in himself enough to take it on."

"What does he do? Let me guess—something in technology."

I shook my head. I was proud of Kal but wasn't eager to share his profession. When our family had needed money, he'd found a legal way to make more than I was capable of bringing in. "He's a dancer."

"Ballet?"

I wrinkled my nose. "Exotic."

His eyebrows rose. "Your brother is a stripper?"

I stopped walking and turned to face Gavin. "My brother's paid off more of my mother's bills than I have. He tried to do it through regular jobs, but he happens to have the kind of body women drool over, and they're willing to pay a lot of money to see it. He hates the job, but he does it and sends money back to my mother."

Gavin frowned. "That's still necessary?"

I held his gaze. "To my brother it is. His feelings about the Corisis are—complicated. I'm hoping that will change once my mother accepts them." We walked in silence for a few minutes, then I said, "I'd like to meet Jared and thank him for lending us his yacht."

"I can arrange that." He looked slightly uncomfortable by the suggestion, then smiled. "Jared won't be surprised at all when I tell him we're together."

Together. I loved how that sounded. "Tell me about Jared." He was the only friend Gavin spoke of, but not in the same lighthearted way I talked about Teagan.

As we continued on the historic trail, Gavin told me how his father had hired Jared on because, as his father said, even a top runner needs to pace himself against someone else. The beginning of the story made me not like Gavin's father very much, but by the end of the tale I was less sure. I liked that Hamilton had helped Jared start his own company and that he'd encouraged Gavin and Jared to work together rather than against each other. On some level, Gavin's father knew his son needed to make connections, even though he'd raised him not to trust them.

Hamilton Wenham sounded as complicated as his son was. "You and Jared are still close?"

"Yes," he said, then added, "He and I are very different, but we understand each other."

I nodded. "That's how I'd describe my friendship with Teagan. She's a little on the paranoid side and a very private person. She sees me as flighty but loves that I could make friends with a stone."

"You've known her since elementary school?"

"Practically. We met in detention at middle school. She was there for hacking into the school's server and adding mustaches to the photos of all the teachers she didn't like. I was there for—"

"Let me guess, talking too much."

I pulled him to a stop and faked outrage. He was right, but I wasn't about to give him the pleasure of confirming it. "It's like you don't want to have sex tonight."

He chuckled and smoothed his hands down my arms. "Do you require a formal written retraction, or will this do?" The toe-curling kiss he delivered would have made any woman forgive him.

When he raised his head, I let out a shaky breath. "Forgiven."

In my ear he growled, "Don't give in so easily. I have a few ideas on how we could make up later."

That's all it took for me to think of a vivid scenario or two myself. "Then consider me still angry, oh so angry. So angry that when you reach for me, I might bolt away, just to see if you can catch me."

Laughter lit his eyes. "Taxi."

We shared a laugh.

In the silence that followed, I grew serious. "I like you, Gavin Wenham."

"I like you too." He kissed me briefly, then put a hand on my back and encouraged me to start walking again. "Now get those legs moving. We said we'd do the whole tour, and I don't like to half ass anything, but I also can't wait to get you alone."

"Yes, sir," I said with a laugh and then picked up the pace of my steps. It was his attention to detail and his dedication to finishing each task completely that made me just as eager to finish the tour.

CHAPTER TWENTY-FOUR

GAVIN

I picked my father up from his new estate in Newton. I grew up in a top-floor penthouse in the business district without a stretch of grass in sight. All of a sudden my father thought he needed a ten-thousand-square-foot house with a pool, a tennis court, and—holy shit—a tree house.

A fucking tree house. My father was definitely having a breakdown.

I expected to be kept waiting while he finished whatever he was working on, so I parked beneath the shade of the porte cochere. The front door of the house flew open, and he was beside my car before I had time to reach the passenger door.

"Dad."

He smoothed a hand over his tie. "How do I look?"

I frowned. He was in one of his signature steel-gray suits. Was I missing something? "Like you always do. Why?"

His smile took me by surprise. "It's not every day I meet my future daughter-in-law."

I raised a splayed hand. "Easy there, Dad. We are not at that stage yet."

He cocked his head to one side. "You're taking me to meet her family, and you expect me to believe you're not serious about her?"

I sucked in a fortifying breath. "I'm serious about her, but I don't know where this is going yet."

"Jared told me he thinks this is *the one*."

"Jared hasn't even met her yet."

"He says the two of you have spent a lot of time together recently."

"We have, but we're still figuring things out."

My father often put forth his opinion before fully hearing mine, but this time he seemed to hear me. "So, I shouldn't ask her how many grandchildren she's willing to give me?"

"Please don't." I pulled open the passenger door. He slid in, and I slammed it shut. I didn't trust this version of my father. He was too happy, too playful. God, I hoped it wouldn't be a mistake to introduce him to Riley's family while he was in this condition. As soon as I was behind the wheel of the car, I restarted the engine and asked, "Are you taking any new medications, Dad?"

"No. In fact, the doctor lowered the dosage for my high blood pressure meds because I am not wound up all the time. I'm getting things done, but I'm not worried about them anymore."

"I'm glad, Dad." My sources said things were not going well at Wenham Global, but that was a conversation for another time. "I still think taking a little time off will be good for you."

"I'll have no trouble stepping away, now that I know things are clicking into place. I'm in the process of buying the adjoining property. That house is slightly smaller, but it has a barn as well as a playground."

Oh, my God. "Please don't talk about this with anyone you meet today."

My father gave me an annoyed side glance. "Why are you talking to me like I'm a child?"

I sighed. It wasn't my intention to offend him. "You're going through a lot right now. I get it. And to make yourself feel better, you're making some impulsive purchases. I understand that as well. Just tone it down a little."

"'Tone it down.'" My father echoed my words. "I used to say that to you."

"All the time."

He looked out the window of the car, then turned back to me. "I thought if you were stronger than I was, no one could ever hurt you the way your mother hurt me, but I was wrong. I should have let you splash in puddles . . . laugh as loud as you wanted to."

"I'm fine, Dad. And you are too. We just need to get through this."

"There's nothing to get through, Gavin. This is me now." He cleared his throat. "I know you have kept in touch with your team at the company. I'm not upset. All I want now is to see you happily married and taking over for me."

I wasn't sure which part of that made me feel trapped, but I loosened my tie a tad and took another deep breath. There were several topics we needed to discuss, but we were quickly approaching Riley and Fara's apartment building, and I hadn't told him what I needed to about her. "Dad, there's something you should know before you meet Riley's mother."

He smiled. "I hope it's that she's my age, beautiful, and single. If so, I'm okay with all of that."

I groaned. Was my father still even in there? "No, it's about who Riley's father was and how her history with him will make today difficult for her. I want to make sure we all support her in a way that doesn't make her feel awkward."

The smile left my father's face. "I'm listening."

"It's a complicated story but one that's important to know, I think, to navigate through today effectively. Fara Ragsdale had two children from a man named Antonio Corisi."

My father's next breath sounded like a hiss. "I know who he was. No one mourned his death."

"Then you can imagine Fara doesn't have good memories of him. He was abusive to her, to the point that she's still recovering from how he hurt her."

"Emotionally?"

"And physically. His last beating left her with a broken spine. She struggles still with physical activity but is hopeful that her next surgery will relieve some of her pain and give her greater mobility."

After a pause, my father said, "I'm sorry. I didn't know."

"There's no reason you would have. Because of Antonio, she raised her children alone and afraid. She equates money with potential abuse. Meeting the Romanos is a big step for her. Go gently around her, Dad. For me."

My father's jaw was tight. "Of course. Corisi was a sociopath. I met him a few times and had no desire to do business with him. There was something dead in his eyes. When his wife went missing, everyone assumed he'd killed her. I remember feeling sorry for his children. One stayed with him—the daughter, Nicole, if I remember. His son, Dominic—"

"Yes, I know. Dominic is Riley's half brother."

"Does Riley have any contact with him?"

"Only recently, but yes."

"Antonio disowned him. He built his fortune on his own."

"What's important, Dad, is that Fara is afraid of him. I'm not quite sure what she's afraid he'll do to Riley, but his name alone is enough to upset Riley's mother, so don't bring it up." I gripped the steering wheel tighter. "There are a few more things you shouldn't mention. Riley and Sebastian Romano look a lot alike. Sebastian is also biologically from Antonio."

"Sounds like one hell of a complicated family. You sure you want to marry into it?"

"Dad." I used his name as a reprimand.

"I'm joking." My father chuckled, then sobered. He took a moment, then said, "I'm proud of you, Gavin, proud of the man you've become. I thought saying it would lessen your drive, but I realize now I should have said it all along. You have risen to every challenge I've put before you and somehow come out with a kinder side than I ever demonstrated. I won't offend Riley, scare her mother off, or bring up anything awkward. I'm just grateful you're taking my advice and settling down—"

"I'm not—" I stopped because I didn't know where things with Riley were going. "I don't want to rush this, Dad, and ruin it." I paused for a breath, then added, "I don't want you to either."

"I completely understand. Consider me *toned down.*" A mile or so later, he asked, "Is she beautiful?"

"Riley? Stunning."

"I was inquiring about her mother."

My head whipped around and I swerved the car but corrected quickly. *"Dad."*

"Still just joking," my father said. Then in a lower voice he said, "Mostly joking. I'd like someone to share that big house with, but this time I'm looking for a friend more than a lover."

He sounded so serious that I was temporarily at a loss for what to say. I really didn't want to imagine my father with Riley's mother. Eventually, I went with, "I'm sure you'll find someone."

"I still want to have sex. I mean, I'm not dead. But this time I'm also looking for someone with some substance and a sense of humor."

I shot him a side glare. "Are you messing with me, Dad?"

"A little, Gavin. Just a little."

I wasn't sure at first how I felt about that. If my father truly wasn't returning to who he was before, or was becoming who he'd been before my mother left him . . . this would be the new norm. I glanced away from the road and caught him smiling.

I didn't hate it.

CHAPTER TWENTY-FIVE

RILEY

After greeting Gavin and his father on the street and introducing our parents, I pulled Gavin aside. "Thank you for coming in a regular car."

He kissed me briefly. "How's your mother?"

"Nervous but trying not to be. Mr. Tuttle wasn't happy when I told him you'd be driving me instead. I didn't invite Dominic, but I did ask him if we could have dinner with him soon. One fire at a time. I hope that's okay."

"That's fine. What did he say?"

"He's looking forward to meeting you."

"I'm sure he is."

Wait, had I missed something? "I probably should have invited him today."

He shook his head. "Like you said, one fire at a time. You're right to let this be about your mother."

"And us."

He gently kissed me again. "And us."

I glanced over to where our parents were talking. "Did you say anything to your father?"

"I did."

Hamilton only partially matched the mental picture I'd made of him. He was well dressed, impeccably groomed, and shared the same strong features as Gavin. What I hadn't expected was the warmth in his expression while he spoke to my mother. Her laugh took me completely by surprise. It was one I hadn't heard before. Lighthearted. Almost flirtatious.

My jaw went slack, and my gaze flew to Gavin's. "Your father is flirting with my mother."

Gavin rolled his eyes skyward. "I'll talk to him again."

I laid a hand on his arm. "No. It's okay. As long as he's not just doing it to be nice."

Gavin's attention turned to his father. "No, it's sincere. Ever since he decided I needed to be married to be happy, he's been . . . lonely, if that makes any sense."

"It makes a lot of sense." I didn't want to, but I had to ask. "Hey, you're not going to ask me to marry you just to get your father's company, are you?" I tried to sound like I was joking, but my question hung heavily in the air between us.

Placing a hand on either of my hips, he pulled me to him. "Funny thing is, I don't know if I want to run the company. My father has tossed around the idea of selling it, and it's a real possibility to me now. He'd make sure I received back the money I've invested, and it would be enough to fund a few more building projects."

"You'd be following your passion."

"Yes, I would be." He kissed me again, this time deeper, and for a moment I forgot where we were. When he raised his head, I stepped back—aroused and confused. For a man who'd said he would never settle down, we were rushing full speed ahead. We'd just introduced our parents, for God's sake.

I had to remind myself we were still in the testing zone. He hadn't proclaimed he wanted to spend the rest of his life with me—he said meeting everyone would be how we would decide if our lives would fit together.

What if the day ended with him deciding they didn't?

My stomach twisted at that thought.

His expression turned concerned. "What's wrong?"

Voicing my thoughts would have added pressure to an already emotionally charged day. "Nothing. Just hoping today goes well."

He tucked me close to his chest in a long hug. "Me too."

I wasn't quite sure how to take that.

I rode in the back seat with my mother on the way to the helipad. Hamilton made pleasant conversation the whole way. He asked enough questions to show an interest in my life but not enough to be uncomfortable. When he spoke to my mother, it was in a softer tone than I would have expected, and I was grateful.

As the helicopter pilot assisted my mother into her seat, I stepped closer to Gavin's father. "Mr. Wenham."

He smiled down at me. "Hamilton."

"Hamilton, thank you for being so kind to my mother."

"She's an easy woman to be kind to."

"Not everyone thought that."

His eyes darkened. "I know." He searched my face. "Would you be uncomfortable if the evening ended with my asking her to lunch tomorrow?"

I shook my head. I didn't agree with some of the things Hamilton had done, but there was no denying that Gavin looked up to his father, and I could see why. Hamilton might not have raised Gavin in a way I could understand, but he hadn't done it to be cruel. He'd probably thought he was protecting his son from being hurt the way he'd been. A man like that would understand how the past still held power over my mother.

At least I hoped so.

CHAPTER TWENTY-SIX

GAVIN

The Romano house was as wild and wonderful as Riley had described it. Camilla and Basil Romano met us at the door, then introduced their four sons, their daughters-in-law, and a slew of children I memorized the names of.

It had taken one shared helicopter ride for my father and Fara to be chatting like old friends. He stayed at her side through the introductions, then wandered outside with her to explore the gardens.

When Riley stepped away to help Camilla with something, Teagan and Gian cornered me. They were both quite pleasant when I'd been introduced to them moments before, so I wasn't sure what had them looking so tense.

Teagan lowered her voice and said, "Riley tells us everything."

"I see."

Gian cut in. "She's very important to us. We just want to make sure this is real."

"Why wouldn't it be?"

Teagan said, "We know about the deal you had with your father. I swear to God, if you're playing her, I will empty every bank account you have—domestic and foreign."

Gian's eyebrows rose. "You can do that?"

She shrugged. "I'm pretty sure." She seemed to think about it, then nodded. "I could figure it out."

I raised both hands in mock surrender. "No need to learn a new skill on my account. Riley and I are still figuring things out, but it has nothing to do with my father."

Teagan nodded, then leaned in again. "She dropped out of school to help her mother. If she wants to go back to school, would you support that decision?"

"Of course."

Gian leaned in. "Has she told you about Kal?"

"Yes."

"What are your thoughts on that matter?"

Feeling like I was walking through a minefield, I went forward with care. "Regarding his career or his feelings about the Corisis?"

Teagan folded her arms across her chest. "Either. Both."

I shrugged. "His career is his business. I respect his reasons for choosing it. As far as him not being ready to meet the Corisis, I respect that as well, but I would like to see him returning Riley's calls. She misses him."

Teagan visibly relaxed. "I like you."

"Me too," Gian added.

I smiled. "So, I passed the test?"

Teagan exchanged a quick look with Gian. "We were too obvious."

Looking more amused than upset, Gian waved his hands. "I told you we should ease the questions into a larger conversation."

Teagan wrinkled her nose in a way that reminded me of Riley. "That was the plan—in my head." She looked at me. "Could we pretend that this conversation was executed much more smoothly than it was?"

I laughed. "Sure." Deciding to turn the tables a bit, I asked, "So, Gian, Riley told me you're working on a side project, something not related to your wine shop."

Without missing a beat, Gian said, "Marry into the family, and I just might tell you."

I surprised myself by joking that I would do that.

Then I swayed on my feet.

Do what? Marry Riley? Is that what I wanted? Why I was there?

The realization that it was made it impossible for me to follow what Teagan and Gian were saying. I was too busy processing that I couldn't imagine my life without Riley in it. I'd made the wish, stated my desire, and now was taking focused action toward making it happen.

Holy shit.

"I think we broke him," Teagan said.

"He'll be fine," Gian reassured her. Then he met my gaze. "You're fine, right? Nod once if we didn't scare you off."

"I'm fine."

"Thank God," Teagan said. "We weren't trying to upset you; we just had to make sure you were the real deal."

The real deal. That was what Riley had once told me she was hoping to find. Was that what I was? For the first time, I felt confident that I could be.

Riley returned to my side and gave Gian and Teagan a funny look. "Did I miss something?"

"No. Nothing," Teagan said, looking so guilty I felt a little sorry for her.

Gian looked just as guilty. "Just getting to know Gavin."

Riley's hands went to her hips. "So neither of you interrogated Gavin?"

When their eyes widened, I said, "They didn't ask me a single thing I wouldn't have expected loyal friends of yours to ask. You're lucky to have such good friends."

Riley relaxed and slipped beneath my arm. "I am."

Gian and Teagan shot me grateful looks that I responded to with a subtle nod. I liked them . . . and that they cared enough to grill me.

As the evening progressed, the noise of the house became less overwhelming. I enjoyed watching the Romano men laugh with their wives, chase after their children, and talk things out with their parents as if they were friends. I loved watching my father pull out Fara's chair and stay at her side like a protective admirer. We all sat together at a long table, shared a few bottles of wine, and laughed over story after story. I felt welcomed, and my father had never looked happier.

Riley kept meeting my gaze as if she wanted to ask me something but was holding back. I thought about the conversation we'd had regarding the visit and regretted making it sound like our future hinged on its outcome. It didn't.

The Romanos were open with their affection for each other. Love was easy for them. They accepted me almost instantly.

Christof offered to teach me how to cook a favorite family dessert, and I laughed until I realized he was serious. Mauricio took me aside to offer suggestions on how to win Riley's heart. I dismissed his advice at first, but some of his suggestions weren't half-bad. Most romantic gesture? According to him, anything that would prove I knew Riley better than anyone else did.

"Don't give up. Sometimes it takes more than one try," his wife joked as she joined our conversation, and Mauricio didn't appear bothered at all by her amusement.

The most reserved of the Romanos was Sebastian. When he asked to speak to me on the side, I braced myself for a possible repeat of my conversation with Teagan and Gian—or, worse, a talk about Dominic. Instead he said, "If you come around enough, you'll eventually hear my father say he was just as happy back in the beginning, when all he had was one store, us, and homemade wine. He means it. I didn't believe him when I was younger, and I paid a heavy price for that arrogance." He looked across the room at his wife. "I was given a second chance to get it right, and I'm doing everything I can to do just that. You and Riley seem to be headed somewhere serious. My advice? If you're ever given a choice between listening to your unborn child's heartbeat or going to a business meeting, choose your family every single time. There will always be another opportunity to make money, but the time we have with those we love? You don't get a second shot at that."

I opened my mouth to say something, then closed it. There really wasn't anything I could add to that. He spoke like a man who'd experienced a great loss, and because of that, his words echoed in my head long after we returned to the group.

I'd never seen myself as a family-oriented kind of guy, but after spending a day with the Romanos, I started to wonder if I wasn't wrong. Take away all their material possessions as well as their success, and they would still consider themselves blessed because they had each other.

After dinner, my father sat with Fara, Camilla, and Basil in the living room. Riley came to stand beside me and slid her hand into mine. "You'd never know they just met today."

I pulled her closer and kissed the side of her head. "Our parents?"

"All of them. They click."

"Like us."

Her hand tightened on mine. "So maybe our lives can mesh."

"Yes." I turned her in my arms and gazed down into the hopeful eyes of the woman I was falling hard for. Before she came into my life, I would have said I had everything I wanted.

She'd turned me around, upside down, and changed my view on so many things. No matter what I did for a living, I wanted to end the day at a home as full of love and laughter as the Romanos' was. What I wanted was clear to me, as clear as my feelings for the woman at my side.

I love her.

CHAPTER TWENTY-SEVEN

GAVIN

Two weeks later

Riley was seated on a stool in front of her bathroom mirror, applying her makeup and, sadly, fully dressed. Our eyes met in the mirror, and I bent to kiss her neck. "I'm looking for my damn wallet," I said.

"Is it in the living room?"

"I looked there."

"You checked in both? My side too? We shed a lot of clothing there when we got home last night."

I flushed as I remembered how wild it had gotten. "I bet it's there."

"We told Dominic we'd be at his place at noon. Did you get your calls done?"

"I did." My father had said I could return to Wenham Global, but I was seeing positive changes at the Terraanum and was beginning to seriously question if I wanted to return at all. I'd already started preliminary plans for creating a park. To do it well, it would be necessary to demolish the storage garage, but I was looking into purchasing a lot nearby and relocating everything there. The details of the project were still up in the air, but it was slowly coming together.

"Are you nervous?" She gave me a look that brought out my protective side.

I walked over to her and went down on my haunches in front of her so our faces were level. "No, are you?"

She bit her bottom lip. "I shouldn't be. You're important to me, and nothing he can say would change that. He's important to me, too, and even if you don't like him, that won't change anything either. All I'm trying to say is that I really want today to go well."

"I'm sure we'll get along fine." *As long as he doesn't offer to pay me off again.*

"I told him how well you got along with the Romanos. I'm not sure if that made the situation better or worse. I should have invited him."

"It might not have worked out as well if you had. Your mother was already quite nervous. It was a step forward, though." I kissed her lips gently, then stood. "Don't worry. We've got this."

She wiped a tear away from the corner of her eye and smiled. "Thank you. I don't know why it's so important to me, but it is."

I shrugged. "You love him."

"And I lo—" She stopped and turned bright red. "I care about you a lot, as well."

I kicked myself for not telling her then that I loved her. The words were on the tip of my tongue. Instead I bent again and said, "Me too. I'll do everything I can to make sure today goes smoothly."

She nodded. "I know you will." Then she turned and began to brush out her hair.

As I walked to the living room, I thought about how much my life had changed in such a short amount of time.

Every day with the same woman should have sent me running back to my old life, but it was the opposite. It felt natural to be with Riley—as natural as breathing. I'd had a door installed on the wall that connected our closets, which meant she and I were sharing the top floor of the building.

Living together. It should have been enough, but I wanted more.

I found my wallet beside the couch I'd bent Riley over the previous evening. When I first saw how Riley's side was decorated, I couldn't say I was impressed. Ultramodern, glaringly white. I preferred my side. However, now that there probably wasn't a foot of it we hadn't had sex in, I could honestly say I loved the furniture. So much of it was the perfect height to incorporate into our romps. Sometimes slow and easy, sometimes wild and impatient. Always good. Better than I ever imagined sex could be.

I'd already looked into the feasibility of taking down another dividing wall. When I mentioned the idea to Riley, she just smiled. I could see in her eyes that she wanted to give me a little shit for it, but she didn't—more proof that she was a nicer person than me and that I likely didn't deserve her.

That didn't mean I was going anywhere, though. I'd made my decision.

My phone buzzed with a message as I bent to pick up my wallet. *Jared.*

We need to talk. Do you have a min?

I called him instead of responding. "What do you need?"

"It's not about me; it's about your father. You dropped the ball on this one, Gavin, and I'm surprised. The board is meeting to remove your father."

Shit. I'd counted on having a little more time. "When?"

"This afternoon. They're pushing for a vote of no confidence."

"I can't go. I have plans."

Jared's voice rose. "You have plans? *Plans?* Unless they're for open-heart surgery, you cancel them and you get your ass to that meeting and end this. With you there, they'll back right down."

"I'll call my team. Maybe they can get the meeting postponed until tomorrow."

In a tone thick with sarcasm, Jared said, "Reschedule a coup? Exactly how stupid has being in love made you?"

"I love her." I hadn't told her yet, but after saying it once aloud, it got easier. "I love her, and because of that I'm not going to disappoint her today. Whatever is happening at my father's business, it can wait a day."

"I'm not sure it can. If they vote against him, they may well vote against you. Even if you decide to sell the company, an upset like that at the top will cost you."

"I understand the risk, but my mind is made up. I'm confident that the team I have in place will quell the storm . . . and if they can't, it doesn't change where I need to be today."

"You're crazy."

"No, I finally see things clearly. My priorities have shifted. Life is about more than work. It's about who we are, the connections we make."

"Are you stoned? You're not making any sense."

It didn't feel that way at all to me. Everything was clear. Sebastian had it right. My father did as well. "No, I just finally know what I want. If I have to choose, I'll choose Riley every single time."

"I hope she's worth it."

"She is."

A movement across the room caught my attention. Riley was standing there crying. I ended the call with Jared and rushed across the room to her. "Riley."

"I love you, too, Gavin," she said as she threw herself into my arms.

"I know."

She leaned back to look up at me. "Go help your father keep his company. We can reschedule Dominic."

I ran my hands through her hair. "No. There always has been and there always will be emergencies at the company. I meant what I said to Jared—I choose you."

We were late to lunch with Dominic.

215

CHAPTER TWENTY-EIGHT

RILEY

I don't think my feet touched the floor as Gavin and I made our way to where Mr. Tuttle was waiting for us. I had a huge smile on my face as I waved to Keith and Bill at the security desk. I wanted to yell to them, "He loves me!" but of course I didn't. They would have approved if I had, though. Gavin's employees genuinely liked him, and that said a lot about a man's character.

Gavin wasn't who I'd thought he was at first; he was a million times more loving. He was loyal, supportive, and often funny when he wasn't trying to be.

Fred opened the door for us. It might have been the way Gavin was openly holding my hand or the fact that he also had a big goofy smile on his face, but Fred caught my eye and nodded in approval.

It was real. No more waiting. I'd fallen in love with a man who loved me back. *"I choose you."* I shivered with giddy happiness as I relived hearing those words.

This is it. The real deal.

Take a good look, ladies and gentlemen: I have found the man I want to spend the rest of my life with, the future father of my children, my other half. Teagan thought he was perfect for me. The Romanos adored him. Dominic would love him as well. I just knew it.

Moments later, seated next to Gavin in the back of the car, I squeezed his hand in mine and said, "Do you think you could say it one more time?"

"What?"

"That you love me."

He cuddled me closer to his side. "I love you."

"I love you too."

He chuckled. "I believe we've gone over this."

"I might tell you every day."

His mouth danced over mine briefly, then he said, "I might say it right back."

I sighed in contentment, but a thought picked at me. "Are you sure about not going to the meeting for your father? I'm sure Dominic would understand if we explained it to him."

He took a moment to answer. "My father built the company. It was his dream, not mine. I would have taken it over and worked myself into a grave doing something I had no real passion for. I enjoy the real estate business. I like designing a building, putting all the pieces together, making everything run smoothly. I can see you and me opening apartment buildings in other cities. With an additional focus on community."

I loved that future. "And your father?"

"He didn't get where he is by being a pushover. They might think they can boot him out, but he won't go before he's ready. My guess? He's preparing to sell to Jared, but Jared won't buy it unless he feels he's helping us out."

I laid my head on his shoulder. "What if you're wrong?"

"I'm not, but even if I was, it wouldn't matter. I understand now what my father meant about waking up. There's no risk of me going back to who I was before I met you. This is me. It always was. I just didn't realize it. I do now, thanks to you."

I looked at him from beneath my lashes. "Thanks to me?"

He chuckled. "Yes, you." His expression grew more serious. "I want to offer your mother an apartment on the first floor of the Terraanum."

"We couldn't afford it."

"It would be a gift."

"She wouldn't accept it."

"What if it was part of an employment package? I'll be opening a community center in the building. You'd be the perfect person to run it. Your mother is so good at making people feel welcome. The two of you could design the play areas and schedule activities as well as fundraising events. It's time the Terraanum starts becoming a community."

"Fundraising? I don't know how to do that."

"Yes, you do. You're a natural. It's no different than gathering old clothing from the brides you worked with. We'd find good causes, you'd gather people who you might want to contribute to them, and you work your magic."

"My magic?"

"You have a way of connecting with people on a real level. I don't doubt for a moment that you could host an annual fundraising event in every city we build in."

I imagined that and realized it held real appeal. "I would love that. I really could be good at it."

"I know you could."

"My mother would love to get involved in something like that."

"That's the plan."

"It would get her out of the house, out into the world, and be a real confidence builder for her."

His expression was gentle. "I hope so."

He'd not only heard me but had also brought me what I needed more than anything else—a way to help my mother that would leave her with her pride. I threw my arms around him and hugged him so tight. "I love you."

He hugged me back. "Although we've already established this, I don't mind hearing it again and again."

The start of our visit with my brother and his family began as most of my visits did. Judy and Leonardo came out to greet us.

Little Leonardo shyly put out his hand to shake Gavin's and introduced himself.

Gavin leaned down to his level and shook it firmly. "Nice to meet you, Leonardo. I've heard a lot of good things about you."

Leonardo dipped his head. "I haven't heard about you, but that's not necessarily negative evidence."

"Let's hope not."

"Hi, I'm Judy." Judy put a hand on her hip and looked him up and down. "So, you're Gavin."

Gavin took it in stride. "I'm Gavin."

"Do you know how to code?"

"Basic only."

"What's your preference—hashed passwords or encrypted?"

Without missing a beat, he said, "Neither is ideal. Hashed passwords can end up on searchable databases once someone decodes them. Encryptions can be broken. I prefer to add random symbols and letters before hashing a password, which at the very least makes the hacker work harder to gain access."

Judy smiled and in a low voice said, "I see why Gian and Teagan like him."

I hugged her and whispered, "I'm glad, because I love him."

Judy hugged me back so tightly I could barely breathe. When she released me, she was all smiles.

Abby called to us from the door to come in. As we headed up the steps, I asked Gavin, "How did you know what she was talking about?"

"My father made me not just work in every department at our family's company but excel there before I could move on. I spent a good amount of time in the IT department because it's not a strength of mine." The pride in Gavin's voice belied his claim of weakness. I had to give his father some credit: he'd prepared Gavin well for the business world.

Abby greeted Gavin with a hug. Dominic shook his hand. It was all very civil—and promising. I hugged both of them, then took Gavin's hand in mine. Although I hadn't said much to Dominic about him, I wanted to make it clear that Gavin was important to me.

Abby led the way to the sitting room. "Brunch is almost ready. Are either of you thirsty?"

Gavin and I both shook our heads.

"I'll be right back, then. I'll check how close everything is to being done."

"Sit," Dominic said with a wave of a hand toward the couches.

I led Gavin toward one and we sat together, still holding hands. There was a tension in the air I wanted to dissipate. "So, I'm excited to see Judy here. I wasn't sure if she'd be at school."

Judy plopped into a chair next to us. "I wouldn't miss one of your visits. Dad knows to call me."

Leonardo smiled and took the chair on the other side of us. "I canceled a field trip to listen to a lecture on microquasar SS 433. It's believed to be a black hole and a giant star orbiting each other. An idea is being tossed around about what is contained in the outflow from the edge of the accretion disc. No one knows for sure, which is why the topic is so fascinating."

I exchanged a look with Gavin. *I told you he's smart.*

Dominic remained standing and frowned. "We were a little worried when we didn't hear much from you."

"I was busy." I gave Gavin's hand a squeeze. "I've been doing the rounds and introducing Gavin to everyone." There was an elephant in the room. I was tempted to apologize for not inviting Dominic to the Romanos' place, but the way he was acting was making me glad I hadn't.

My mother was never strong on discipline, but my guess was that this was how it would have felt had I been raised by an authoritarian parent. I really did need to have a talk with him. I wanted to be a part of his life, and for him to be part of mine, but I wasn't a child, and I didn't like being treated as one.

Gavin cleared his throat. "So, Riley and I walked the Freedom Trail recently. I grew up in the area, but it was a first for me. Have you walked it?"

"Oh yes!" Leonardo exclaimed. "Did you go into the Paul Revere house?"

Gavin shook his head. "It was closed when we were there."

"We've only been when it was closed," Leonardo said. "Right, Dad?"

"That's correct," Dominic said. "It's easier to secure the building that way."

They really did live a very different life from what I'd ever had, but not necessarily a better one. Money hadn't given them freedom. In some ways it had given them the opposite.

Leonardo continued, "Did you know that no one really knows which horse he rode? It wasn't his. There are all kinds of theories. It's fun to debate the credibility of the sources as well as the ethical implications of taking a horse that might not have been his to perform a service that likely saved many lives."

I loved Leonardo. He was so intense. In many ways he reminded me of Teagan. My guess was that he'd have trouble making friends as he grew up. I hoped he'd find his own version of me. Teagan's high IQ should have made her more popular—it would have if the world made sense. People were afraid of anything different. I'd been raised to celebrate our differences. "I'd love to go back with you, Leonardo. I bet you give a better tour than the people who work there."

He blushed.

Gavin agreed. "I'm in, if you don't mind a tagalong."

Dominic's eyes narrowed, and he folded his arms across his chest. "You're a constant source of surprise, Wenham. For example, I didn't think I'd see you here today."

"No way I would have missed it," Gavin said in an even tone. "Anything that is important to Riley is important to me."

Dominic took a moment to answer, then said, "You'd better be what you appear."

I looked back and forth between them. "What's going on?"

Gavin shook his head. "We're good."

I searched Gavin's face. His expression was tight, but he didn't look angry. I wasn't as happy with Dominic. He appeared to be testing Gavin, and not in the cute way Teagan and Gian had. "Judy, could you take Leonardo in the other room?"

Judy looked confused, but she stood. "Come on, Leonardo. Let's go see if there's anything ready in the kitchen to snack on."

Leonardo followed her out.

As soon as we were alone, I stood. Questions were circling in my head that I could no longer hold back. "Dominic, why did you think Gavin wouldn't be here today?"

At first Dominic said nothing.

I glanced back at Gavin, who was equally silent.

I advanced on Dominic. "I know you care about me; that's not what's in question here. I want the truth, though. Dominic, have you been running off my dates?"

Although he looked uncomfortable, he held my gaze. "Yes."

Until confirmation came out of his mouth, I hadn't believed it. I'd feared it might be so, but I hadn't allowed myself to accept that he would really do it. *Why?*

He pocketed his hands and shrugged. "There's only one way to know for sure if someone is after your money."

My hand flew to my mouth as I imagined all sorts of ways he might have done it. "You didn't hurt them, did you?"

He didn't look sorry. "All I did was offer them a tempting sum if they broke it off with you. Really, you should be thanking me. Anyone who took the money was someone who would have eventually disappointed you."

Gavin stood. "He does have a point." He looked angry, and I wondered if the conversation reminded him that his mother had chosen money over him. "Your delivery sucks, but I understand your intention."

"I don't require your approval, Wenham."

I stepped between them. "Don't talk to Gavin that way."

Dominic raised both hands in mock surrender. "I'm fine with him now. He came today, and that says all I need to know."

He came? "Why did you think he wouldn't?" As a horrific thought occurred to me, my mouth rounded in horror. "What did you do?"

Gavin came to stand beside me. "If you were at all involved in today, Dominic, you went too far."

"I didn't make the situation, Wenham. You and your father did that. All I did was encourage it to peak today."

Gavin leaned forward. "You bastard."

"I needed to know."

"My silence should have been enough."

I broke in. "Your silence? Gavin, what are you talking about?"

Without looking away from Dominic, Gavin growled, "This is between your brother and me. I didn't have a problem with you before, Dominic. I was actually on your side. I have a problem with you now. I warned you to stay the hell out of my family's business."

I couldn't believe what I was hearing. My head was spinning. "Stop. Just stop." They both turned their attention to me. "I want the truth. All of it. No more dancing around what's going on. Which one of you wants to tell me?"

Neither man spoke.

Judy appeared at my side. "Dad, how could you? This is why I'll never tell you when I'm interested in someone. This right here. It's too much, Dad."

Anger rose within me. I was too upset to worry about Judy's hypothetical situation, not when an actual clusterfuck was playing out in front of me. "Dominic, did you offer to pay Gavin off?"

Dominic grumbled. "For fifty million, he would have walked."

Gavin hissed out a breath. "I said that to see what your response would be, not as an actual amount. I don't care how much money you have, Dominic; I can't be bought, and I won't be intimidated. I respect that you think you're protecting your sister, but—"

I threw my hands up in the air and turned on Gavin. "He offered you money to stop seeing me, and you didn't think that was important enough to tell me?"

His cheeks flushed. "I didn't see how sharing that information with you would be helpful."

"Didn't think it would be helpful . . ." I looked at them, standing there nose to nose, two overinflated alpha males who were beginning to resemble the type my mother had always warned me about—men who used their wealth and power to control women. "I'm so angry with both of you right now I don't know what to say."

Dominic and Gavin exchanged a look.

Hugging my arms around myself, I fought back a rising fear that my mother had been right about my brother. "Don't tell me you're also the reason why no brides have been offering me work."

Finally a hint of guilt entered Dominic's expression. "I may have made a few calls, done a few background checks. Your safety is important to me."

"I'll get Mom," Judy said before sprinting out of the room.

I was shaking. Dominic had interfered with my relationships and cut off my income. Gavin stepped closer, but I put a hand up as a sign for him to stop. Before speaking, I took several deep breaths. "Dominic, I realize some of this is my fault. My mother always said people can only control us to the extent that we allow them to. We have to be smart enough to not put ourselves in a position where people feel that we don't have other options except *their* way. I don't like to see people in that light, but you're living proof that my mother is right. I should have said no to the penthouse. Nice as he is, I should have said no to Mr. Tuttle. I don't need you to rescue me, Dominic, and I damn well don't want you thinking you can play God with my life. I love you, but this ends today. If you want to be in my life, it'll have to be on equal terms. You're my brother, not my guardian." I shook my head back and forth. "You broke my trust, Dominic, and it'll take time for us to get back to where we were."

Gavin took another step toward me. I waved him off again. "I don't know if you deserve for me to be as angry as I am right now, Gavin. Maybe I'll get home, have a glass of wine, and decide none of this was your fault. But right now I need a minute, because I'm having a hard time telling the two of you apart. I want to believe that you offered to move my mother into your building to make life easier for her, but she would tell me it's so you could have leverage over me."

Gavin's expression hardened. "If you want to, go. I won't stop you."

I was visibly shaking. "That's what you expect, isn't it? What a sad pair we are. I'll talk to you tonight. I need to go somewhere and just clear my head."

Abby reentered the room in time to see me turning away. "What happened?" she asked quickly. "Are you leaving, Riley?"

I hugged her. "Yes. I'm sorry. I know you planned a nice meal for us today."

She hugged me back. "Don't give it another thought." She looked behind me at her husband. "I'll talk to Dominic."

I stepped back and met my brother's gaze across the room. "You don't have to. I spoke my piece."

Judy met me at the front door of the house and asked if I wanted her to come with me. I was tempted to say yes so I wouldn't be alone, but I said no, because if she'd come with me, my focus would have become making her feel better.

Before I could do that, I needed to sort myself out.

CHAPTER TWENTY-NINE

GAVIN

What the hell was that?

"Your ass should have followed her out," Dominic said after the sound of the front door closing behind Riley echoed through the house.

"Your ass should have backed off when I told you to."

"So this is my fault?"

"It sure as hell isn't mine. I'm not the one having my sister constantly watched, messing with her income, offering her dates money to ditch her, and"—I leaned in to growl—"why the fuck would you want my father's company to fail? I've been nothing but good to your sister. Today was supposed to be a nice day."

Dominic frowned. "First, I didn't mess with your family's company, just the timing of the meeting."

"Oh. Sorry, then—my bad; you're innocent. Fuck you."

Dominic rose to his full height. "No one talks to me that way."

"Somebody needs to, because you're out of control."

"Be very careful. Riley is the only reason I have any patience with you."

"Then we have something in common. Riley's the only reason I'm here."

Dominic was quiet for a moment. "Why did you offer to move Fara into the Terraanum?"

"Because she is living in a building where the elevator doesn't work, which isn't good since she has mobility issues."

Dominic pocketed his hands. "Fara won't even meet me."

"Oh, I don't know why. You're so charming."

Looking flustered, Judy reentered the room. "She's gone. Good job, Dad."

Abby put a hand on her daughter's shoulder. "Judy, be respectful."

"Why?" Judy protested. "So he can buy off anyone who tries to date *me*? Make it impossible for me to get a job when I graduate? And don't even tell me you'll talk to him, Mom. You can talk all you want, but he doesn't listen." She turned to me. "What did *you* do to upset Riley?"

I shrugged. "I'm not entirely sure."

Dominic sighed. "You didn't tell Riley about our conversation; that's how you got clumped in with me."

He was right. *Fuck.* It might have been to make Dominic pay just a little for the situation, but I said, "Hey, you did me a favor. If it was going to end, I guess now is as good a time as any."

He snapped, "If so little is able to break you up, you weren't meant to make it."

Judy gasped. "Mom! Do you hear this?"

Abby gave Judy a pat on the back. "Come on, Judy. We're not helping by staying and listening to this. Neither of them mean what they're saying. Hopefully, when they lose their audience, they'll find their brains."

She was right. I didn't mean what I'd said. I should have left with Riley, should have bolted right out the door after her. Only my desire to see her work things out with her family had kept me there.

Dominic and I said nothing to each other for several minutes. I half expected him to throw me out, but he didn't.

Leonardo walked into the room and took a seat on the couch, sitting back until his feet were dangling. "So, Mom and Judy are not happy with you two. I think I'm lumped in because I'm male, which isn't fair since I haven't even hit puberty yet."

Dominic walked over and sat beside his son. "No one's mad at you. I messed up."

"What did you do?"

It was fascinating to see a softer side of Dominic emerge. "You know how Mom is always telling me that I need to respect boundaries?"

Leonardo nodded.

Dominic added, "I forgot to."

I moved to sit in the chair across from Dominic. "Good intentions, bad delivery."

"Story of my life," Dominic said harshly. He looked across at me. "Did you see the way Riley looked at me? Like I was our father. All I want is to keep her safe—that's the opposite of how he lived his life."

"I'm surprised she left me here." I sighed. "When Riley and I first met, I kept telling her I wasn't good at relationships. I guess she chose today to believe me."

"Women are a real puzzle, aren't they?" Leonardo rubbed his chin.

Dominic ruffled his hair and laughed. "They sure are."

It felt like the right moment to say, "I love your sister."

Dominic looked over at me. "I believe you."

"I understand why you tested her dates, but why scare off her potential clients?"

"Weddings are difficult to secure." He sat forward and hung his head. "And I guess I was hoping she'd see she was capable of so much more."

Leonardo scooted closer to his father. "You meant well, Dad. She'll forgive you."

I wasn't so sure, but I also had a pressing question. "Is there even a crisis at my father's company?"

He shrugged. "Nothing I can't fix. Consider it resolved."

"Don't do anything."

He sent a quick text. "It's done."

For the first time, I understood at least a little how Riley felt around Dominic. "Dominic, have you considered that sometimes it's best to let people figure out their problems on their own?"

A pained expression tightened Dominic's face as he looked across at me. "Growing up, I had no one I could depend on. My children will never know that feeling."

Leonardo wrapped an arm around his father. "You're not alone, Dad. I've got your back."

Dominic ruffled his hair again.

"Riley isn't a child." I stated what should have been obvious.

"I realize that."

"Do you? What you've done will have struck a nerve with her. Fara is afraid you're as controlling as your father was. Riley doesn't want to believe it, but she'll see this as proof that her mother is right." I ran my hand through my hair. "Hell, I'm in trouble by association."

Wise beyond his years, Leonardo nodded sagely. "That's often what happens. I get in trouble every time Judy does something crazy and I don't warn Mom. Snitches get stitches, but accomplices get grounded . . . there's no winning move."

Dominic hugged his son to his side. "I'll talk to Mom."

"You're in enough trouble, Dad. I can handle it. My ethics professor said it will give me character."

I almost laughed, but he wasn't joking. In the quiet that followed Leonardo's statement, I began to hatch a plan in my head. "We can fix this," I said. I thought about the Ragsdales and their family philosophy. When someone stumbled, the others lifted him back up. I'd never had that, but I wanted it in my life. If I was right, the man across from me wanted the same thing. "Together."

"Together?" Dominic seemed to weigh the word in his mouth.

"It's the only way to show Riley that we've heard her." I put my hand out for Dominic to shake.

While we were shaking on that, Leonardo put his hand over both of ours and said, "I'm in."

"Then we will definitely succeed," Dominic said. We all sat back, and he added, "What do you have in mind, Gavin?"

"Riley loves carnival games and has a thing about winning the large prizes. She once told me that she was only interested in 'the real deal,' winning the big bear. If I can get her to talk to me again, I intend to propose to her. Would you like to help me plan how I can make it happen while everyone is together at a carnival?"

Dominic arched an eyebrow. "Are you sure my involvement won't break the rules of whatever new boundaries we're establishing?"

"Dad," Leonardo said, "I think what they want is for you to wait to be asked before you help. And he's asking."

I winked at Leonardo. "You've got it." Then I met Dominic's gaze. "So, are you in?"

CHAPTER THIRTY

RILEY

Mr. Tuttle scrambled to get the car when he saw me exit Dominic's home. I started walking down the long driveway instead of waiting for him. I'd call for a rideshare if I had to, but I had to put some distance between myself and what had just gone down.

Slowing beside me, Mr. Tuttle lowered his window. "Miss Ragsdale, are you okay?"

I kept walking but said, "I'm fine. But I might have just gotten you fired. I'm sorry about that. I just had it out with my brother. I'm sorry if that means you have to find other employment. Or maybe he'll keep you on. I don't know. I only said good things about you."

"Where are you going?"

"Away. Maybe to Lockton. Maybe just somewhere outside. I just need a quiet place to think."

"I don't mind driving you around while you figure things out."

I paused, and he stopped the car beside me. "I couldn't ask you to do that. I might have just cost you your job."

"I doubt that, but even if you did, I always land on my feet." He opened his door and walked to the back door for me. Normally I would have said the same about myself, but I was shaken by my talk with Dominic.

I hesitated.

He added, "I'll even listen—if you need to talk to someone."

My eyes filled with tears even as I smiled. "You're a good man, Mr. Tuttle."

"Benjamin," he corrected and then motioned for me to get inside. "Today I'm just a friend taking you for a drive while you clear your head."

"Should I sit in the front, then?"

"No."

He said it with such finality that I laughed. "Okay, then." I slid into the back seat.

He got into the car as well, then met my eyes in the mirror. "I should tell your brother and Mr. Wenham that you're safe."

I nodded. I wasn't happy with either of them, but I also didn't want to worry them. "Thank you, Benjamin."

He sent off a text, then took the car out of park and drove down the driveway. I glanced back at the house as we pulled away. Gavin was still inside. I had no idea if that was a good sign or a bad one. My emotions were all over the place. I wanted to hop out of the car, run back inside, and throw myself into Gavin's arms. I also wanted to drive far, far away and not look back. My life had made a lot more sense before I met him and my brother.

I sat back and sighed. "I don't know what to do. I'm so angry, but I'm not even sure what I'm most upset about." I put a hand over my face. "My mother sees people so differently than I do. God, I don't want her to be right."

Mr. Tuttle nodded, listening in quiet support.

"Do you think love can happen fast? This morning I was certain it could. Now I'm not so sure. I trusted Gavin, but what if I was wrong to? What if all I'm doing is repeating the mistakes my mother made without learning from them?"

I looked out the window without focusing on anything in particular. I'd often been accused of being too optimistic, but that's how I saw the world. There was no good spin on what I'd learned that day. I felt unusually defeated. "I believe that there is something bigger than us, some kind of plan. What if there isn't one? What if nothing we do makes sense because none of it even matters?"

Mr. Tuttle met my gaze briefly in the mirror. "One thing I learned in combat situations is that your chance for survival instantly diminishes the moment you start doubting yourself. You can't make clear decisions while afraid."

"That makes so much sense. And it explains why I felt like I had to get away. I'm not really angry; I'm scared. My mother is suddenly so trusting. She and Hamilton have been spending every day together, and it's freaking me out a little. He seems like he's had a change of heart and wants the same things she does, but what if it doesn't last? What if it's not real?"

"Trust is a complicated thing. It isn't easily built, but it is easily broken."

I nodded. "Exactly. I trusted Gavin, but when it comes to my brother, he wasn't honest with me." As I thought it over, I added, "He didn't outright lie, but a lie of omission is just as bad, isn't it?"

"I suppose it depends what a person omits and their reasoning."

For one day at least, the walls were down between the front and back seat of the car. I spilled about what I'd learned Dominic was doing to my dates as well as how his "background checks" had essentially stopped me from being able to find work as a bridesmaid. I finished with how Dominic had set up something at Wenham Global to test Gavin. "Gavin said he would always choose me, but when my brother threatened him, he kept that from me. I don't understand. When I left, they looked about to have it out."

Mr. Tuttle whistled. "Not many men would go up against your brother."

"What I don't understand is why Gavin didn't tell me Dominic had tried to pay him off."

"My guess? He wants things to work out between you and your brother."

"But if Gavin can keep something like that from me, how can I not wonder what else he's keeping from me?"

"Like I said, trust is a fragile thing. It's also an individual experience. Did they shatter your trust or just shake it up a little? Only you can decide."

I rubbed my hands up and down my arms. "I don't know. It felt like a huge betrayal in the moment, but now I'm not so sure. I know Dominic only wants the best for me and that he tends to be heavy handed when it comes to helping. And Gavin?" I tried to remember the faces of the men who had stood me up and couldn't. They hadn't mattered. He did. "Gavin outright told Dominic that he couldn't be bought off or intimidated."

"That's a good man."

"I told Gavin I needed time to think, that I'd talk to him tonight."

"But?"

"But I don't know what to say. He offered my mother an apartment at the Terraanum, said she and I could work together to facilitate fundraising and community building in every city he puts up an apartment building in. It sounds too good to be true, which means it is, right?"

"What would his motivation be?"

I weighed his question before answering. "He said it's because he loves me."

"Do you believe him?"

"I want to. I love him, but I can't shake the fear that I might be walking down the same path my mother chose. Her knight in shining armor seemed too good to be true as well, and he was. I want Hamilton to be the man to restore her faith in relationships, but what if she was right all along? Money does affect people, and maybe she and I need to stay in the world we understand."

Mr. Tuttle didn't have a response for that, so I continued, "The funny thing is, I wished for so much of this aloud, and those wishes tend to come true. My mother is finally getting out and meeting people. I should be happy for her, right?"

"I can't say I put much faith in wishes, but I've heard you talk about them enough that I understand why you do. So, I have a question for you. How do you know that showing your mother how to trust doesn't involve facing down your own fears first? Leading by example?"

I got goose bumps as his question washed over me. "But am I leading her anywhere good? How can I tell my mother she can trust Dominic when I'm not sure *I* do? Thank you, Benjamin. You've given me a lot to think about."

"We're approaching the highway. Would you like to continue to drive around, or do you have a destination in mind?"

"Just drive for now. If we end up at a beach somewhere, that would be perfect. I always find the waves soothing."

"You've got it."

We drove in silence for quite a while before my phone rang. *Eugenia.* I groaned. I was not in the mood. I almost didn't answer, but then I reminded myself that she was pregnant, likely highly emotional, and possibly in need of help. What kind of friend would I be if I chose my own meltdown over her possible crisis?

"Hi, Eugenia. How are you?"

"Sorry I've been MIA, but so much has been going on, and I owe it all to you. Seriously, Riley, if you ever need a kidney and I'm a match, just ask and it's yours."

"What are you talking about?"

"I took your advice and told Edward's mother off. I told myself our family, our baby, needed me to be strong enough to stand up for myself. I was polite but firm. I told her that I'm pregnant and that if she wants to be part of the baby's life, there will need to be changes. I said there was no way a child of mine would grow up listening to anyone speak to me the way she did."

I gasped and covered my mouth with one hand. "And what did she say?"

"She didn't know what to say. I don't think anyone has ever spoken to her that way."

"What did Edward do?"

"He stood by my side and agreed with everything I said. She sputtered and tried to threaten to cut him off, and he said"—she sniffed, as if she was crying a little—"he said he'd rather live with me in an apartment full of IKEA furniture than without me in a mansion."

I smiled at that. For Edward there probably wasn't a situation direr than living in a rental with furniture he'd assembled himself. Still, he'd stood up for his wife, and that was huge. "I'm so proud of him."

"Me too. When we got home, we had a long talk, and I realized I was taking a lot of what he was saying as a criticism when he hadn't meant it to be. He also owned up to the role he'd played in letting his mother get as bad as she was. She's been holding his inheritance over his head his whole life, but when he saw how much it was hurting me and imagined her treating our child the same way—he realized no amount of money is worth that."

"Oh, I'm so glad."

"And—hold on to your panties. This is the best part."

"It gets better?"

"She apologized."

"What?"

"To me and to him. And not a stilted one. Neither Edward nor I spoke to her for a week after our talk with her. When she called, we had no idea if it was to tell him we needed to move out of the house she'd given us or to threaten us again. But instead she asked if we could start over."

"Wow."

"I went to her house the other day. Me. All by myself. And she was nice. It was freaky. She's either plotting my death or excited to be a grandmother. I'm hoping it's the latter."

"Me too." I laughed. "I'm sure that's what it is. Oh, Eugenia, I'm so happy for you."

"I couldn't have done it without you. Truly, Riley. You have this way of seeing the best in people and holding them up to that standard—it made me believe I could do this. I needed to trust that Edward loved me and that if I could open his eyes, he'd stand with me. And he did. I'm so glad I didn't give up. Edward and I are stronger than we've ever been. I'm happier than I've been in a long time. Like I said, my kidney is yours if you ever need one. I owe you big."

I was smiling and sniffing back tears. "I'm so happy for you. Lunch next week?"

"I'd love to. We can catch up on how you and your brother are doing."

"I'd love that."

By then I hoped to have better news. Before talking to Mr. Tuttle, I would have said things were horrible, but were they? Dominic. Gavin. Both relationships were teetering, and both hinged on the same issue: trust.

What kind of person did I think Dominic was? Could I actually see him hurting anyone in my family?

Did Gavin really love me? Was his love the healthy kind, or was it whatever my bio father had called love?

To figure this out, maybe I needed to imagine love like a combat situation. Its ability to survive depended on not doubting it.

Doubt had made me defensive.

Scared.

It had sent me running away instead of staying and talking it out.

Doubt had no place in a healthy relationship.

After ending the call with Eugenia, I sent a text to Gavin: I'm sorry.

His answer was almost immediate: Me too. I love you.

I love you too. Mr. Tuttle is driving me to the beach but then I'm going to head home.

Which one?

As soon as I put my doubts aside, the answer was easy: Wherever you are.

I should have told you about Dominic.

Without doubt, I understood why he hadn't. You didn't want to damage my relationship with him.

He does mean well.

I sighed. I know he does. I thought I was angry, but really I was scared.

About your mother moving in. I'll keep the apartment vacant. It'll be ready for her if and when you're comfortable with offering it to her.

My heart started to beat wildly in my chest. Gavin really did love me. He wasn't trying to corner me into a situation where he'd have the upper hand. I'll talk to her about it. Thank you, Gavin. Like me, she might need time to get used to the idea.

I'm not going anywhere. We can move forward at whatever pace you're comfortable with as long as we move forward together.

Together.

When had that become a word he was comfortable with?

I was beaming. Aloud, I said, "Benjamin, I'm going to marry this man."

He smiled back at me. "I don't doubt it."

To Gavin, I wrote, Ditto

He sent back a heart emoji. I laughed. "Benjamin, Gavin just sent me a heart emoji. I think I broke him."

Mr. Tuttle laughed. "Love has been known to reduce a man to that now and then."

I hugged my phone to my chest. "I love how strong he is, but also that he gets as goofy over me as I get over him."

"Do you still want to go to the beach?"

"I do. A little fresh air will be good for me. Plus, being away from him is only scary if I don't trust him to be there when I come back."

Mr. Tuttle nodded in approval and turned on the music. I took that as a signal he was okay with me calling Teagan and pouring out the whole story again.

CHAPTER THIRTY-ONE

RILEY

Gavin was keeping another secret from me. I saw it in his eyes when he met me at the door of his penthouse and carried me to his bed.

It was still there in his eyes the next morning, when I asked him how things had gone with Dominic after I left. He looked like he was holding back a smile and refused to look me in the eye when I pushed for details. He said it was the last secret he'd keep from me.

I tried not to give in to the mild panic nipping at me. He'd apologized. We were in a good place again. Not every secret was a bad one, right?

Dominic called the next morning and apologized for interfering with my private life. He promised to never do it again, then corrected himself and said he'd *try* not to. Then corrected himself again and simply promised to never again pay someone off to stay away from me.

Odd.

I asked him how things had gone with Gavin after I left, and he was as evasive as Gavin had been. Not angry. Not defensive. Definitely hiding something.

The struggle to trust both of them was real. I wished they'd spill whatever the hell they were cooking up.

Dominic asked me to join his family on Martha's Vineyard for the weekend and said Gavin would be welcome. I told him I'd have to ask Gavin and get back to him.

Gavin's smile when I brought the question to him was a guilty, happy one.

I put my hands on both hips and asked, "What are you and Dominic up to?"

"Up to?" he asked with laughter in his eyes.

I wanted to laugh along, but I needed to know. "You're planning something, aren't you?"

"Maybe."

"You and Dominic—together?"

He brushed an imaginary piece of lint off his shoulder. "I won him over."

"But you're not going to tell me what you're up to?"

His smile faded, and he stepped closer. "You're worried."

I was always horrible at lying, so I didn't try to. "I'm sorry."

Gathering me into his arms, he held me close and murmured near my ear, "He and I have planned what I hope is a wonderful surprise for you. I don't want to tell you about it, but I will if you need me to. You and I are a team, Riley. Tell me what you need, and you'll have it."

My heart beat wildly in my chest. "I trust you." I said it, and I almost meant it. Some of my belief in magic, wishes, and love had been challenged, but it was resilient.

He tipped my face up toward his. "I'm not perfect. I made a mistake, and I'm sure I'll make more, but I love you, Riley. I would never intentionally disappoint you. You can believe in me."

"I do."

And this time I meant it.

I wrapped my arms around his neck and writhed against him. The kiss we exchanged was long and heated and made me forget everything beyond how good we were together.

CHAPTER THIRTY-TWO

GAVIN

A few days later, Riley and I were back in one of Dominic's helicopters, flying from Boston to his place on Martha's Vineyard. I opened the intercom to the pilot. "Mr. Tuttle?"

"Yes, sir."

"Your wife told me to tell you not to worry, because she packed your favorite pajamas."

"Excuse me?"

"Isn't this weekend your anniversary?"

"Yes, it is, but she understands that my schedule is unpredictable. We're planning to go away somewhere the next weekend I get off."

"So, I should call her to pack up and head back home?"

"Mr. Wenham, what are you talking about?"

"Have you ever been to Dominic's place on Martha's Vineyard?"

"No, sir, I have not."

With a huge smile, Riley leaned over and took my hand, as if realizing just then what I was up to. God, I loved that woman's smile and could easily imagine spending the rest of my life finding ways to see more of it.

I whispered in her ear, "You'll love this. I set up a whole romantic weekend for them."

Her eyes sparkled with humor. "Without asking him? Should I worry that Dominic is rubbing off on you?"

I feigned looking offended. "This was all me." I raised my voice again so Mr. Tuttle could hear. "A few years back, Dominic bought out a beachside hotel and renovated it into all self-contained suites. Each has its own kitchen and, if requested, its own butler. I requested a butler for you and your wife, as well as a beachside suite on the first floor so you can walk right out of your door to a cabana that's all yours until you fly us back Sunday night."

When Mr. Tuttle said nothing, I wondered if the line had gone dead. I made a curious face at Riley. She made a similar face back, and we both waited.

"Thank you, sir," Mr. Tuttle finally said.

"Gavin," I said.

"Sir," Mr. Tuttle countered with finality.

Riley covered her mouth to muffle her laugh. I found myself laughing along. She said, "Stop before you get us in trouble."

I put an arm around her shoulders and pulled her in for a kiss. "What's he going to do? His wife was so excited when I spoke to her. She booked every moment of his time the whole weekend." I kissed her forehead. "Besides, he doesn't scare me. Okay, maybe he does just a little. But let's see how tough he is when his wife is there."

"Please turn the intercom off, *sir*."

Startled, I hit the button, then burst out laughing. Riley did as well.

"Busted," she said.

I kissed her again. "There's no one I'd rather be in trouble with."

She settled her head on my shoulder. "When are you going to tell me what this is about? We're staying at Dominic's hotel, that much I have. But it's more than that. I know it is because you can't stop smiling."

I decided it might be best to give her a little bit of a heads-up. "Obviously, Dominic and his family will be there."

"Obviously, since they invited us."

"My father is joining us. He's flying your mother over."

"Wait, my mother is coming? She didn't say anything about coming." She sat straight up, her eyes wide. "She knows Dominic will be there?"

"Yes. I would never spring something like that on her."

"And she's okay with it?"

"She was after I spoke to her about my visit with him. It helped that my father as well as Teagan and Gian swore they wouldn't leave her side. I'm confident that once your mother sees Dominic with his children, she'll see that he's nothing like his father."

"You're right." Riley burst into happy tears. At least, I think they were happy, because she was smiling and flapping her hands. "You are the most amazing man. You really are."

I wiped away her tears and kissed her. "I wouldn't be for just anyone, but ever since you tried to get between me and my coffee, I've kind of had a thing for you."

She laughed.

In the silence that followed, her expression grew serious. "Mom is finally going to give Dominic a chance. I wish Kal could be there to see it."

I didn't tell her that he was also flying in but was arriving the next day, because I didn't want to promise something that might not happen. He'd been a tough one to convince, and I wasn't certain he'd follow through and show up.

We landed on a helipad beside Dominic's private hotel. Our things were whisked away to our suite, and we were led to an outdoor area where people were gathered.

Teagan and Gian waved to us from a table they were sharing with Fara and my father. We headed over to see them first. "What's wrong with my father?" I asked as we approached.

"He looks fine to me."

"He looks all flushed and smiley. I hope he's not drinking. He doesn't touch the stuff normally."

"He doesn't look drunk," Riley said, then lowered her voice. "You think he's falling for my mother?"

"Oh, my God, he is."

When we reached the table, Teagan and Gian greeted us with hugs. Fara rose to her feet with the assistance of my father. He was sporting a silly grin, and she was blushing.

I bent and whispered in Riley's ear, "Do I look like that around you?"

"Just like that," she whispered back.

Riley hugged my father, then bent to greet Fara with a kiss to her cheek. "I'm so glad you decided to come."

"Me too," she said and then blushed again. "I was nervous, but with Hamilton here I feel like I can handle it."

Seeing my father care for Riley's mother was heartwarming. It spoke to how sincere he was regarding the changes he wanted to make in his life.

My father said, "Fara was telling me you offered her an apartment in your building, but I'm hoping she'll consider commuting to work."

Fara added, "Hamilton has been so kind. My surgery is scheduled for the week after next. He offered to set up an area at his house for me to rehab. I'm considering it. I'm sure he'll get sick of seeing me hobble around, but he says he needs the company."

He took her hand in his. "Riley, your mother has no idea how beautiful she is—inside and out. She's the one who will get sick of me hovering over her."

Fara blushed and gazed at him in wonder. "Hamilton, you are too sweet."

"No one has ever accused him of that before," I said.

Riley elbowed me in the ribs. "People change."

My father kept his attention on Fara but said, "I didn't change; I woke up. All it took was two funerals and one date with this lovely woman to free me from the anger I'd been carrying around."

"You freed me too." All eyes, Fara smiled at him. He leaned over and kissed her temple. I'd never seen him look happier. "I would love to commute to Boston from your home, Hamilton."

My father nodded to me. "When you're up to it, we can take that apartment at the Terraanum as well. You could work with Riley. I'm sure Gavin could use some help with his plan to expand."

"Dad—" I almost said I didn't need his help, but I caught Riley's gaze, and she was beaming with joy. My father and I were redefining our relationship. He'd probably drive me insane, but that didn't stop me from liking the idea of having him in my day-to-day life. "That sounds wonderful. We'll talk about it more on Monday."

My father took me by surprise with a tight hug. "I love you, Gavin."

Wow. This side of my father still took some getting used to. I didn't hate it, though. In fact, the more I got used to it, the more I hoped this was who he'd always be. "I love you too, Dad."

Still smiling, my father stepped back and held out the chair for Fara to sit, and they resumed whatever conversation we'd interrupted.

Leonardo came over wearing swim trunks. "Have you seen my dad? We're supposed to go swimming."

Gian said, "I think he went back to his room to change. Your mother went with him."

Leonardo plopped down in an empty chair next to Fara. "If they're together, it'll be a while."

Out of the mouths of babes. I barked out a laugh.

"Where's Judy?" Riley asked. "I bet she'd go in with you."

"Knowing her, she's probably seeing if she can break into the office safe." His shoulders slumped. "I guess I'll wait."

Riley's mother said, "Leonardo, Hamilton and I can sit by the pool and watch you swim, if you'd like."

Leonardo's expression lit up. "Really?"

Fara turned to my father and gave him a sweet smile. "I'm sorry, I should have asked you. Do you mind if we move over by the pool so he can have a swim?"

Looking more like a smitten teenager than a man in his sixties, my father stood and said it sounded like a great idea. "I love children," he added.

"I do as well," Fara gushed as she rose again to her feet. "I can't wait for grandchildren."

"That's another thing we have in common," he murmured. "I intend to spoil them rotten."

I coughed, and Riley shook her head at me. Hey, if I hadn't discouraged him, my father would have spilled the beans right there.

After our parents wandered away, Riley slid under my arm and hugged me. "If Leonardo is already comfortable with my mother, that means she must have met Dominic already."

"And things must have gone well for her to look as happy as she does."

"Thank you for this, Gavin. I can't believe you made this happen. I can't tell you how much this means to me."

I wiggled my eyebrows and growled in her ear, "Maybe you could show me later."

She smacked me in the stomach playfully, and we exchanged the kind of look two lovers do when they can practically read each other's minds. *Oh, what a dirty mind my woman has. I love it.*

CHAPTER THIRTY-THREE

RILEY

This has to be a dream.

Even after a night of lovemaking, I was up early, too excited about life in general to waste a moment of the day. I went out onto the balcony and watched the staff as they bustled around putting up tents. Cars were pulling into the front of the hotel, one after the other, as if people were gathering for an event.

I went back to sit cross-legged beside Gavin, who was still sleeping. "Gavin?"

He groaned. "Sleeping."

"What do you have planned for today?"

"Sleep."

I pinched him. He rolled over onto his back. His eyes wandered over me. "You're wearing too much clothing."

"I'll make you a deal. I'll take it all off if you tell me what you have planned for today."

He ran a hand along my leg. "I'll make *you* a deal. Get naked, and let's do something that'll take your mind off asking about it."

I laughed. "How is that a good deal? I'm dying of curiosity."

He tumbled me down onto his chest and kissed me, then rolled so I was pinned beneath him. "Deal with it." He kissed my neck.

I laughed. "That's not very nice." Actually, it felt very nice, but I was determined to at least get a hint out of him.

"I never claimed to be a nice man." As he kissed me, his hands moved my robe aside to reveal more skin for him to explore. His mouth closed over one of my nipples as his hand slid down my bare stomach to cup my sex.

You know what? I can wait to find out.

A few hours later, showered and changed, Gavin and I emerged to have breakfast with our parents as well as the Corisis at one large table in a lounge with a view of the ocean. It still felt surreal to see my mother sitting at a table with Dominic and his family—as well as with Hamilton.

Antonio Corisi was dead. It was past time that the damage he'd inflicted be put to rest as well. The more I watched Hamilton with my mother, the more I believed that people came into each other's lives for a reason. He was strong enough to make her feel safe. She was loving enough to bring out the gentle, attentive side of him. They were each a little broken but leading each other back.

I met Gavin's gaze when he looked up from a conversation he was having with Dominic and Abby. The love I saw in his eyes sent my heart racing. I'd started off guiding him through this relationship maze, but somewhere along the way, he'd started guiding me.

We'd become friends, then lovers, and now . . . I was beginning to believe he was ready to take things to the next level. I definitely was.

"Dad, can I go down and see if the booths are set up yet?" Leonardo asked.

Judy shushed him, then whispered something in his ear.

I cocked my head to the side in question, but Gavin pretended he didn't know what Leonardo was referring to. The sound of helicopters approaching filled the air.

Gavin took my hand in his and brought it up to his lips for a kiss. "Are you ready for your surprise?"

A huge smile spread across my face. "I am."

He stood, helping me to my feet. "Then let's go."

Feeling like I was walking in a dream, I practically floated down the stairs with him to the beach. As we reached the bottom, a grassy area came into view, and my mouth dropped open. About twenty carnival-game booths had sprouted right in the spot where there had been nothing the night before.

As we approached them, people began to gather around us. My parents. Dominic and his family. The Romanos. I started to get misty eyed when I saw Eugenia with Edward. They were holding hands, looking as happy as they'd been at their wedding.

More and more people arrived. Some I recognized, some I didn't, but they all seemed excited to be a part of what Gavin had planned. Somehow he'd even gathered the other brides I'd worked with. I was all smiles as I waved to each of them.

Jared winked at us as we passed by him, and he bent to say, "I knew where this was headed from the first time he mentioned you."

I winked back and said, "Hamilton told me you're single, but he's working on that. If you hurry up, we can all raise our children together."

Gavin laughed and clapped a hand on Jared's back. "You did buy the company. You know the deal involved in taking it over."

"We'll see," Jared said, then stepped aside as others came forward to greet us.

I made the mistake of searching the crowd for Kal.

Gavin dipped his head down near my ear. "You okay?"

Not wanting to take away from the moment, I nodded quickly. I could call Kal later and share the news. I had a pretty good idea where this was headed, but I still asked, "What are you up to, Gavin Wenham?"

His smile warmed my heart. "You once told me you like to win the big bear. Today is your chance to do just that."

I blinked back happy tears. "So you gathered everyone I know to watch that?" *Sure.*

"Unless you don't think you have the skills to make it happen."

"Oh, I have skills." We made our way closer to the games. At the top of each booth was an enormous stuffed bear. "Which game should we do first?"

"It's entirely up to you."

I spotted one of my favorites. "How about the water gun game?"

"Sounds perfect."

We separated at the booth to each choose a gun. I glanced his way and asked, "What happens if I lose?"

"I win."

Yeah, I got that. That wasn't what I was asking. "Okay, smart-ass, what happens if I win?"

He winked at me. "I do too."

It was a little disconcerting to have the attention of so many people on us as I raised my water gun, but they faded away as I looked into Gavin's eyes. "I love you."

He chuckled. "I love you, too, but could you squeeze that trigger, because I'm nervous over here."

I could not imagine loving anyone more than I did him in that moment. "No need to be; you know what I'll say."

"Just shoot."

I turned and took aim, then pulled on the trigger and shot as much water as I could into the hole in the target across from me. Gavin did the same. Above the targets, two horses raced toward a finish line. They were neck and neck for most of the track until they neared the finish line, and my horse won.

The booth attendant announced I was a big winner and disappeared to retrieve my prize. He returned a moment later with a stuffed panda bear the size of Gavin. Held between its gigantic paws was a tiny velvet box—and my heart leaped to my throat.

Gavin accepted the bear, then looked a little uncertain about how to navigate retrieving the ring. He seemed to consider asking me to hold it, then thought better of it.

I burst out laughing when he rearranged the bear's legs so it appeared to be kneeling before me with the ring box held out.

"Riley Ragsdale," Gavin said. "Will you marry me?"

I laughed again. "Maybe. First, I need to clarify which one of you is asking."

He retrieved the ring from the box and dropped the bear to the ground behind him. "If he's competition, he's out of here." Stepping closer, he took my left hand in his and held out the ring in his other. "Let's start over. Riley Ragsdale, I didn't know what my life was missing until you came crashing into it. You shook me up, woke me up, and showed me what was possible. I want to spend my life yelling out wishes with you, then making them come true for us."

I used my free hand to wipe a happy tear from my cheek. "I want that too."

"Then marry me, Riley. We'll have a herd of children, ship them off to my father's house every weekend, and use that time to make more grandchildren."

Fara called out, "Try for twins."

Gavin whispered, "Is there a technique for that?"

"I have no idea," I answered with a laugh. In a louder voice, I said, "Yes, Gavin—yes to all of it. When we first met, I knew you were looking for something. I'm so glad it ended up being me."

We shared a laugh, he slid the ring onto my finger, and we kissed as those around us applauded. I was smiling and felt giddy when I turned back toward the crowd and spotted Kal.

In my ear, Gavin growled, "Go."

I didn't care who was watching or what they thought; I ran to my brother and hugged him tightly. "You came."

As he hugged me back, he said, "Of course I did. I'd never miss a moment like this."

Tears were flowing down my cheeks, but I couldn't stop them. "I know it wasn't easy for you to come back, and some of what's going on must be confusing, but it's all good. Tell me you'll stay long enough to see how good."

He nodded, then said, "Get back to your fiancé. I'm not going anywhere. We can catch up later."

I gave him one last hug, then rejoined Gavin. He handed the panda bear off to a staff member, and together we made our rounds, hugging all those who had come to congratulate us. When we reached our parents, my mother took Gavin's face in her hands and said, "I knew you were meant to be my son."

Gavin smiled down at her. "I couldn't ask for a better mother."

His father cleared his throat. "Or father."

I wrapped my arms around Hamilton and gave him a tight hug. "Do I get to call you Dad?"

"I would be honored." The smile he beamed at me was so full of joy that I almost burst into tears again.

Fara added, "Gavin, you can call me whatever you're comfortable with."

Gavin seemed to consider his options for a moment, then said, "I've always wanted a mother who could cook golf balls."

My mother laughed and put a hand on her hip. "You had to go there?"

I moved to Gavin's side. We laced our hands together, and in a sweet voice I said, "Mom, I've found the man of my dreams, and we are going to live happily ever after together—but he can be a little stinker sometimes."

Gavin gasped in mock surprise, brought a hand to his heart, and proclaimed, "Never." Just before he swooped in for a quick kiss.

I didn't believe this "never" any more than I had his previous ones. When he said never, he meant always.

THE END

Want to keep reading? The series continues with *He Said Together* (The Lost Corisis, Book 3).

ABOUT THE AUTHOR

Ruth Cardello is a *New York Times* bestselling author who loves writing about rich alpha men and the strong women who tame them. She was born the youngest of eleven children in a small city in northern Rhode Island. She's lived in Boston, Paris, Orlando, New York, and Rhode Island again before moving to Massachusetts, where she now lives with her husband and three children. Before turning her attention to writing, Ruth was an educator for two decades, including eleven years as a kindergarten teacher. Learn about Ruth's new releases by signing up for her newsletter at www.RuthCardello.com.